CHRISTMAS MOURNING

ANDREA FRAZER

Christmas Mourning

ISBN 9781783751501

This edition published by Accent Press 2014

This book is for Colin Crouch, the best and most inspirational English teacher I have ever met: a man who taught me to open my eyes and see a whole world of possibilities I never knew existed.

Other books by Andrea Frazer

<u>The Falconer Files</u>

Death of an Old Git
Choked Off
Inkier than the Sword
Pascal Passion
Murder at the Manse
Music to Die For
Strict and Peculiar
Christmas Mourning
Grave Stones
Death in High Circles
Glass House
Bells and Smells

<u>Belchester Chronicles</u>

Strangeways to Oldham
White Christmas with a Wobbly Knee
Snowballs and Scotch Mist
Old Moorhen's Shredded Sporran
Caribbean Sunset with a Yellow Parrot

<u>Holmes and Garden</u>

The Curious Case of the Black Swan Song

DRAMATIS PERSONAE

Old Village

Kerry Carmichael – wife of DS 'Davey' Carmichael, and her sons, Dean and Kyle

Rosemary Wilson – Kerry's aunt, and proprietor of 'Allsorts', Drovers Lane

George and Paula Covington – owners of 'The Fisherman's Flies' public house

Alan and Marian Warren-Browne – formerly of the post office; godparents of Kerry

Rebecca Rollason – proprietor of the Castle Farthing Tea Shop. Husband Nick, son Tristram (3)

Brigadier Godfrey and Joyce Malpas-Graves – The Old Manor House

Albert Carpenter – a village elder, of Woodbine Cottage. Great-nephew, John.

New Village

Digby Jeffries – ex-BBC, of Michaelmas Cottage, Carsfold Road

Robin De'ath – ex-Channel 6, of Pastures New, Carsfold Road

Cedric Malting – playwright, of The Nook, Carsfold Road

Alice Diggory – ex-English teacher, of Hillview, Carsfold Road

Henry Pistorius – ex-BBC radio, of The Old School House, Sheepwash Lane

Warren Stupple – physics teacher at Market Darley, of Pilgrim's Rest, Sheepwash Lane

Helena Stupple – his wife. Two sets of twins: Emily and Amelia; Sholto and Octavius

Dr Hector Griddle – In charge of Blue Sky, a rehabilitation centre based in the old vicarage

The Officials

Detective Inspector Harry Falconer of the Market Darley CID

Detective Inspector 'Davey' Carmichael of the Market Darley CID

Rev. Searle – officiating clergyman in St Cuthbert's for 24th and 25th December

Superintendent Derek 'Jelly' Chivers, PCs Green, Starr, Proudfoot, et al.

Prologue

The village of Castle Farthing had been positively bustling, as far as changes in residents went, over the past eighteen months, and as many had left so many more had moved in, and it wasn't quite as sleepy as it had been when the village had been struck by the tragedy of murder in the summer of 2009.

The four new houses that were being built at the time that those events took place were now finished and occupied. As there was no intention of installing a full-time vicar for the village again, the vicarage had been sold off by the church, the garage had been taken over by a large chain of petrol stations, and its little shop now provided some very unwelcome competition for Rosemary Wilson's shop, Allsorts.

Sheepwash Lane had been particularly hit by the departure of previous residents, and three in a row now had new owners: The Old School House, The Beehive and Pilgrim's Rest. Alan and Marian Warren-Browne had retired from the post office and bought The Beehive, once the home of Clive and Cassandra Romaine, and were delighted to have the property, as it had a studio building in the garden which they had turned into a rumpus room-cum-playroom for their goddaughter Kerry Carmichael's two sons.

The Old School House had been purchased by a widower who, rumour confidently had it, used to be involved in the broadcast of agricultural programmes on the radio but, for the locals, there would always be Martha Cadogan's shade out in the garden somewhere, tending her beloved plants.

Pilgrim's Rest, the former home of Piers and Dorothy Manningford, was now inhabited by a lively family of six, and its proximity to The Old Manor House had considerably

1

increased the Brigadier's intake of pink gin and the frequency of his tantrums when the children were laughing and shouting in the garden.

The vicarage, against furious local opposition, had been acquired by an organisation that dealt in the final stages of rehabilitation for ex-drug users and alcoholics, and events at the village hall, which was adjacent to the property, had dwindled since the property had been in use in its new guise.

As for the four new houses, two either side of the Carsfold Road where it bifurcated to go round the village green, these were occupied thus: Michaelmas Cottage housed Digby Jeffries, who had been something to do with the BBC; Pastures New was occupied by Robin De'ath (pronounced, naturally, as *Deeth*), who had worked for a less well-known television broadcaster; on the east side of the road, Hillview was the home of a retired English teacher, Alice Diggory; The Nook, by the amateur playwright, Cedric Malting.

With Henry Pistorius in The Old School House and three of the four new houses containing residents from a similar background, debate had become more lively, and the competition between these four had been furious as to who should be top dog when it came to prior importance in their respective fields.

What with the opening of the new rehabilitation centre, newly named 'Blue Sky' (all the residents of which were barred from the village's only public house, The Fisherman's Flies, by order of the centre's resident doctor), life had become very different from what it had been in the past, and Castle Farthing was slowly and reluctantly becoming used to the changes that had occurred in its midst.

The post office, although run by a young couple now and not closed as many thought it would have been, was still a lively place for people to meet and gossip as they waited their turn in the queue, and the Castle Farthing Tea Shop did a livelier trade than it had in the past, mainly due to the residents of 'Blue Sky', as they were banished from the pub and there was little else to do in the village. Rebecca Rollason, who ran it, had always found them courteous and polite, and would not have dreamt of refusing their custom because of their pasts.

DS Davey Carmichael and his wife Kerry had almost finished the joining of Kerry's formerly rented home, Jasmine Cottage, and its neighbour, Crabapple Cottage, and were really appreciating the extra space it had given them, not only for themselves, but for Kerry's two sons, Dean and Kyle, too. With the addition of the two dogs to their family – Mr Knuckles and Mistress Fang, the latter in pup – the arrival of a stray cat which they had adopted, and the imminent arrival of their own baby, they had noticed little about the change in the population, being much too busy with more important things: creating the perfect nest for their family.

Cosy little villages tended to stay the same in cosy fiction, but real life simply isn't like that. Castle Farthing had changed considerably, and was due to change again as the cataclysmic winter of 2010 approached, as unsuspected events closed in around the little village.

Chapter One

In Castle Farthing on this Christmas Eve, all was aglow with myriad lights, all twinkling in the cold air and filling it with a rainbow. George and Paula Covington had outdone themselves with their decorations this year and, apart from the many varied strands of lights attached to the outside, they had added an enormous inflatable Father Christmas and an equally huge inflatable snowman, both of which were lit up from within.

From the Christmas trees outside the pub doors, every colour imaginable sparkled from the fibre-optic trees (with added strings of light and decorations) that they had placed outside the doors of the public house, and an equally large Christmas tree did the same job inside, the roaring log fire providing an extra welcome to customers in this bitter weather.

Even the castle ruins from which the village had originally been given its name (the 'farthing' thought to be the toll charged to pass down the road through the old castle grounds) had been seasonally tarted-up, and, for the first time, were strung with sturdy outdoor lights in an assortment of colours.

The lights strung round the village green also did their bit to add to the seasonal atmosphere, and every cottage sported a brightly lit and decorated tree in its front window. Castle Farthing looked like a Christmas card, the impression heightened by the snow that had threatened earlier in the day and had eventually begun to fall at about two-thirty, delighting those on their way to the church for the crib service, for St Cuthbert's had a locum this Christmas, and services would be heard in its ancient walls at this time of the year for the first time in two years.

5

In the next few hours, however, everyone back in their houses hiding from the cold and the rising wind, the snow had begun to fall in earnest, the flakes large and soft as duck down, falling faster and faster in ever increasing volume, and Castle Farthing, unbeknownst to most, now had six inches of blanketing white decorating it, too, and the sky was heavy with more to come.

Wednesday 1st December – morning

Detective Inspector Harry Falconer was sitting at his desk finishing off a provisional report on the crime figures for November, when a whirlwind entered the room; the door flying back on its hinges to bang and rebound from the metal filing cabinet behind it, and then slammed with a shudder that ran through the whole room and a giant of a figure crossed over to the desk and flung itself into the chair on the other side of it, exclaiming, 'That *bloody* man!'

'Carmichael!' retorted Falconer, in horror, for he rarely heard Carmichael swear. 'Whatever's got into you? What man? Calm down and tell me all about it, and we'll see if we can't get it into some sort of perspective for you.' And damn you for interrupting when I thought I'd just got a handle on these figures; I'll have to start all over again now when you've got it out of your system, thought Falconer with a mental sigh.

'That one I've mentioned a few times to you: the one that's moved into the village: the one that's trying to get his finger into every pie, and who's been upsetting Kerry. You remember, sir?'

'I certainly do. What's he done now?' The inspector hoped it wasn't anything too heinous, but Carmichael didn't usually get all het up about nothing.

With a renewal of the anger he had demonstrated on entering the office, Carmichael's face grew red, and he made strangling motions with his huge hands, declaring, 'I could kill the man myself, saying such things to a pregnant woman.'

At the rise in the volume of his voice, a uniformed officer

poked his head round the door to see that everything was all right, and withdrew when he realised that it was only the DI and the DS in there.

'Come on, you! Let's get ourselves off to the canteen, get some hot tea into you, and talk about this calmly. Just simmer down, and you can tell me all about it, but without the murderous gestures, if you don't mind,' Falconer suggested. Then, perhaps he could get back to what he had been doing, in peace. Let the younger man get it out of his system .

'Sorry, sir, but he just makes me so mad!' replied Carmichael, blowing on his hands now, which were blue with cold as he wore no gloves.

'And get your hands by that radiator for a couple of minutes before we go. I don't want you throwing scalding tea everywhere, especially over me, just because you've got no feeling in your fingers. My arm's only just recovered from that knock with the baseball bat I got, and I don't want to follow it up with a nasty case of Advent burns.'[1]

Falconer had received a nasty blow to his arm during an attack from a suspect in their previous case, and was still taking painkillers and painstakingly following the exercises the physiotherapist had shown him after that injury.

A few minutes later in the canteen, his enormous hands wrapped round the special pint mug that Maggie behind the counter kept for him (*she was soft-hearted, and proud of it!*), Carmichael took a noisy slurp of the almost-boiling liquid, squinted his eyes in pain and appreciation, and began his tale of woe.

'That chap I told you about over the last few weeks: he's getting worse, and it's really upsetting Kerry,' began Carmichael.

'What's he said this time?' Falconer asked him, taking a tentative sip of his coffee and finding it to his liking.

'Yesterday he cornered her in Allsorts and told her some horror stories about pets lying on newborn babies' faces, and

---

[1] See *Strict and Peculiar*

smothering them, backing it up by saying that he worked for the BBC and had heard all about such events. He only shut up when the owner, Rosemary Wilson – you remember Kerry's aunt, don't you? – came over and heard what he was saying. She had him out of that shop so quick his feet didn't touch the ground.'

'Is that all?' asked Falconer in all innocence, finding the story quite mild, and not realising what a hornets' nest he was stirring up.

'*All*?' shouted Carmichael, drawing eyes from all over the canteen.

'Shhhhh! Calm down, Carmichael, otherwise I'll be able to sell tickets to this conversation.'

'Well, when was the last time you spent a lot of quality time with a pregnant woman?'

'OK, you've got me there.' The answer was never, so perhaps he'd better find out just why his sergeant was in such a rage about it. Capitulating, he continued, 'You win; but what about it?'

'Their hormones are all over the place. The littlest thing upsets them out of all proportion, and they're convinced that everything's going to go wrong with the pregnancy, the birth, and for months after that.

'The closer to the birth they get, the more ridiculous and outrageous the fears, but there's no rationalising with them. Kerry's getting herself into a right tizzy now there's only just over a month to go, and this idiot just feeds her fears and creates new ones she hadn't even thought of.'

'Is it really that bad?' asked Falconer. He'd always considered Kerry Carmichael a very grounded person, not easily upset or knocked off balance.

'You should see her, sir. Sometimes she just cries, and there's nothing I can do or say to help her, and quite often it's because she's bumped into *him*, and he's set her off again.'

'And what is *his* name?'

'Digby Jeffries. He lives in one of those four new houses just to the south of the village green. He's an old codger, or I'd have asked him to step outside to settle the matter long before

8

now.'

'Come on, Carmichael. We can't have you assaulting old-age pensioners. That wouldn't do the reputation of the police a jot of good. Have you tried to have a word with him and told him what effect he's having on Kerry?' Wise words, Falconer thought, but was then disabused.

'Yes! He actually gave this horrible little giggle, then said he was just passing the time of day, and was I sure it wasn't *me* being over-sensitive?'

'Sounds a right arse. Is there anything I can do?'

'I don't think so, sir. At least, not yet. I'll try talking to him again, and see how far I get,' Carmichael finished, and heaved a huge sigh. He really didn't need this hassle. And, in fact, neither did Falconer. Not only did he have his monthly report to finish, but there had been a spate of burglaries of garden furniture and statuary that was trying him to the limit, and no one yet had reported a sighting of the van that might be transporting these heavy items from gardens to God knows where.

Monday 6th December – afternoon

Even though the weather was bitingly cold and the roads slippery, Carmichael had stated that he was going home for lunch, giving no reason other than he thought it might be a good idea. He'd been in a subdued mood for the final half-hour of the morning, but would offer no reason for it. After his departure, Falconer had sent out for sandwiches, not wishing to brave the severity of the temperature if he could avoid it, and spent a quiet hour with his current reading matter – statements about the stolen garden accoutrements.

The hands of the old-fashioned wall clock had no sooner reached two o'clock when it seemed that time was repeating itself, and Carmichael stormed into the office again like an avenging angel, his face purple and twisted with fury. This time, without waiting to be asked, he burst into speech in a sort of strangled scream.

'He's done it again! She rang me just before lunch, but by

the time I got there, she was in a right old state. Something's got to be done about him!'

'I presume you're referring to Mr Jeffries again?' asked Falconer in a quiet, calm voice. There were so many suspect vans registered locally that it had been like looking for a needle in a haystack, and he was quite glad of the interruption.

'Yes I *bloody* well am! Mr *bloody* Jeffries had better watch out, or I'll strangle the *bloody* life out of the old villain!' This time, Carmichael's voice was a low and dangerous growl.

'Calm down, Sergeant. Just take a deep breath or two, sit down, and count to a hundred, or a thousand, if it helps, then see how you feel. Would you like me to have a word with this trouble-making old codger?' asked Falconer, as Carmichael sank reluctantly into his chair. 'Nothing official, you understand, but maybe I could drop into The Fisherman's Flies with you for a half sometime, and you could point him out to me. I presume he uses the pub. Gossipy old-woman types like him usually do, to spread their poison and pick up new ammunition.'

'Please, sir,' agreed the sergeant, tears forming in his eyes, now that his fury had abated, and with real anguish on his face, 'but not just yet. Let's leave it a couple of days, and see if he gets bored with taunting her.' His soft heart was breaking for Kerry, who usually coped with everything that life could throw at her without turning a hair. It could only be the effects of the pregnancy, but that didn't make the situation any easier.

'OK, so what horror story did he have for her this time?' asked Falconer, dreading to hear what this interfering old ferret had come up with this time to frighten a woman within a few weeks of giving birth.

'It was all about the number of newborn babies who are mutilated or killed by jealous pets who were in the household before they were born.'

'Monstrous! Silly old sod obviously needs to take up a hobby, or maybe start writing horror stories to stop him getting under the skin of other people.' This chap really knew how to stir up the emotions, choosing just the right material and delivering it at just the right time. He must be well-practised. Maybe a word from someone a little higher up the food chain would sort him out.

Friday 10th December

The raging roar started this time, presumably in the foyer of the station, and Falconer could hear it getting louder and louder as it approached his office. The office door nearly came off its hinges this time as it was flung open. Carmichael rushed through and headed straight for the nearest wall, beginning to bang his fists on it while uttering obscenities and threats.

Deciding that distance was the better part of valour in this case – Carmichael was in one hell of a temper, and had very big fists and lightning reflexes besides – he spoke slowly and calmly, hoping to distract his sergeant from his assault on Market Darley Police property. 'I presume Digby the Mouth has had another little dig. What did he say this time?' he asked, laying aside the paperwork he had been trying to clear from his desk.

It took a few minutes for Carmichael to stop thumping at the plaster, gather himself together, and sit down in the closest to a civilised manner as he could manage, given his current emotional state.

'I was in the shower this morning, and Kerry only opened the door to collect the milk, and there he was; just happened to be walking past – my big, fat, hairy arse, he was. This time he'd dug up even more horror stories, and told her a tale of big babies – referring to my size, obviously – being the cause of a lot of internal damage to the mothers, sometimes even maternal death.

'I had to go over to the shop to get some more milk. Kerry dropped ours, still in its bottle holder, with horror at what he was telling her. I took her over to her godparents at The Beehive, to spend the day there – though Marian seemed in rather a weird mood, and not really pleased to see us – then dropped the boys off at school. But, on the drive here, when I'd

11

had time to take in what had actually happened, I felt my temper start to rise, and as I approached the station, I knew I'd have to get inside, or risk behaving the way I just did outside and have to be restrained.'

'Thank God! I thought it might have been something I'd done,' said Falconer, more to make the younger man smile than because it was true. This sort of occurrence was becoming tediously repetitive. 'We're going to have to do something about this. We don't want Kerry to go into premature labour just because this joker gets his kicks from making other people feel uncomfortable or scared. And you say he's like this with everyone?'

'Yes. 'Can you make it tonight, and come to the pub with me? If he's there, maybe you could say something to him to make him stop.'

'No worries. I'll follow you home later, and we'll just drop in and see if he's in there. All I can do is my best, but I'll try to put the frighteners on him if I can.'

'Thank you, sir. Honestly, I don't know how I keep my hands off him.'

At Falconer's request, Carmichael telephoned Kerry at her godparents' home that afternoon and told her that he would be bringing a visitor home that evening, but not to worry about food, as Inspector Falconer was going to pick up fish and chips for them all on the way. It would save his wife cooking, and she was so very tired now at this advanced stage of pregnancy.

When they had done what they could for the day, Falconer followed Carmichael's battered old Skoda, both cars stopping once so that Falconer could be given instructions for what the other members of the family would like, then they headed straight for Castle Farthing. They had gone slightly out of their way to the chip shop on the Upper Darley parade for although there had been a tragic occurrence there just after Easter,[2] it still produced the best fried food in the area.

---

[2] See Battered to Death – A Falconer Files Brief Case

Kerry was back in her own home and greeted them with the table already laid for five, a pot of tea brewing in the centre, two plates of bread and butter, and all the condiments needed for a meal of this sort, but her face was puffy and her eyes swollen and red with weeping.

It simply wasn't fair, thought Falconer, that such a previously happy couple should have their simple existence blighted by the spite of a silly old man, whose obvious delight it was to tease and frighten the weaker and more vulnerable members of the community, and he felt his ire rising just at the thought of setting eyes on him.

Carmichael had immediately taken his rotund wife in his arms and begun kissing her hair and murmuring words of comfort to her, while she told him that she thought there was something seriously wrong with Auntie Marian. She'd been strange all day – sort of distracted and forgetful, and now she was really worried about her.

Carmichael did his best to explain that it was probably because Kerry was so sensitive and had been upset, that she was seeing something that simply wasn't there in her godmother, and that they should just concentrate on their own worries before taking on those of other people. She'd feel a lot better when both Christmas and the birth were over, and she must just try to keep calm for the remaining weeks so that her blood pressure didn't go too high.

For want of anything better to do, Falconer looked round their developing home and realised what a good job they were doing, turning two cottages into one. Where walls had once been, separating the space into tiny boxes, now there were sturdy RSJs holding up the structure, and making large open spaces that were much more conducive to life in the twenty-first century rather than the nineteenth.

The chimney that had been shared by both properties was now a central fireplace (surrounded by safety-guards, of course), the space opening out into what had been the cottage next door, to either side of it, making one room out of what had once been two tiny parlours and two minuscule dining rooms.

13

Both kitchens had also been joined together at the rear, and a downstairs shower room added into the mixture. The only indication that this had once been two dwellings was the presence of twin staircases, placed centrally where the two cottages had once divided, but, as far as the boys were concerned, this only added to the fun of their home, as the two landings had now been joined too, and they could now race up one staircase, through the new opening on the landing, and down the other stairs – a grand game!

This evening a hearty log fire burned in the grate and the atmosphere was cosy, the first few Christmas cards on display, adding to the atmosphere, as did the huge wicker basket of logs waiting to provide heat throughout the evening.

Falconer took himself off into the kitchen, extracted two enormous roasting tins from the storage drawer beneath the oven, and loaded the contents of his still-steaming packages into them. He'd bought enough to satisfy even the appetite of a Carmichael, Davey, DS. As he did so, he thought of his first sight this evening of the two boys, Dean and Kyle.

They were both squeezed into the seat of one armchair, the older boy with his arm around the younger, the younger one with his left thumb in his mouth, his right hand picking at the wool of the front of his jumper. To him, this was demonstration enough of how badly affected the boys were by their mother's distress. Usually, at Carmichael's entrance, they threw themselves at his legs, chattering away about their day and what they had done. Tonight they had sat in silence, cuddled together in the same chair for reassurance. He must do something to help.

After a few more minutes of comforting his wife, Carmichael loosed his embrace and found Falconer looking at the cards on display on the sideboard, apparently unperturbed by Kerry's display of distress, and her fears for her godmother, branded as just another symptom of raging hormones by her husband.

'Sorry about that, sir,' he mumbled, as he walked towards the kitchen, cheered to find that Falconer had turned on the oven and put the food in to warm. 'I'll just get the plates out.'

The food proved to be a good reviver of spirits, being the boys' favourite; for Kerry, something she hadn't had to cook; and, for her husband, lots. Just lots! That was fine by him. After the meal, however, when Kerry was clearing the table and shooing the boys upstairs to the bathroom before putting on their pyjamas, Falconer sat down opposite his sergeant, and said,

'We simply can't put up with Kerry getting herself into that state. Tell her we're off for a quick drink, and you can point this old joker out to me, while I think what on earth can be done about him. You say you've already had a word with him, and that's had no effect. Well, that says something for the thickness of the man's hide. If you'd had a word with me, I'd be terrified.'

'But I bet you can be more scary than me, sir. You've got this sort of … presence of menace when you're angry.'

'Have I?' queried Falconer, being totally unaware of just how intimidating he could appear when he was in a fury.

'It must be your army training, sir, because you scare the wits out of me sometimes.' Then, completely abandoning the subject, but leading to matters that arose from it, he called out, 'Leave the washing up for me, Kerry love, and I'll do it when I get back. We're just slipping over to The Fisherman's Flies for a quick one. I won't be long.' As he pulled on his warmest coat, a hand grabbed at his trousers, and he looked down to see Kyle standing there with an excited expression on his face. 'Got a surprise for you, Daddy,' he whispered, looking shyly at Falconer as he did so, 'but you can't have it until tomorrow.'

'Lucky, lucky me!' exclaimed his stepfather. 'I'll look forward to that all night. Now, you push off upstairs and get into the bath, because I think your mum's very tired, and would like to have a rest in front of the fire.'

'OK, Daddy, and …'

'What?'

'I love you,' said the little boy, flushing with the embarrassment of saying this in front of Uncle Harry, who didn't know about this little nightly ritual.

'I love you too, son. Now, off you go upstairs. Little angels,' he commented to Falconer as he reached to open the front door for them.

The wind took their breath away, blowing straight from the north with needles of ice in its breath, which stung their cheeks and closed their eyes in self-defence. There must have been a light dusting of snow between their arrival and now, but under this, where the temperature had dropped even further, was ice, and the going underfoot was treacherous.

Ignoring what anyone might say should they be seen, Carmichael put his arm through Falconer's so that they could help each other balance, for the pathway to the green was like a skating rink. Ears, noses, and fingers were red and stinging when they reached the pub's door, which was only across the green, and Falconer felt for anyone homeless who was outside on a night like tonight.

Inside, the heat of the log fire and the lights and good cheer lifted their spirits. Falconer got them a half-pint of shandy each, as neither was much of a drinker, and they settled down at a table that had a good view of the whole bar.

'That's him, down there!' muttered Carmichael, pointing discreetly at table level. 'Sitting with his 'new village' cronies, all previously involved with the media in some way, and so very smug because they consider themselves so much better than the 'turnips' who have lived here for generations.'

'But *you're* an incomer,' Falconer commented, as Carmichael had been a resident of the village for less than a year, and had only moved in after his wedding at New Year.

'I know, but I'm bred from the same soil. There's nothing hoity-toity about me, or any other of our neighbours, no matter how much money they've got or what they've achieved in the past. We're all just villagers. But these incomers, they're a breed apart, and they look down on everyone else, thinking themselves something special just because of what they did for a job.'

'Give me a rundown, then. There're five of them at that

table: four men and a woman. Put yourself in 'obs' mode, and tell me what you know, and what you see,' said Falconer, hoping to avoid a return of the anger that had completely overtaken his normally mild-mannered and polite sergeant that afternoon.

'Can you see the one that looks just like a garden gnome?' asked Carmichael, a storm clouding his brow with emotion.

'Yes! I see just what you mean. He only needs a little red hat and a fishing rod, and you could put him at the side of your garden pond any day of the week,' replied Falconer, still leaning towards a light-hearted manner, but Carmichael had been spot-on with his description. Even sitting down, he could see that the man indicated was not tall, but he was on the tubby side, with white hair and a white beard, and he seemed to be hell-bent on having his say within the group, his right index finger being waggled in the air for emphasis.

'That's Digby Jeffries, one-time employee of the BBC,' explained Carmichael, through clenched teeth, 'and the one on his left is Robin De'ath, ex-Channel 6. They're like a pair of terrible twins, lording it all over not just the locals, but over the other incomers as well.

'See that big man opposite Jeffries? He's also ex-BBC, but only radio, and the World Service to boot: Henry Pistorius. How they like to put him down because he was nothing to do with television. He holds his own, though. He's more than a match for them, and sometimes they come off the worse for tangling with him.'

'What about the scrawny fellow and the grey-haired lady?' asked Falconer, now genuinely interested in the characters that Carmichael was describing.

'The little chap is Cedric Malting, and he seems to have no character whatsoever.'

'What's he doing with the group of mighty incomers, then?' asked Falconer, getting into the mood now.

'He says he's a playwright, and can list quite of number of plays he says he's written, but none of them has ever been published or performed on a professional stage. A couple of them have had an amateur airing, and he thinks that puts him on a level with the others, but they look down their noses at him most of the time.'

Falconer forbore to mention the comedic sketch on class that had featured John Cleese, Ronnie Corbett, and Ronnie Barker, because he thought it unlikely that Carmichael would have seen a programme from such a long way back. But it made him smile, nevertheless, to think about the similarities between this and what Carmichael had just said. 'And what about the woman?' he asked, rekindling his interest after his little sortie into memory.

'She's a retired English teacher: tells them all about the appalling standard of English currently in use in broadcasting and in the media in general, and yearns for the days when English grammar lessons will be re-introduced into the school curriculum. Fat chance!'

'And you'd like me to have a little word with our *friend* Jeffries?'

While they were talking, however, the noise level from the table under scrutiny had risen, and the finger-wagging Jeffries was now waving his arms about in the air, and getting into a very agitated state. Henry Pistorius was also similarly roused and half-standing from his former sitting position, leaning across the table and hissing in anger.

At this point, George Covington appeared from behind the bar and approached the table, calling, 'Now, now, gentleman. No need for any bad feeling. Either drink up and make up, or I shall 'ave to ask you to leave these premises, for I won't 'ave no trouble in my bar.'

Digby Jeffries rose to his feet, pulled his coat from the back of his chair, dragged it on, and stumped his way to the door, without a word to any of the others he had been sitting with. As the door let in a blast of arctic air, Henry Pistorius burst out laughing, and the whole bar heard his deep voice comment, 'Piddling little pip-squeak!'

As George made his way back to the bar, having reassured himself that peace had broken out at the table Digby had left,

Falconer beckoned him to their table.

'What was all that about, then, George?' he asked.

'Police takin' an interest, are they?' asked the landlord with a gust of beery breath.

'Not really. Just nosiness, I suppose,' explained Falconer, not wishing to disclose why he had an interest in anything that upset Digby Jeffries.

'I'm not exactly sure, but if I know my Digby, I expect 'e was name-droppin' again. 'E's always doing it; I can almost 'ear the clangs from be'ind the bar. "When I met this celebrity ... When I was working on this show with ... When I was at so-and-so's party, I bumped into ..." 'E never gave up with the self-aggrandisement, and I expect the others just got tired of 'is boastin' and braggin'.

'Old 'Enry and that Robin 'ave achieved a lot more in their careers, I 'ear. That Jeffries, it turns out, was just a floor manager, but 'e keeps that to 'imself, and is wringing 'is BBC connections for every drop 'e can get out of them. It's not my place to tell anyone else what 'e actually did do, so I stay out of it. I reckon 'alf of his stories are made up, the other 'alf exaggerated out of all recognition, but 'e still thinks 'e's cock of the walk because 'e was BBC television staff.'

'Thanks very much for that information, George. I do believe it's put some powder in my flask. That man's been upsetting Carmichael's Kerry no end recently.'

'That man's upset just about everyone in the village. Tell 'er to take no notice of 'im. 'E's all wind and piss, when you get down to it. Tell him to stuff whatever 'e's been sayin' where the sun don't shine. I've just about 'ad enough of 'im. If 'e causes any more trouble in 'ere, I'm goin' to bar him, and that's a fact,' the landlord informed them.

'It doesn't quite work like that with pregnant women, though,' Carmichael stated lugubriously.

'Well, you got troubles of your own, lad. Give 'im a smack in the gob if 'e upsets 'er again. That should sort 'im out good and proper. None of us will tell on you.'

'I wish it were that easy,' sighed Carmichael.

'Well, don't you worry! 'E'll get 'is comeuppance one of these fine days, and I 'opes you're there to see it,' was George Covington's final comment on the matter, and throwing the drying cloth, which he habitually carried everywhere, over his shoulder, he strolled back behind the bar.

'I have a suspicion that George is right, you know. It didn't look as if he was flavour of the month over there. There must be a lot of other people who feel like you, and one of them is going to crack. Just make sure it's not you. And tell Kerry if she catches sight of him again to hide and not come out till he's gone,' Falconer advised him, draining his glass. 'Shall we go back to the cottage now, so that I can say goodnight to Kerry? I doubt he'll be back in here tonight.'

'OK, sir. And I'll try to keep my cool in future.'

Chapter Two

Saturday 25th December – Christmas Day, 2 a.m.

There were no stars and no moon to shed light on Castle Farthing. Only the light from the village green, children's bedrooms, landings, and from those careless enough to leave their Christmas lights on overnight, lit the centre of the village. The sky, though invisible, was still pregnant with snow, and a wind from the north-east howled in chimneys and eaves as it scoured through the little community, sculpting and shaping the surfeit of snow that had already fallen with more skill and artistic sensitivity than any human hand could have achieved, or eye envisaged.

At that hour, there were still footprints visible in the whiteness, evidence of some human movement and some activity carried out, but the ever-falling curtain of white soon filled the depressions and erased any trace of their existence. By daylight, no one would know that anything at all had occurred out in the open in the earliest hours of Christmas Day.

But there had been a lot of activity. There were a number of sets of prints which had been ploughed in the virgin covering which all led to the church, but one less leaving it. Anyone taking an overview of the village at this time would have seen from whence the footprints had come, and been able to work out with a fair degree of accuracy the chain of events which had led to the inevitable.

Doors had opened and closed quietly, not even spotted by the most dedicated youngster, still on watch for the arrival of Father Christmas, and later another set of footprints had joined the original tracks that had been made before the busy distraction in between.

Only the elements had been witness to what had happened, and as far as the human population was concerned, they were deaf to the voice of the elements, the elements being incapable of communication on mere human matters.

Friday 17th December

Carmichael had been making his entrance to the office for a week now with no more foul tempers. He had, however, raised a fair head of steam in Falconer. The 'surprise' that the boys had mentioned when Falconer had visited the Carmichael household had turned out to be a random-coloured knitted hat with ear-flaps and a sort of Mohican sprouting of multi-coloured wool from the nape of the neck to the front of the hat.

The boys said that they had saved their pocket money for it, because Daddy's head got so cold. Carmichael, touched more than he could express, had hardly had the thing off his head, and he looked extraordinarily like a gigantic chicken to his colleagues. No one would be able to take him seriously were he to talk to them with that on his head. Falconer had forbidden him to wear it when on official business, but he had it on every morning when he came into work, and replaced it on his head every evening when he left. Much to Falconer's embarrassment, he also wore it in the canteen, and raised many a smile and chuckle by doing so.

Carmichael considered that things like that hat made the world a happier place, and if there were enough of these little things, the world would be the better for it.

Falconer considered sitting at a separate table.

Later in the day, Carmichael raised the 'bogey' of Christmas. 'I asked you ages ago to spend it with us, sir – last December, if I remember rightly – and you said you would.'

'I know I did,' replied Falconer, desperately looking for a way out of his so-long-ago promise, 'but what about my little pride of felines? Don't they deserve Christmas as well?' he suggested, hoping to play on the soft side of Carmichael's nature.

'They can have Christmas any day of the year, sir, with respect. They're hardly crossing off the days on a calendar, are they?'

'No.' He had a feeling he was going to lose this one.

'Christmas Eve, Christmas Day, and Boxing Day,' said Carmichael, rubbing his hands together with glee. 'You can stay over, or go back to your little furry friends at night: your choice.'

'Three days?' queried the inspector, his voice higher than its normal pitch with panic at the thought of three days in the Carmichael household, with two tiny dogs, one of them pregnant, a cat, two boisterous children, a pregnant woman, and the great galumphing galoot that was his sergeant.

'It would be such a help to Kerry, although she doesn't realise it. Christmas will be so much more work for her, and if I try to help her she always refuses and does things herself. With you there, I can say we'll do the clearing away and the washing-up, and she can hardly turn down an offer from my superior officer, can she?' the sergeant pleaded.

Bugger! thought Falconer, and agreed with a heavy heart. He knew he'd enjoyed his brief window on a Carmichael Christmas the previous year, but he was looking forward to getting back to his own routines with no other humans involved. He'd already turned down invitations from both his parents and his aunt Ursula, and was looking forward to a bit of seasonal peace and quiet, never mind goodwill to all men: cats were less demanding, and a morsel or two of seasonal meats would work wonders as a bribe to *their* peace and quiet.

'With the weather like it has been, we might even get a white Christmas this year. It's certainly looking that way,' said Carmichael with longing in his voice, and Falconer's spirits took another nose-dive. That was the last thing he needed; to be snowed in with the Carmichaels until God knows when.

'With my luck, we probably will,' was Falconer's only comment, and for a few seconds, he lowered his head into his hands and said a little prayer that this should not come to pass.

That evening, Digby Jeffries entered his house with a smile of triumph on his face. That talk with Alan Warren-Browne, one of the former church wardens, had done him a huge favour and, with the knowledge he had gleaned, he had been able to achieve an ambition he had held gleefully to himself for the last few months.

Gossiping in the post office, the general store, and out and about, he had learnt that during the years when St Cuthbert's had had its own vicar, there had always been someone to play the part of Father Christmas at the crib service for the children on the afternoon of Christmas Eve. Further probing had discovered that this had been carried out by the same man for decades: one Albert Carpenter of Woodbine Cottage, the last in the row which ended at the boundary of The Old Manor House's grounds, and included the two cottages that the Carmichaels now owned.

Albert Carpenter had not been averse to having the occasional visit from Jeffries, and he had learnt that the old man intended to continue this role while he still had breath in his body. He was currently eighty-nine years of age, and getting decidedly unsteady on his feet.

What an opportunity! Jeffries had thought, and had then worked on his well-honed technique of extracting information from people to ascertain from the ex-postmaster the name of the vicar who would be conducting the Christmas services in Castle Farthing this year.

Just a little more wheedling and prying had produced an address for the retired vicar; one to which he had hastened that very day to raise the subject of the man behind the red suit. Albert Carpenter was obviously of unsound health, claimed Jeffries, citing recent visits to Albert's home, and his advanced age; this being the case, he volunteered his own services, real white beard included, along with the promise not to trim it this side of the festivities.

Rev. Searle had fallen for his taradiddle hook, line, and sinker, and Jeffries had been duly appointed to the role with alacrity when he claimed he also had the outfit, used in years gone by in his former parish of residence.

This was in fact an outright lie, as he had bought his costume before offering his services in that previous parish and been turned down flat, having been informed that there was a waiting list to play the role and he would just have to await his opportunity in the fullness of time – which meant 'never', in the then incumbent's opinion. Said incumbent was always uneasy in Jeffries' company, and had a few shrewd suspicions that would preclude the man for ever from the role.

The red suit had hung at the back of his wardrobe ever since, being placed in the same position when he moved to Castle Farthing, and had hung there ever since. He had, of course, used it for his grandchildren's Christmases but, now he was divorced, he was not being included in the arrangements for the festive season this year, this being his ex-wife's year as the honoured guest.

Poor red suit! Always the bridesmaid and never the bride! Now it had an opportunity to have a proper public airing, and not just in the living room of wherever he had happened to spend Christmas.

Of course, he'd said nothing to Albert Carpenter. Let him presume all he wanted. By the time that old codger had dusted off his no doubt ancient costume, it would be far too late. The die was cast.

Hugging this fact to himself, he headed straight for his bedroom, where he undressed and tried on the costume, posturing and posing in front of the cheval-glass, and booming, 'Ho, ho, ho!' in a variety of volumes and pitches. When he bored of this, he moved the long glass to where he could see his side of the bed, and used a well-plumped-up feather pillow as a child, cradling it on his knee, and practising his 'spiel' for use in just a week's time. How he was looking forward to it.

Eventually he came out of what had seemed like a semi-trance, and thought, Oh, you'll dance to my tune all right, because if you don't, I'll stop playing; and when I stop playing, the Heavens will fall.

Always a bumptious little man, he had begun to turn spiteful, bullying, and domineering in his mid-fifties, and this was the main but by no means the only reason that his wife had left him. As a young man, he had been the life and soul of any party, but as he aged and realised he would never progress beyond what he was, he had turned sour and bitter, and the only things that made him happy were upsetting others and getting the better of anyone; it didn't matter who it was, as long as he came out on top.

While Jeffries was thus employed, several other inhabitants of Castle Farthing were cursing his name and the very day he had arrived in their midst.

In his anticipation of triumph, and while waiting for the appointed time for his meeting with Rev. Searle, he had divided his time between several of the local establishments, his mood infused with a particularly high level of spite.

In The Rookery in the High Street, right next door to the tea shop which she ran, Rebecca Rollason was in tears, telling her husband Nick of the scene Jeffries had caused that lunchtime in her establishment. He had only ordered a cup of coffee, and she usually insisted that something to eat – even if it was just a toasted teacake – was purchased with a drink, during this sometimes very busy period, but she had said nothing to Jeffries because he was a local.

This elicited no loyalty to her, however, as he had called her over after a couple of sips from his cup, and declared, in an unnecessarily loud voice, that she had used instant coffee. All the faces at the other tables had turned in their direction, as she explained that she only used the very best Costa Rican beans, and ground them herself.

This cut no mustard with this particular customer, though, and she found herself getting into quite a heated discussion about the source of this particular drink. Eventually, with a red face, she had led him behind the counter and into the small kitchen, and shown him the unground and ground beans. His flippant comment – 'Oops!' – was made out of earshot of anyone else in the establishment, and several customers had left in the time it had taken to convince him of the veracity of her ingredient.

'And when I think what I could have said about him, if I hadn't been so polite! The Lord only knows what those customers will think of the place, the fuss he made. It was obviously pure spite, for my coffee tastes nothing like instant. And it was the way that he did it. Not just calling me over and whispering in my ear, but calling out like that, so that everyone in the tea room could hear. He manipulated me into taking him behind the scenes, knowing that people would leave, and with an erroneous impression of my standards.'

Her husband Nick took out his handkerchief and dried her tears, offering what words of comfort he could muster. He was a farmer, a recent change of occupation as he had been thoroughly sick of his former work in the insurance business, and his talents lay in his fitness and strength, and in his hands, for he was not a natural wordsmith. 'Don't you be the one to start the rumours, love. You just keep your dignity. He'll get his comeuppance one of these days, you mark my words. You're not the only one who's seen things.'

'I don't know how I kept my mouth shut,' she wept.

'There, there, love,' he spoke softly to her. 'Your regulars know your standards, and no one has ever queried them. Anyone who was there, and who has tried your coffee, must know what good stuff it is, and if they don't, then they don't deserve to drink it.'

'But what shall I do?' she wailed.

'Stop all this silly weeping – there – you've woken Tristram now.' Tristram was their three-year-old son. 'They've been putting up the tree on the green for the last couple of hours. I should think it would be about time for them to turn the lights on. Shall we get Tristram down, just this once, and all wrap up and go out to have a look?'

That did the trick, for now, but Rebecca Rollason was already harbouring a deep grudge in her heart for the needless spite that had been directed against her that afternoon, considering what she knew about the man.

Alan Warren-Browne was seething about treatment of a very different sort, but from the same source, and was only now calm enough to tell his wife Marian about it.

'I was quietly queuing in Allsorts, when I went to fetch some more painkillers and butter for your shortbread, when I found that objectionable little gnome behind me. Before I knew what was happening, he had worked out of me what I was going to buy, and then started making the most obscene insinuations about the frequency and duration of your headaches.

'He'd obviously been told about them, and asked me if you'd suffered from them on our honeymoon, and he nudged me twice, winked twice, and then actually said, 'Nudge, nudge! Wink, wink!' As if that wasn't enough, he said he knew a lot of men who had been denied their conjugal rights, but that he knew a woman in Market Darley who would oblige for a very low price. And then he had the cheek to add, 'if I didn't already know her'! I could have punched his lights out.

'And to think he worked all that information out of me without me suspecting a thing,' he added, changing the subject completely, then returning to it without batting an eyelid. Marian knew what he was talking about. Didn't she?

'Most of the people in the queue – the shop was of course in the middle of a mini-rush – knew us, but there were a few from Manor Fields that I'd never set eyes on before, and what they thought of his little pantomime is nobody's business. He's either a very spiteful man, or he has a twisted sense of humour: probably both, because I don't know anyone else who has a good word to say about him.

'And now *I've* got a headache, *too*. Damn and blast the man!'

Rosemary Wilson, Kerry Carmichael's aunt, who ran Allsorts, had done something very out of character for her. She had taken herself off to the local pub for a drink to calm herself down. She had witnessed the little incident with Alan Warren-Browne in her shop earlier that day, and had also not long been privy to the information that Jeffries had been terrorising her niece with horror stories of pets and babies and childbirth. She felt fit to burst if she didn't find someone to talk to about it and get a couple of relaxing drinks down her neck at the same time.

Glad to see that the object of her disapproval was not in the bar, she ordered herself a large sherry, and espied the Brigadier and Joyce, just settling themselves at a table near the log fire. They would do, she thought, and made her way over to them to ask if they'd mind if she joined them.

The Brigadier was in a fine old fury, confirmed not just by the colour of his face, but by the way he just threw his pink gin down his throat and slammed the glass on the table, calling out to the bar for a refill.

'What's eating you?' asked Rosemary, innocently enough, and was then bowled over by his angry tirade.

'That bloody man! That bloody dreadful little ... little ... cad! Bounder!' he began, banging both his fists on the table.

'Come along, Godfrey. Remember your blood pressure. Calm down before you start talking, or you'll just work yourself up into a right old tizzy,' advised Joyce, his wife, putting a hand on his arm to pacify him.

At that moment George Covington the landlord approached the table with a glass on a tray. 'I made sure it was a large 'un,' he stated, before transferring the glass to the table, and winking at Joyce conspiratorially.

'Thanks, old man. Just shove it on this evening's slate, and I'll settle up later,' replied the Brigadier, having blown down the boiler considerably to give such a polite answer.

'Come along,' cajoled Joyce. 'Tell Rosemary all about it, and it'll make you feel better.'

Rosemary interrupted at this point, to say, 'If it's the same man who's got me all wound up, I can tell my story afterwards, and then we can make a little wax doll of him and stick pins in it together.'

This lightened the atmosphere somewhat, but the Brigadier

looked as if he was actually taking her suggestion seriously for a moment.

'It's that blasted Jeffries man. The one who's always boasting about his time at the BBC, and all the celebrities he was on first name terms with: kiss my arse and all that.'

'Ditto,' confirmed Rosemary, and the Brigadier relaxed enough to give her a small smile.

'There you go, Godfrey. Now you two can have a nice bitching session and make each other feel better.'

'I wouldn't put it quite like that, Joyce,' he replied, but, nevertheless, put his elbows on the table and leaned forward, so that he could tell his tale without the chance of there being too many eavesdroppers.

'The blighter just turned up on the doorstep earlier. No telephone call to let us know he was coming. No appointment, no invitation. Nothing! Always doing that. Damned bad form, in my opinion.' The Brigadier spoke in a rather telegraphic way, which was a habit which became more pronounced when he was cross about something. Tonight he was beyond cross.

'Walked straight into me billiards room when Joyce opened the door without a bye-your-leave or anything. I was settin' up a battle scene on the baize,' (the Brigadier was an inveterate collector of model soldiers and re-enactor of battles), 'when the blighter just waltzed in and asked me which battle it was.

'I, of course, ignored his enormous lapse in manners, and replied in as courteous a manner as I could muster, under the circumstances. Bounder stood there with his head on one side for a moment or so, then told me I'd laid it out all wrong.

'Damn it all! I've been laying out that same battle scene for more than forty years, and he just swans in and tells me I don't know what I'm doing.'

'Godfrey's going to do a battle re-enactment on the snooker table in the back room here, the day after Boxing Day,' Joyce explained, to enlighten her husband's listener as to the point of what he had been doing, when he had been so unexpectedly interrupted.

'That was it, as far as I was concerned. I told him he was a bloody ignorant nincompoop, grabbed him by the scruff of his neck, propelled him out of the house, and dumped him on the doorstep. Spoilt my day; and I'd been looking forward to having a dress rehearsal, too. Blackguard! By Gad, I'd like to give him a damned good thrashing!'

'I told him just to ignore the fellow, but you know what Godfrey is. He spent hours after that, checking the details in what must have been about a dozen different books, and in the end I dragged him down here to cool off. What about you, Rosemary? Tell us your tale of woe,' said Joyce, looking at her husband's colour and seeing that he felt better already for having told someone else about this upsetting little incident.

'It's my niece, Kerry. You know? The one that's married to a policeman and lives in Jasmine Cottage?'

'Go on,' urged Joyce, and Rosemary began her story of Jeffries' cruel attempts to put the wind up a pregnant woman, then recounted her tale of Alan Warren-Browne's uncomfortable encounter in her establishment earlier that day. 'And to think, if it hadn't been for him, that terrible old man would never have got permission to play Father Christmas in the church this year.'

At a table at the far end of the pub, there was a similarly acrimonious conversation in full swing regarding the same person that was being discussed at the table near the fire.

There were only four people sitting round it, and these were Henry Pistorius, Cedric Malting, Robin De'ath, and Alice Diggory. Conspicuous by his absence this evening was Digby Jeffries, and he was the sole subject of conversation. Without his presence, they could all be honest about the way he treated them individually, and were getting things off their chest with enthusiasm.

'I can't believe the sheer cheek of the man,' Alice Diggory said, shifting in her chair in a wriggling motion as her anger took form. 'He was always telling me that he knew much more about English grammar than did I. I wrote a piece for the Parish Council magazine recently, and he lectured me at inordinate length about my use of grammar.' Although the church was no longer in regular use, the magazine had been kept going as a means of keeping the villagers in touch with events planned in the locality.

'Of course, it was all a load of old codswallop. I don't know where he was taught English, but I should imagine it was in one of the old secondary modern schools, for he had no idea even about singulars and plurals. Kept saying things like, 'The BBC are,' instead of 'The BBC is'. I tried explaining to him that the BBC was '*a* corporation', and therefore, singular. He, of course, insisted that, as it had so many employees, it was plural. No amount of example, like 'the crowd *is* on the pitch', and 'the members of the crowd *are* on the pitch' convinced him.' She was getting in a high old state just talking about Jeffries.

'He dismissed all my objections, saying that I had become out of touch with the language since I had retired, whereas it was obvious that he had no basic schooling in the subject. I could have slapped his silly, smirking face. At the end of it he suggested I invest in a good grammar book and brush up on my subject. I don't think I've ever been so cross with anyone before. He's got a skin like a rhinoceros!'

The other two, who had listened with interest, tried to placate her as she had become quite worked up with recounting the tale, and Cedric Malting launched into his particular grievance as a means of solace to the angry woman.

'You've no idea how much he belittles me. I've written more than a dozen plays over the years, and I'm proud of all of them. Three of them have been put on, to full houses, I might add, by amateur dramatic societies, and got good reviews in the local papers.

'He pooh-poohed that, of course, emphasising the 'amateur' status of the actors, and said I could not count on any degree of real success until the BBC had not only bought, but broadcast something I'd written. He couldn't see beyond the bloody BBC. You would have thought that no other broadcasting service in the world existed. He called me an amateur hack who ought to give up gracefully, and read plays written by some of the great playwrights of the twentieth century to learn from them.

'He's never even read, let alone seen, one of my plays, yet he made those sweeping swingeing criticisms, based on nothing whatsoever except his own inflated ego and his sense of superiority. I went home after that conversation and kicked the front step until I'd taken the top off the leather of my shoe, just imagining it was him I was damaging.'

'Oh, you poor thing!' cooed Alice, putting a hand on his shoulder to comfort him. 'I'll look at your plays anytime. At least I can speak the lingo grammatically, and give you a fair opinion based on my experience of teaching English grammar, language, and literature. Just drop something round anytime, and I'll look at it straight away.'

'Thank you very much, Alice, dear,' replied Cedric, looking quite uplifted by this generous offer. 'I'd be happy for you to read my work.'

Henry Pistorius broke up this tender little moment with his own grievance. 'What about me, then,' he said, in his deep and carrying voice. 'I could match him, BBC for BBC, but because I worked in BBC Radio, mostly on the World Service, he had me down as a third-class citizen. He looked down on the four best-known radio stations, but his view of anything else – local stations and the World Service – well, he thought they were less than dust.

'Nothing I could say would sway him on that. He put what I did throughout my entire career on a par with hospital radio. Can you imagine how that made me feel?'

'I can, actually!' It was Robin De'ath who had spoken. 'It was just as bad for me, because although I worked in television, it was for Channel 6. He thought the channel produced nothing but dross and sensationalism with a good dose of rubbish thrown into the mix.

'It might have been a bit like that when it first hit the air-waves, but over the last five or six years it's done some very in-depth and hard-hitting documentaries and exposed a lot of sleaze in many quarters. He seemed to view me as some sort of tea-boy. He looked down his nose at me, and there were times when I wanted to tap his claret for him.'

'Why do we put up with him, then?' asked Alice, with absolute logic.

'I've absolutely no idea,' answered Henry, and the others offered answers along exactly the same lines.

'I propose,' said Henry Pistorius, raising his glass, 'that we expel Digby Jeffries from our little social circle. He shall be *persona non grata* from henceforth.'

'I say, Henry, that's a bit strong, isn't it? It could be very awkward in a small village like this,' Alice challenged him.

'Well, I'm not going to socialise with him any more. It only makes me angry. You others must do as your consciences dictate.'

'I'm with you,' agreed Robin De'ath, but from the other two there was no decision vocalised, and they sat staring into their drinks in an embarrassed silence.

Chapter Three

Only five days before Christmas Eve, the Carmichael household was a seething mass of anticipation, excitement, last-minute bustle, and bursts of Christmas carols and songs, Slade's 1973 seasonal offering proving the most popular for all the family.

Carmichael was sitting at the base of the Christmas tree, which had this year been placed under the stairs to stop the dogs and cat from knocking it over every time they swept through the house. He was wrapping up a few presents for people in the village, and stopped to remark, 'We'd better give Slade and Wizzard a miss if we're going to the crib service. We'll need to know proper carols for that, so I think we ought to practise a few. Shall I put on a CD?'

'Yes,' the other three chorused, and he rose to sort out the music.

'Did I tell you that I spoke to Uncle Harry, and he *is* coming for Christmas?' he asked, ingenuously.

The two boys cheered, but Kerry asked, 'How long have you known that, you secretive monster, you?'

'Only since Friday,' he answered, and Kerry threw a cushion at his head.

'You might have said something on Friday, so I could have got in a bit of extra shopping yesterday.'

'A bit of extra shopping? Whatever for? You've got enough food in this house to feed the five thousand, and the inspector's only one more mouth, not a plague of locusts. We'll be absolutely fine, and we'll have loads left over when all of us have eaten – and I include the dogs and the cat in that statement.'

Kerry put down a second cushion that she was intending to hurl at him, and thought for a moment. 'You're right!' she admitted, after a short silence. 'Everyone does exactly the same thing and always gets far too much in, then some of it goes to waste. I won't buy another thing until after Boxing Day.'

'That's my girl!' Carmichael said, with a smile, then added, 'I doubt you'd get through many shop doors, the size you've suddenly grown to.'

Kerry picked up the cushion again, and aimed it at his stomach with pin-point accuracy.

'Oof! That was a heavy one!' her husband exclaimed, as the missile caught him in the midriff.

'I'm thinking of having one of them stuffed with bricks, for just this sort of occasion,' his wife retorted. 'Now, get that CD on, so that we can sing along to some real old-fashioned carols.'

Over the strains of 'Silent Night', Carmichael made a rough inventory of their preparations for the festive seasons, and began to tick things off on his fingers as he recited, 'Tree – decorated: check. Paper chains and bells: check. Christmas cards strung on walls: check. Presents wrapped and under tree: check. Silly seasonal ornaments strewn all over the place: check.'

This last item earned him another cushion-missile.

The Falconer household was much quieter and more grown-up in comparison. The inspector had no paper chains, tinsel bells, or silly seasonal ornaments. He had holly and trailing ivy in a couple of vases, a small sprig of mistletoe suspended over the door to his living room (ambitious to the last), and his cards sensibly kept in order on a cardboard card-tree.

For his Christmas tree, he had taken special precautions this year as last year, even with only the three cats, he had been forever picking it up and tidying the baubles. This year, with a fourth cat added to his menagerie, he had screwed a white plastic-covered hook into the ceiling above where it stood and attached a length of almost invisible fishing line to this. The other end of it he had firmly tied round the central mass of the tree, thus securing it firmly, and he hoped this little wheeze would at least keep it upright, even if he did have to replace some of its baubles with irritating frequency.

This year, he had added to his household the silver-spotted Bengal, Meep (or Perfect Cadence, as she was registered), and he could hardly blame his quartet for being fascinated by this once-a-year contraption that offered so many objects to pat and paw and steal and gnaw. If he were a cat, he knew he'd be the worst offender of them all.

The thought of Meep jogged his memory, and he went to get his camera to take a few shots of her as she patted a bauble. She had come into his possession in June, previously the property of a murderess, and he had promised faithfully to look after her.[3] Knowing how he felt about the cats he already had, he transferred the prints to his computer and printed them off on photographic paper.

Taking a padded envelope from the drawer in which he kept his stationery, he parcelled them up and addressed the envelope to Ms B. Ironmonger, then added the name of the women's prison that held this individual. Although he had no duty to do this, he did it out of compassion. There were precious few happy moments in a prison, but this little packet would provide a heart-warming moment or two this Christmas.

This dealt with, he cleared his mind of those past unhappy events and went up to his bedroom, where he had concealed in his wardrobe, several presents for his feline companions. Although he felt a bit of a fool going to such lengths, he wanted to wrap them in secret, so that they would be a real surprise for the quartet on the day. He understood that he was anthropomorphising, but could not help himself. With no children to spoil, these furry personalities were his only indulgence, and his particular soft spot.

In The Fisherman's Flies in Castle Farthing, George and Paula Covington were clearing up after the lunchtime session. As they

---

[3] See *Murder at The Manse*

collected and washed glasses, disposed of empty crisp and other snack packets, and wiped down the tables and the bar, George aired his today's grievance to his wife.

'I've a good mind to bar that Digby Jeffries! Do you know what 'e said to me this lunchtime?'

'Wossat?' asked his wife, not paying him any particular attention.

''E only went an' accused me of watering the Scotch; that's what 'e went and did. Then 'e ordered a pint o' bitter, as if to prove 'is point, and had the blasted cheek to tell me that my pipes weren't properly cleaned, 'cos 'is beer was cloudy.' George was highly indignant at this snipe at his integrity as the licensee of a public house.

'Cheeky bugger!' replied Paula. ''E needs 'is ears given a good boxin', that's what 'e needs. I reckon 'e's upset just about everyone in the village since 'e moved 'ere.'

'Well, I'll overlook it 'cos of the festive season, but come New Year, any more nonsense like that, and 'e'll be out on 'is ear. I'll bar the bugger, you see if I don't.'

'And I'll be right behind you, George,' replied Paula. 'There's several times 'e's been in 'ere when 'e's tried to cop a feel, and I'm not gonna stand for it any longer. Dirty old sod needs 'is 'ands cut orf, if you ask me.'

'You never said anything before! Why not?' queried her husband.

''Cos I didn't want to cause any trouble, but I've been 'earin' things about 'ow 'e treats other people, and I've decided that enough is enough. Our takin's'd probably go up if 'e wasn't in 'ere so much, upsettin' other folks who only came out to enjoy a quiet drink.'

'That's a plan, then,' agreed George, effectively putting an end to that topic of conversation, then immediately opening it again to tell her about the Brigadier.

'I 'ad a phone call from the old Brigadier yesterday afternoon. I never said anythin' about it, because I managed to get it sorted out, but as we've been on the topic, it seems that that old git Jeffries had dropped in on 'im without an invite, and given 'im a lecture on the battle 'e's goin' to re-enact for us in the back room. Told 'im 'e didn't know what 'e was doin', and the old boy was so upset, 'e only wanted to cancel the whole thing.

'Well, I told 'im not to take any notice of old motor-mouth, Mr Know-it-All, and managed to persuade 'im to go ahead as planned. It's only when you talk about it, that you realise just 'ow much trouble one man can cause. We've 'ad nothin' like that in this village since old Reg Morley popped 'is clogs.'

''E didn't actually pop them naturally, though, did 'e?' commented Paula, and they shared a few moments of silence as they remembered the tragic events that had occurred in the village in the summer of the previous year.

Chapter Four

Friday 24th December – morning

Unusually for one so prompt, Carmichael was late arriving at the station, and offered his apologies to Falconer with an air of suppressed glee, bouncing on his toes with excitement, and his face lit with an inner glow of anticipation, as he smiled like a lunatic for no obvious reason.

'Come on, spit it out! What have you been up to now?' asked the inspector, beginning to feel anxious about his planned visits to the Carmichael household.

'Just a little surprise present for the family,' explained Carmichael, and seemed to be overwhelmed with mirth at this simple statement.

'What are you plotting now?' This boded no good for Falconer's Christmas.

'It's a secret, sir,' his sergeant replied with maddening simplicity.

'Will I like it?' This needed further investigation.

'It's not for you, sir,' beamed Carmichael, starting to click his fingers and boogie on the spot.

'I'm not going to like it at all, am I, Carmichael?'

'Not for me to say, sir. Now, about the arrangements for later. You know how this lot get on Christmas Eve,' Carmichael began. 'Everybody not on duty just parties the afternoon away if they're not a designated driver.'

'Yes,' was Falconer's tentative reply.

'Well, we don't really drink, do we, sir?'

'No-ooo ...' Falconer was getting more and more suspicious.

'So, I thought we could just toddle off about one-ish, after an early lunch, so we could get back to ours to be in good time for the crib service at three. We're all going to that, and I thought you'd like to come along as well.'

'OK!' This didn't sound too awful. 'But we'll have to take a diversion to my place, so that I can change the cats' water, top up their food, and clean out the litter tray.'

'No problem, sir. So, it's a date!' And at this, Carmichael began to get that look in his eyes again as he sat down at his own desk, boogying in his seat and making it creak ominously. There was only so much strain that a standard office chair could take, and Carmichael was a heavy load to bear.

As an afterthought, he added, 'We can go to Midnight Mass as well, if you like. Kerry's Auntie Rosemary said she'd sit in and listen out for the children.'

'That would be nice, thank you, Sergeant. It's probably my favourite service of the year, and most years the only one I can get to.'

During the morning, the locum vicar, Rev. Searle, arrived at The Fisherman's Flies where he was going to take a room for the night. He intended to conduct a full family Eucharist on Christmas morning, before returning to his empty bungalow in Carsfold. His wife had died some two years ago, and both of his children were going away for Christmas, giving him good reason to take up the opportunity to preside in St Cuthbert's and relive a little of his past when he had been a respected and useful member of a community.

He was looking forward to the three services he would conduct, and the company he would have, instead of the still silence of the bungalow with only the odd burst of seasonal television and radio to interrupt its quiet. Without a wife or parish, his life was now solitary. No parishioners turned up at his door asking for advice or help, no phone rang to book a wedding or a baptism, even a funeral.

There were no more PCC meetings, no more choir practices; in fact no more anything. He had been feeling particularly surplus to requirements when he had been asked if he would come to Castle Farthing for these two days, and that man who had visited him to ask about playing Father Christmas had made him swell with a little seasonal warmth and anticipation.

And the landlord of the pub in which he had booked a room had been most welcoming, and asked him if he would like to join them for Christmas dinner. All in all, this would probably be the best Christmas he had spent since his wife had passed on.

His room was clean, aired, and welcoming, and his only worry was at the sprinklings of snow that occasionally flurried down. On reflection, though, what did it matter if there were a lot more snow? He had no one to rush home to, and he could certainly afford to stay on a bit longer in this genial hostelry with the remuneration he would get for his services.

Plumping his suitcase on to the bed, he looked around him, and his face broke out into a rare smile. The room reminded him of the one he had stayed in at his grandmother's as a child, up here in the eaves as it was, and he felt an unaccustomed wave of happiness wash over him. It grew a little stronger as there was a sharp knock at his door, and Paula Covington entered, bearing a tray with fresh coffee and biscuits for his elevenses.

'How very thoughtful of you,' he commented, taking the tray from her and setting it on the bedside table.

'All part of the service, Vicar. Just call if you need anything. I'll be in the bar, bottling-up for the lunchtime rush. We'll probably be rushed off our feet this dinner, and we'll definitely be overrun tonight. Still, at least at closing time we can send them on their way to you, so that they can have a damned good singsong before they go home,' she commented, thoughtlessly condemning him to the anticipation of the arrival of a horde of drunks at his Midnight Mass.

She said nothing about George's plans to open for a short period after the late service, so that everyone could have a last snifter, as they didn't have permission for this and would be doing it on the sly.

Falconer and Carmichael finally arrived in Castle Farthing at a quarter to two, the sky already darkening and the flurries of snow getting more frequent and heavier. As they got out of their cars, Falconer looked around him at the village in its festive clothing. The parish tree was a marvel of lights and heavy-duty tinsel, the shops and pub were alight with colour too and through each cottage window glowed the electric rainbow of Christmas tree lights.

With the slight covering of snow in the failing light, the village looked like a life-size 3D greetings card. Someone had even scraped up the modest offering of snow and made a tiny snowman by the village pond, so tiny that its carrot nose was as long as the whole figure was high, and was doomed to fall to the ground in the very near future.

The village pond itself was covered in a very thin layer of ice. In some parts it was so thin that it gave access to the few ducks that braved an afternoon swim in these temperatures; it was much thicker in others, where they would slither and slide, confused as to why their natural element had suddenly become their enemy. Unless the temperature went up considerably, these poor aquatic birds were condemned, for a while, to be the laughing stock of anyone who was out and about watching their antics.

Having been left on his own outside to contemplate the scenery, Falconer was suddenly exhorted to come on in before all the heat went out through the front door. There was no hall, and one stepped straight into the living room, thus there was no way to keep the heat in the living room once the door was open.

Grabbing his bag from the passenger seat, which was filled with presents for the family who had so kindly bullied him into spending Christmas with them, he made his way swiftly into the house, to be engulfed in a sea of people and animals, all anxious to greet their honoured guest.

When he was free from the melee, he handed his holdall to Carmichael to put his contribution to tomorrow under the tree with the rest of the presents, and looked round him. His first impression was that he had strayed into a department store's Christmas grotto. Every surface was crammed with novelties and ornaments manufactured specifically for the season of goodwill.

Carmichael, he noticed, had to adopt a gorilla walk in the room, so many decorations were there hanging from the comparatively low ceiling of the cottage. And the tree must have had several strings of lights twined round it for it to glow so brightly; he felt he almost needed sunglasses to look at it.

At the foot of the tree, and climbing up its trunk (for it was a real fir tree) and into the bottom-most branches, were piled wrapped gifts, large and small, and in great number. Carmichael was surely the Ghost of Christmas Present, with all this largesse of the season.

Holly was pinned to the picture rail and a sprig of mistletoe hung from the doorway into the kitchen, and Falconer made an early decision not to go into that part of the house unless there were no adults present. For one thing, he didn't think he could reach Kerry's cheek to kiss her because of the roundness of her figure and, for another, he didn't trust Carmichael's sense of humour further than he could throw a grand piano.

The two boys were already scrabbling about under the tree to 'cop a feel' of the gifts, trying to identify the contents of each of the newly added presents, and Kerry settled her bulk, one hand in the small of her back, the other on the arm of a comfy chair, and sighed with exhaustion.

Christmas was not the time to be heavily pregnant, and her resources were severely drained with the extra weight she was carrying, combined with all the work involved in creating a magical Christmas for her boys and husband, as they had never before spent this part of the year as a married couple, and she wanted it to be really special.

Noting her tiredness, Falconer hastened to assure her that he was not there to add to her load, more to lighten it, as he and Carmichael would do everything they could to help her. Arriving at the chair with a footstool, her husband agreed with this sentiment, and carefully elevated her slightly swollen legs into a higher position to rest them.

'I can manage,' she claimed, but her eyes had dark circles

under them from the lack of sleep that the last stage of pregnancy always brings. The unborn baby is so large that its movements are a constant source of wakefulness at night, and the engaging head an unwelcome pressure on the bladder, meaning more sleep disturbance as it boogied and danced.

'You know you don't have to come to either the crib service or the midnight mass,' Carmichael informed her. 'No one will criticise you for needing a bit of extra rest, and we two men can easily cope with these two monsters,' he said, reaching out his hands and ruffling Dean and Kyle's hair, 'at the earlier one. They'll be dead to the world during Midnight Mass, and it would save your Aunt Rosemary a trip across the green in the biting cold.'

'Davey,' she responded, 'You are a mind-reader. I really didn't fancy going out, especially because of how slippery it is after those snow flurries. I'd hate to fall, at this late stage,' she said, massaging her bursting belly with her right hand. 'If I hurt the baby, I would never be able to forgive myself. And anyway, I think my Braxton-Hicks contractions are starting, and that's always an uncomfortable time.'

'Your what? Your contractions are starting?' Carmichael was suddenly all arms and legs. 'Where's your hospital bag? Can you babysit while I take Kerry to the hospital? This is all too early and unexpected. The nursery's not quite ready. What should I do first? Should I ring up your godparents and your auntie? What about other relatives? What about Father Christmas?'

'*Shut up*!' the normally quietly spoken Mrs Carmichael yelled, to quench the cascade of questions that fell from her husband's lips. 'I said Braxton-Hicks contractions. They're the practice contractions that can start a while before the baby's born.

'If you'd ever managed to get the time off to come to the antenatal classes with me, you'd know what I was talking about, but I know that your work has to come first because of its very nature.' Kerry's voice had softened; she knew her Davey only meant well.

Carmichael meanwhile was left silent and turned to stone, as he took in this information, both his hands frozen in the act of running them through his now tousled and wild hair. 'So you're not actually in labour?' he finally recovered his voice to ask.

'No, nor am I likely to be for a good while yet. Calm down and swing yourself back into normal Christmas Eve mode, Davey. Take a chill pill,' she instructed him, and smiled up at his dazed expression. 'Your first-born isn't going to be a Christmas baby, believe you me.'

Carmichael's enormous form collapsed like a broken ironing board onto the sofa, his head extended over the arm one end and his legs overhanging the other. 'Thank God!' he sighed, extracting a clean handkerchief from his trouser pocket and wiping away the cold sweat that had broken out on his forehead and top lip.

'Davey Carmichael, I do believe we're going to have to have a dress rehearsal before I actually pop so that you don't get yourself into such a state when it's for real. If I stay home this afternoon, I'll write a script of what we should do when I do go into labour, then, when it's actually time, you can take the list and tick off things as we do them. If you get yourself into a tizzy like that when it's really happening, you're not going to be safe to drive me to the hospital, now are you?'

'No,' he replied, in agreement. 'Fatherhood's harder than I thought, and it hasn't even started yet.'

'Oh, yes it has, Davey. Just look at those two darling boys, and consider the sterling job you've done since I've met you, bringing them up. You've made a profound difference to their lives, as well as mine, you can't deny that: and you'll be just as good when this little one's born. You'll just have to get used to how small he or she is, but that'll change in no time.'

'Hmph!' Falconer cleared his throat and pointed at his watch.

'Good Lord! Look at the time!' Carmichael was up off the sofa in one bound, grabbing coats, hats, and scarves for the boys and for himself. 'If we don't get going, we're going to miss the start of the service, and that would never do.'

47

He rushed to open the door, and stopped dead, exclaiming with utter surprise, 'Good grief! Crikey! While we've been in here talking, it's been snowing like mad out here. Come and look,' this last request unnecessary, as the boys had rushed to his side, and Falconer was trying to peer beneath his armpit, as he was far too short to look over his humungous sergeant's shoulder.

There was a good six inches of snow on the ground, and it was still falling fast, not showing any signs of abating. 'I'll never get home in this,' wailed Falconer, now haunted by the thought that he would have to spend the night here, *chez Carmichael*, in Castle Farthing.

'No problem, sir. We've got a guest room ready made up, and you're very welcome,' Carmichael reassured him.

'But what about my cats? Who's going to feed and water them?'

'Have you got your next-door neighbour's contact numbers?' asked his sergeant. 'Just give him a ring, then, after the service, and ask him if he would be so good as to feed and care for your pets while you're here. Let's get going, though: time's getting on, and the service will be starting in five minutes.'

Chapter Five

Christmas Eve – late afternoon and evening

The trek down the High Street from the row of cottages to St Cuthbert's in Church Lane was much more difficult than anyone had expected. The snow was blizzard-like, and the keen wind was strong and tried to tip them over sideways. Collars were pulled up, hats pulled down, and hands shoved as deeply into pockets as they would go. The boys very sensibly pulled their scarves right across their faces, so that only their eyes showed.

And the going was slow. With the prolonged duration of low temperatures, the ground underneath the snowfall was slippery and treacherous, and the two adults and the children linked arms in an attempt to achieve a greater amount of balance than they would have had as four individuals. Their progress was also slowed by Carmichael, who kept stopping and putting out his tongue in an attempt to catch snowflakes on it, when all he got for his efforts was a good buffeting by the wind, and so much snow in his face that it made him cough.

'Come along, Carmichael, and act your age. You're supposed to be the father figure here,' Falconer chided him, and he did as he was bid. As they got closer to the church, they could just discern other figures, likewise struggling, so it looked like they weren't the only ones who were going to be a little late.

As they reached the left-hand turn into Church Street, they could discern a trio of figures through the blinding curtain of blustering, swirling snow, and they identified themselves, as George Covington's voice roared through the efforts of the wind to carry away his words.

'Ahoy there! We've got the vicar between us,' he bellowed. 'Poor chap couldn't stand up when ' e went outdoors, so we're givin' 'im a hand: two, in fact. Paula's on 'is other side. If we get much more of this, we'll have to dig our way to Midnight Mass, won't we?'

As he finished this explanation, three shapes materialised out of the gloom, and proved, indeed, to be Paula and George Covington, with Rev. Searle between them, the feet of the shrunken little cleric barely touching the ground, more dragging through the top surface of the snow.

The vicar was making fussy little protests about how late he was, and giving a fair impression of the white rabbit from 'Alice in Wonderland'. Unable to consult his watch by reason of the hold his two minders had on him, and the prevailing weather conditions, he continued to mutter away, speculating about people waiting outside the church in this dreadful weather, and then wondering if anyone would turn up at all in such inclement conditions.

'There're four of us here, Vicar, and the Covingtons make six, so at least the church won't be completely empty,' Carmichael reassured him in his loudest bawl, as they became aware of other dark shapes fighting the snowstorm and heading in the direction of St Cuthbert's. 'And by the looks of things,' he added, 'Castle Farthing's not going to let you down. I can see other people headed in the same direction.'

Rev. Searle finally looked up from his muttered monologue, observed that what the young man had said was correct, and immediately cheered up. It would have been tragic if he had been given this opportunity to conduct Christmas services, only to have it snatched away from him by appalling weather and a consequently empty church.

As the bedraggled inhabitants of Castle Farthing entered St. Cuthbert's, they were greeted by the sight of Digby 'Father Christmas' Jeffries in full regalia at the front of the church, wire-rimmed spectacles replacing his usual horn-rimmed ones and 'ho-ho-ho'-ing away in the hammiest manner possible. As they took their seats, this apparition raised a red-mittened hand in greeting, then put his hands below his cushioned belly to begin another round of 'ho, ho, ho'.

The children arriving giggled, their parents turned away in embarrassment and disgust. Old Albert Carpenter had played the part with such dignity in the past, only appearing at the end of the service at the vicar's behest, and quietly handing out little gifts to the children with the minimum of fuss. It was evident, from their first entry into the church, that Albert's Santa was to be sorely missed this year. Digby Jeffries seemed to be intent on taking over the major role in the crib service, playing it with all the gusto and bad taste of a department store Santa in an American movie.

Although the starting time was long past, people continued to arrive and soon the church was almost full. Warren Stupple sat at the aisle of one row, his twin sons and all his Cubs in uniform ranged along the pew beside him, their parents who were not still at work in the pew behind. Across the aisle sat his wife, their twin daughters beside her, followed by the Brownie pack, all in their uniforms, again, with parents behind them.

The Carmichael group sat near the rear of the church, just in case Kerry's waters broke and she sent a message to the church. They were thus the first to hear the noise from outside. Through the howling wind came the sound of a human voice, raised in anger. ''E'll not take your place, Uncle Albert. We'll soon rout 'im!'

Those further forward were not aware of whatever was approaching the building, but Falconer left his seat and strolled to the still open door to see exactly what was about to descend on this happy little Christmas Eve group.

As the vicar opened the service, his elderly voice struggling to fill the building, Falconer closed the door, putting himself in the porch, and able to see what was just arriving out of the whirling white snow. It had been the voice that alerted him to the arrival of someone not in the best of moods. What actually emerged through the storm was a man built like a brick out-house, pulling strenuously on a rope which was looped around his middle. So swathed in outdoor garments was he that he was unrecognisable, but the little figure behind him on the sledge that he pulled through the knee-high depth of snow was evidently a second Father Christmas, and a very angry one at that.

The big man halted at the huge wooden door and laid down his rope, puffing as if steam were about to issue from his body. The little man behind in the red suit leapt from the sledge and promptly toppled over in the depth of snow. 'You 'old your 'orses, Uncle Albert, and I'll get you inside. Just stay where you are.'

Stepping out to join them and make his presence known, Falconer arrived just in time for the little man in red, who was now being borne the last few snowy feet in an undignified fireman's lift by his relative, to enquire in a querulous, high-pitched voice, ''Ave they got yon fake Father Christmas in yon church?'

'Indeed they have,' replied Falconer, going along with the fantasy. 'And you, I take it, are the real one?'

'Damned right I am. Put me down! Put me down, yer great lumpen fool! I gotta git inside to do me dooty!'

The larger man set him gently upon his feet and pushed the church door open for the older man to enter, and Rev. Searle's carefully planned and scripted crib service suddenly went to hell in a handcart.

'You git outta my church, you old imposter, you!' screeched the old man, hobbling as fast as he could down the aisle towards Digby Jeffries. 'You bain't Father Christmas, I am. I allus 'as been in this 'ere church, and I ain't 'avin' my place taken by no upstart incomer. Git out of 'ere this minnit, afore I brains you.'

'I have sought and received permission to be here today in this capacity, and I shall not be dissuaded from the role that I have been entrusted with,' was Digby Jeffries' dignified, if slightly ungrammatical reply, even if it was cut off as he finished speaking by the arrival of his rival, who tugged furiously at his beard to try to unseat it. It being real facial hair, Albert then tore at Digby's red hat, throwing it to the floor and stamping on it.

'You git outta my church this instant, or there'll be trouble,' the querulous elderly voice continued, pulling at Digby's abdominal area and exposing the pillow resting behind the front of the red jacket. 'You ain't no Castle Farthing Father Christmas. That's me, that is, and always has been. Git, afore I 'as yer eyes out!'

The old man might have been small, but he was wiry and still strong for his years, and Digby retreated from this onslaught while Rev. Searle vainly called for order. It took the combined efforts of Falconer and Carmichael to pull the one man off the other, and escort both now-rumpled figures into the vestry, where they could be neither seen nor, hopefully, heard, and there Carmichael left them to return to his children to enjoy the service in peace. In the sudden silence that followed the slamming of the vestry door, the voice of the vicar could be heard, attempting to re-start his stalled service.

'What's all this about?' hissed Falconer, in the vestry, trying to keep his voice from penetrating to the main body of the church.

'I had to bring him, didn't I?' came the bass rumble of the man mountain who had propelled the old gentleman to the church. 'He's getting on a bit, and this might be his last Christmas. It would be too cruel to deprive him of what might be his last chance to play his part.'

As Digby Jeffries inflated his lungs in preparation for mounting his high horse, Albert got in before him, and complained that he had played the part of Father Christmas to the children of the village since his father had given up the role, but that this year this effing incomer had come along and snuck behind his back to a vicar who didn't know what was what in these parts, and had consequently stolen the part from under his nose.

To the strains of 'Away in a Manger' Digby tried, in as dignified and pompous manner as he could muster, to explain why he was a much better choice for the role, being of a more solid build (despite the cushion) and not so well-known to the children and, therefore, more believable.

At this, Albert Carpenter flew into a mini-rage, scolding the man for putting himself in the position where a child might want to sit on his lap, but would be too frightened to do so, because he or she didn't know him.

'But they don't actually know Father Christmas, do they?' asked Jeffries, logically.

'No, you fool, but they thinks they do, so they needs someone who they feel comfortable with. Any fool could work that one out. Have you seen how the little ones cry in the big stores in the town when they sit on some strange man's knee and he asks them what they want Father Christmas to bring them? Well, they don't do that here, because they knows me, and what's more, they trusts me. Huh!'

Falconer decided that it was time he restored order, and silenced the combatants with, 'Shut up, both of you! Now, listen to me: this year there are going to be two men in red suits giving out the presents to the children. You can stand – or sit – together, and take it in turns to hand over a present. No! No argument! What I have said is final, and if you don't agree, I'm going to eject both of you from this church. Which of you wants to be responsible for the children *not* getting a present at the crib service? Nobody? Good! Now, behave yourselves.'

As the voices in the church wobbled out the final verse of 'Once in Royal David's City' in a mixture of piping young voices and a few booming low ones, Falconer glanced at the large man who had conveyed Albert Carpenter to the church through the storm. He had introduced himself as Albert's great-nephew, John, and the two of them escorted their 'prisoners' out of the vestry and to the rear of the church, where a sack of wrapped presents stood by the door.

'Now, share those out between you, and keep it zipped or there'll be trouble, and you wouldn't like me when I'm angry,' hissed Falconer, determined that this last tradition of the service should pass in peace and harmony.

Rev. Searle blessed them all and, with the innocent faces of the children and the twinkling lights of the tree, all looked calm. Falconer and his new ally stood by their respective Father

Christmases to make sure it stayed that way, both of the red-clad men still in deadly competition, the lenses of their respective wire-rimmed spectacles locked in resentment at the presence of the other.

Carmichael held his little family back until everyone else had gone before they approached the door, this being a very fortunate situation for Dean and Kyle, who each received a present from both Father Christmases, neither of whom wanted to cede the last bestowal of a gift to the other.

'I take it your great-uncle won't be coming to Midnight Mass?' asked Falconer of the man who was not quite as big as Carmichael.

'If he does, he comes as Albert Carpenter, and not in some stupid fancy costume,' was the received answer and, after escorting the elderly man back to his seat on the toboggan, they left, the runners of the wooden vehicle leaving deep ruts in the footprints made by its puller.

The snow had ceased to fall, and for a while the sky must have been clear, but there were new clouds lowering over the village, pouring slowly across the skyscape with the promise of more snow to come. That which had fallen was already deep enough for Carmichael and Falconer each to lift a child on to his shoulders to carry them home and save them the struggle of moving forward in such difficult conditions.

'You'd better ring your neighbour when you get in, sir. I can't see any chance of you getting home tonight,' advised Carmichael.

'Neither can I. I'll do it as soon as we get in. Golly, I'm frozen. Have you got any cocoa in the house?'

'Cocoa, hot chocolate, whatever you want. That's a topping idea, sir; it'll warm us up a treat.'

'Why were there two Father Christmases, Daddy?' asked Kyle, his question echoed by Dean.

'I expect it was because we haven't had a crib service there for some time, and that was to make up for when we didn't have one.' answered Carmichael, diplomatically.

'Then why was they fighting?' asked Dean.

'Yes, and one of them swored, Daddy. We heard him,' expanded Kyle.

'Who wants marshmallows in their hot chocolate?' asked Carmichael, cleverly changing the subject so that no more awkward explanations were necessary.

Others, released from the rather chilly confines of the church, manfully (and womanfully) made their way to The Fisherman's Flies for a drink to celebrate the arrival of Christmas, and George Covington made sure that his establishment had a roaring fire to greet them.

Customers took their usual seats, Alice Diggory, Cedric Malting, and Robin De'ath settling down while Henry Pistorius went to the bar to purchase their first drinks. By habit, he ordered one for Digby Jeffries, who had not left the church with them, though Henry had no doubt that he would turn up to smugly celebrate his triumph at being Father Christmas, even if he'd had to share the honour with that withered old man.

Returning to the table with a tray, the other three were discussing the undignified jostling for the role of the red-suited man, and Henry took his seat with the knowing contentment that he was going to enjoy this conversation. 'So, what've you been talking about?' he asked in feigned innocence.

'The laughing-stock that old Digby made of himself, refusing to yield his role to that poor old man who probably hasn't got another Christmas in him,' replied Alice, summing up succinctly their conversation since they had sat down. 'We think it's absolutely disgraceful, behaving in that way. What does he think it did for the kiddies, seeing two Father Christmases giving out presents? Disgraceful! He should have given up the idea immediately, and slipped out quietly through the vestry door before there was a chance for any sort of scene.'

'Well, you know Digby,' commented Henry. 'He always has to be top dog, no matter what the collateral damage.'

'Goodness knows what the parents thought. He hasn't done himself any favours by insisting on staying,' added Robin De'ath.

'That's because he's incapable of thinking about anybody but himself,' interjected Cedric Malting, so keen to get a censorious word in that he inadvertently dribbled his beer down his front.

At this moment, appropriate, as everyone at the table had had their say, Digby Jeffries entered the pub, a blast of freezing wind following him in. He was still in his red uniform, and his face was aglow with triumph. 'HO-HO-HO!' he shouted across the room and raised a hand in greeting. 'Here comes Santa Claus!' and then looked surprised that he was not either showered with greetings or given a rousing cheer.

'Look at him!' said Henry Pistorius, clearly disgusted. 'He hasn't even got the sensitivity to realise that all the locals know that old fellow as Father Christmas. He must have been playing the part since time immemorial. He probably gave out the presents to their older kids, and to some of them as well. He practically *is* Father Christmas in Castle Farthing, and a newcomer trying to usurp his role will not have gone down well.'

'He's got the sensitivity of a house-brick. It'll be impossible to persuade him that what he's done is completely out of order, so I suggest that we don't even waste our breath trying,' sniffed Robin.

'That's going to be easier said than done,' sighed Cedric Malting. 'Look! Here he comes with a tray of drinks, and the crib service is going to be his only subject of conversation. You wait. I'd put my shirt on it.' Cedric won his bet.

'That was a grand job I did today,' Jeffries began, handing out the drinks. 'Did you see the expressions of wonder on those kiddies' faces?' he asked proudly.

'I think you'll find that those faces were expressing astonishment rather than wonder. How would you have felt at that age, being confronted with two Father Christmases?' asked Henry Pistorius, in his pragmatic way, immediately breaking their agreement not to discuss the subject.

'Henry's right, you know. It must have been terrifying for them. You surely can't imagine that that row in the vestry was unheard in the body of the church. Why, Albert Carpenter was shouting fit to bust before the end. Not only did the poor little ones have to put up with working out why there were two men in red suits, they had already heard them almost coming to blows off stage, as it were.' Alice Diggory had become incensed at the thickness of the man's hide.

'Coming to Midnight Mass, are you?' Robin De'ath asked, always one to try to stir with the largest spoon available to him.

'Definitely!'

'More soberly dressed, I hope.'

'Absolutely not. I shall keep on my costume until I go to bed tonight. After all, I can only wear it one day a year, so I might as well get the maximum pleasure out of it.'

'You're a fool, Jeffries. It'll only bring more trouble down on your head,' advised Cedric Malting.

'Bullshit!' he retorted, and applied himself to his drink.

At the next table sat Alan and Marian Warren-Browne, doing little other than eavesdrop unashamedly on the quartet beside them, when the latch on the door to the staircase gave a clunk, and Rev. Searle tottered through, now in 'civvies'. Alan waved him to join them, as seemed only polite, as he was an ex-church warden. 'What can I get you, Vicar?' he asked as the old man eased himself into a chair.

'That's very kind of you, young man,' he replied, raising a smile from both the Warren-Brownes which said more than words could express. 'I'll have a dry sherry, if it's not too much trouble.'

Alan went to the bar to fetch his drink while Marian congratulated him on a very nice Crib Service, not being so crass as to mention the little matter of the Father Christmas twins. This certainly animated the old man, as he had not taken a service, let alone a Christmas one, for so long, and after effusive thanks for her appreciation, he called out in his still almost pulpit-strong voice, 'Hello again, Father Christmas. Grand job you did back there. I should think that, if they decide to open the old church here again for Christmas, you will be one of the first people they get in touch with. Congratulations on your absolutely grand costume.'

Jeffries swivelled round and beamed at the old cleric. 'Any time, Rev., any time. If you ever find yourself in need of a Father Christmas, don't hesitate to get in touch with me – Christmas bazaars, parties, or services, I'm always available.'

The others at his table winced with embarrassment, and turned the conversation to the weather. Anything was better than Jeffries constantly slapping his own back, and it *was* unusually early for snow in these parts.

Alan Warren-Browne returned to the table with Rev Searle's dry sherry and hinted to Marian that they had promised to drop in on the Carmichaels, Kerry being their god-daughter, and them having presents to deliver before the morrow.

Marian was unusually quiet and he asked her if she was all right, only to receive the reply, 'You know.' And he did, and tried to distract her with their plans for Christmas dinner. They were planning to have Rosemary Wilson round to visit them; the keeper of the local shop, Allsorts, and Kerry Carmichael's aunt. Neither household wanted to intrude on Davey Carmichael having his boss round for the day. Kerry had enough to contend with, with her pregnancy, two excited children (three, if you included her husband), two dogs, one of them pregnant, and a stray cat that had made its home there.

The decision to leave was made for them when Jeffries motioned the vicar to join their table, and welcomed him as an honoured guest in their midst. 'Come on, love,' said Alan. 'Let's get these presents delivered so that you can have a little nap before we go to Midnight Mass, or you'll be crippled with one of your headaches tomorrow and miss all the fun.'

Back at Jasmine Cottage there had been another incident, unexpected by all those under that roof with the exception of Carmichael himself. As soon as Kerry had gone into the kitchen to begin making the hot milky drinks, an absolute cascade of barking and howls had sounded from the back garden, making her cry out in surprise.

Carmichael had already risen from his chair and gone to the

back door, from whence he ushered in the biggest dog that Falconer had ever seen. 'That isn't your *little* surprise, is it?' he hissed urgently to his sergeant, his fingers automatically crossing as they had done when he was a child and wishing for something not to be true.

'Of course it's not,' Carmichael hissed back, then called for everyone's attention, a totally superfluous act, as he already had the eyes of all the family on both him, and the dog that looked as big as a race horse.

'This,' he declared, 'is Mulligan.'

'Not the Moores' dog?' asked Kerry, naming one of their neighbours in the terrace.

'Spot on, Kerry,' replied her husband, a dopey smile on his face, as his own pets sniffed inquisitively at the new arrival and the mountain of canine flesh beheld them benignly.

'So what's he doing here?' she asked in puzzlement. 'Davey, just *what* have you done?'

'I got a phone call from them just before we left for the Crib Service,' he explained. 'They were supposed to be going to their daughter's tomorrow – she lives in Shepford Stacey – but with the weather closing in like it has, their daughter just turned up on their doorstep in the Range Rover, and told them they'd better come immediately, or they'd be snowed in.

'As they hadn't intended to stay away overnight, that left them with the problem with what to do with Mulligan at such short notice. Their daughter can't have him because she's very allergic to dogs.'

'That's what *she* says,' interjected Kerry, thinking that she might develop a sudden allergy to dogs if threatened with one as big as Mulligan as a house guest: then realised that it was already too late to even contemplate this plan of action, as Davey had evidently invited Mulligan to spend the night with them.

'So,' continued her husband, 'I said he could stay the night with us. I was sure you wouldn't mind.'

Yes, she'd been perfectly correct. He had, the big soppy dope!

There was complete silence as all present absorbed this interesting information.

'What if he rolls on one of the other animals?' asked Falconer, an expression of deep misgiving on his face. He wasn't fond of dogs, but they seemed to find him irresistible.

'He won't. He's as gentle as a baby, aren't you, Mulligan?'

The dog looked up at the sound of his name, then espied Falconer and began to taste the air with his nose in interest. There was someone over there that he just had to go and meet. His life wouldn't be complete without an introduction to this man with the fascinatingly attractive smell.

'What if we're all snowed in and he has to stay till New Year?' asked Kerry, appalled at the thought of having to dodge this huge animal in their home's relatively small rooms – small compared to Mulligan, at least. 'You'll have to look after him. I've got enough to do, especially since I've become the size of an elephant. I just can't take on any more work.'

'He'll be no trouble at all,' replied Carmichael, unhooking the leash with which the dog's master had left him tethered in the garden. 'I just love Great Danes, don't you, sir?'

Sir didn't reply, as he was underneath Mulligan, fighting for air, while the dog gave his face a rather too vigorous wash with its tongue. Carmichael rushed over and hauled the dog from its prey, telling it to sit while he held its gaze with an extended forefinger. 'Uncle Harry doesn't want to play, Mulligan. Lie down and leave him alone,' he ordered, and the dog retreated to the rug in front of the fire, whining in frustration.

The visit by the Warren-Brownes was short and sweet, as Marian said she was feeling under the weather and wanted to get home for a lie-down before Midnight Mass. After she left, Kerry expressed her worry at her godmother's health.

'She hasn't looked well for ages,' she said. 'She doesn't seem to be with it, and her skin's almost translucent. Uncle Alan says it's because she's not eating properly, but I'm not so sure. I'm going to try to get him on his own after Christmas and give him a good quizzing to see what he knows that we don't.'

'I should let sleeping dogs lie if I were you,' replied Carmichael. 'If there's anything else wrong with her, they'll tell us in their own good time. Now, Mrs Carmichael, I don't want you going to Midnight Mass tonight. I want you to put your feet up and have a jolly good rest while we're gone. I don't want you going into labour and having the baby on Christmas Day. Who'd cook the dinner?'

He ducked and laughed as she threw another cushion at him, something that was becoming habitual, due to her inability, so late in pregnancy, to get up and box his ears for him. Who'd cook the dinner, indeed!

The church was full for Midnight Mass, no more snow having fallen in the meantime, and the vicar conducted a very enjoyable service, his enthusiasm shining out through his eyes and echoing in his voice.

The only fly in the ointment was, as anticipated by some, Digby Jeffries, still in his red costume and sitting prominently in the front row, brazen as only a man with his impenetrable hide could be.

At the end of the service, many of Castle Farthing's population had managed to find a little something to wrap for the reverend gentleman, a gift in appreciation at his coming out of retirement to put the Christ back in the village's Christmas, and these he received with visible gratitude as they were handed to him as the faithful left the building to trek home through the snow.

The only out-of-tune note during the service had been his announcement that he would be leaving the church doors unlocked, as he had done every Christmas Eve night since he had been ordained. 'For,' as he put it, 'if there is no room in God's house for a stranded wayfarer on the eve of his son Jesus' birth, how could a church call itself the house of God.'

He declared that he'd never been robbed yet, doing this, and he was sure that everything would be as right as rain in the morning as he would leave it this evening. Unfortunately, however, in the event of further snowfall, he would reluctantly have to cancel the Christmas Day service.

A word from Falconer before the party left did nothing to change his mind about leaving the building unprotected, and they left the church ahead of most of the other members of the congregation, in Carmichael's rush to get back to see how Kerry was faring in their absence, with her unexpected new friend, Mulligan.

Others without such worries headed towards The Fisherman's Flies for a last drink before Christmas Day dawned, George Covington having opened especially for this purpose, with the hope that none of the local constabulary should visit the area during this illegal little gathering, and he locked the pub doors so that he could claim that it was a 'lock-in'.

A light falling of snow after the service had done its best to erase the plethora of paths that had indicated the presence of so many people gathered in one place but, that seeming to have been the purpose of the weather, it soon stopped, a smooth blanket whiteness having been restored.

Back at Jasmine Cottage Kerry proved to be fine, but things did not go so well for Falconer. As he made his way upstairs to the room designated to him, Mulligan was as close behind as it was physically possible for him to be, his nose pushed firmly into Falconer's backside while the dog sniffed happily and wagged its tail, and Falconer whimpered for assistance.

'Sorry, sir. There's nothing I can do about it. He's such a big dog he could probably batter his way into any room he chose. I'm afraid you're just going to have to put up with him as an overnight guest tonight. Don't worry though; he'll be going home tomorrow evening.'

So will I, thought Falconer, and thanked God that he had only one night to spend under the roof of his crazy sergeant.

An overview of Castle Farthing at two-thirty am would have revealed the presence of later visitors in the fairly deep snow, leading both to and from the church. There was definitely one more set of tracks leading there, than there was leading away …

At three o'clock, the wind arrived with a roar, and thrummed through the overhead wires and howled in the eaves. In its wake it dragged the snowstorm, which fell in a blizzard, intent on holding the little village in its sway for some time to come. Within an hour, it would have been impossible to discern that there had ever been any disturbance to the recently trodden whiteness leading to and from the church.

By morning, the village was snowed in, the drifts leaning all the way up to cottage windowsills and completely covering the bench on the village green and cars on the road. Not a sound was to be heard, as the snow fell relentlessly, while the savage wind had now calmed and moved on to wreak havoc elsewhere.

Chapter Six

Christmas Day – morning

Falconer was jerked awake by the excited yells of the boys at six o'clock. They had evidently found their stockings, and wanted the whole world to know about it. What Falconer didn't want the whole world to know about was the fact that he had woken up with his arms round Mulligan's neck, Dr Honey Dubois' name on his lips, and doggie dribble on his pillow.

In fact, so rapidly did he move away from the dog that he half-fell out of bed, and had to make a grab for the animal's body to stop all of him landing on the floor and rousing Carmichael to come in to see what had happened.

As he collected the sum of all his parts squarely on the bed again, he became aware of a banging noise emanating from downstairs, and hastily pulled on some clothes so that he could investigate the source of this inexplicable row on such a morning. He descended the stairs to find Carmichael busy constructing a huge wooden-framed, wire-sided cage in the sitting room. The two dogs and the cat were sitting attentively watching him as he hammered away, whistling through his teeth while he did so.

'What on earth are you doing?' Falconer asked, and Carmichael jumped at the sound of his voice, so absorbed in his task had he been.

'Merry Christmas, sir,' he greeted the inspector. 'My surprise present is three chickens, hidden in the garden shed for now, and I'm constructing their chicken house for them.'

'Inside?' asked Falconer.

'It's warmer in here,' explained Carmichael, as if stating the bleedin' obvious to an idiot.

'So you're happy for them to be *inside* chickens, are you?'

'Don't be silly, sir. When it's built, I'll put it out in the garden for them.'

'How?' Falconer watched Carmichael's face as he looked, first at the almost completed chicken house, then at the size of the back door.

'I see your point, sir. Would you mind giving me a hand to take this thing to bits? I'll have to do it later, when all the presents have been opened.' The young man had turned the colour of holly berries, which was very appropriate given the season of the year.

They had only just finished this task when the boys came tearing down the stairs to show off all the wonderful things that Father Christmas had brought them in the night. They were in a high old state of excitement, and both of them groaned when the telephone rang.

As Carmichael went to answer the summons, Falconer pulled a curtain aside to see what the weather was like. Although it was still dark, he could see from the few street lights around the village green and the multi-coloured glow from the Christmas tree that there had been a much heavier fall of snow during the night, and they appeared to be well and truly snowed in.

Across the green at The Fisherman's Flies, which was fully illuminated, he could see that the snow was over halfway up its doors, and the bench on the green had disappeared under its thick covering and was now hard to discern, so thick was the snowfall. There was no sign of either moon or stars, and it could be assumed that the sky sported more snow-laden clouds, just waiting to deposit another load on the surrounding landscape.

Panic immediately set in. He'd asked his neighbour to feed the cats the night before, in the certainty that he would be able to go back to his own house later today. Now, that looked a physical impossibility, and he grabbed his mobile and rang his neighbour, in the hope that he would be able to feed his little furry family until this avalanche of snow was either tamed, or

66

disappeared. There was no way the roads would be clear yet, and no guarantee when the local authority would get around to arranging emergency snow ploughs and road-gritters on such a date.

He ended the call completely reassured that his neighbour would play Mother Goose to his little darlings until such times as he could get home, and would even sit with them every day to give them a little company and dispel any loneliness they might feel, just as Carmichael re-entered the room.

'Family, to wish you Merry Christmas?' Falconer enquired with a relieved smile, now that his little crisis had been solved.

'No,' denied Carmichael with a grave face. 'Murder! In the church. That was George Covington on the phone.'

'What's happened?'

'It would appear that Rev. Searle, although he'd cancelled today's service, insisted that it was necessary for him to get to the church somehow, to say morning service anyway. George, ever obliging, dug a passage through and escorted him there, knowing that the church had been unlocked overnight, and anxious to check that it hadn't been burgled.

'Well, it hadn't been burgled, but Father Christmas was still in there. Nailed to a cross, and as dead as a doornail.'

'*What?*' shouted Falconer. 'Would you mind repeating what you just said? I think I must be hearing things.'

'In the church. Father Christmas. Nailed to a cross. And dead as a doornail.'

'That's what I thought you said! But what cross, which Father Christmas; and when did all this happen?

'The cross from the Strict and Particular Chapel in Steynham St Michael that I told you about ages ago. It was moved to the church in Castle Farthing for safe-keeping, and kept in the vestry,' Carmichael explained fairly calmly. 'And the dead man is Digby Jeffries, still dressed in his Father Christmas costume.'

'Nailed?' queried Falconer, hoping that he really had misheard this piece of information both times.

'Yes.'

'Oh, my God!' It was lucky that Falconer had had no

breakfast yet, or he might have had an unexpected rebate. It was usually Carmichael's stomach that suffered from queasiness, but that one word, 'nailed', had caused his own insides to turn over. It was just so savage.

'Shall I inform the station, sir?' asked Carmichael, this being standard operating procedure.

'I suppose you'd better,' replied Falconer, as the lights suddenly cut out and they were plunged into darkness.

There was the sound of someone scrabbling in a kitchen cupboard, and the hiss of a stream of swearwords, almost drowned out by the cries of surprise from the boys, who could no longer see what they were playing with, and Falconer was surprised to identify the voice of the swearer as Kerry's. She must be under even more strain than Carmichael thought, and this was just the last straw for her. Falconer took a moment to wonder idly if his sergeant knew how freely and comprehensively his wife could cuss.

A match was struck, and the wick lit of, first one candle, then another three. 'I always keep some handy, because we get so many power cuts out here in the villages,' she explained, her voice now sounding back in control.

Carmichael's voice confirmed what Falconer's mind knew it must. 'Phone's out, too. I'll have to try my mobile.' (A pause.) 'Dammit! No reception on that either. Have you got your personal radio with you, sir?'

'I'm afraid I left it in the office. What about yours, Carmichael?'

'I handed it in yesterday because it was broken. I've just used my mobile: you try yours in case that can still get a signal.'

'Dead. The transmitter must be having trouble. That's that, then.'

'What are we going to do, sir?'

'Light a fire to keep warm, sort out some more candles or oil lamps, and then review the situation. And just thank God that you've got an open fire and a gas cooker, so we shan't freeze and we shan't starve either.' Although there was no piped gas in the villages, Falconer knew that Carmichael had insisted they have a cooker that would run happily on bottled gas, and the cylinder for this was cunningly concealed behind one of the cupboard doors in the kitchen.

'Shouldn't we go over to the church? George is probably waiting for us.'

'Then he'll just have to work out that we're not going to get there in a hurry, won't he? After making this place warm and light, it's going to take us ages to dig a pathway through all that snow. It must be thigh-high or more, and it's definitely a shovel job.'

'But how can we start an investigation without any equipment?' Carmichael was beginning to panic.

'By improvising, Sergeant. When everything we can do here is done, we start to gather the equipment we can use that is available in a normal household.' Falconer crossed his fingers behind his back, when he said the word 'normal'. There was nothing normal about this household.

Mulligan chose that moment to come lolloping down the stairs, reminding them that they'd have to put up with his company for the foreseeable future, and Falconer, ever forward-thinking, called out, 'Make sure that any candles and lamps are put up high, so that that monster doesn't knock them over with his tail, or accidentally eat them in mistake for a 'light' snack.'

'Very funny, sir!' Carmichael, like Queen Victoria, was not amused. This wasn't how he'd planned his first married Christmas with Kerry and the boys.

His mood lightened, however, when he discovered a spark of life in last night's fire, and remembered that he'd filled the log basket before going to bed the previous night. With a smug smile of satisfaction, he dropped a few twigs on the embers and received a cheer when within seconds these caught and produced flames. 'And for my next trick,' he said, adding some fairly thin logs, 'I shall produce heat.'

The boys cheered, but Falconer had his mind on more serious things. 'We'll just have to improvise a murder kit from what we can find about the house. Have you got a camera,

Carmichael?'

'Yes, and a video camera as well.'

'Excellent! Now, we'll need a tape measure, some sort of pipette, and some fine powder. Any offers?'

'I've got my retractable DIY rule,' offered Carmichael. 'And I've got a pipette for giving the dogs medicine, and some baby powder. Are they any use?'

'Perfect! Now, what about lighting?'

'George Covington's got some of those spotlight things that builders use, that he puts up in the pub garden if there's something going on late into the evening,' Carmichael remembered.

'And just where do we get the power to run them?' asked the inspector. 'In case you've forgotten, we've got no electricity.'

'Bottom!' said Carmichael, with feeling.

'We'll just have to rely on good old-fashioned candle power for now, and maybe see if we can get a few oil-lamps down there, if there's not enough light. And I can record things on my mobile. At least that functions OK, even if I can't use it to summon help, although I'll have to go easy on the battery,' finished Falconer. 'There's nothing we can do about the absence of a doctor, so we'll just have to use our own judgement and record things as precisely as we can. Boys! Have you got any sticks of chalk?'

'Yes, Uncle Harry,' they chorused, and scrambled off in search of them, hunting through their bedroom by feel. The adults downstairs knew that was what they were doing, because they distinctly heard Dean say, 'Ugh! That's a wax crayon!' and Kyle call out,

'I've got some. At least, it tastes like chalk!' Those boys were really using their initiative in difficult circumstances.

As Kerry laughed at this, she remembered she had a vanity case that they could use to keep all the stuff together and, offering this into the mix, went off to fetch it with one of the candles for light, then made her ponderous way back downstairs, depositing the case in Falconer's arms before lumbering off to the kitchen with a cry of, 'I must get the turkey on, or it'll never be cooked before bedtime.'

Fortunately, Carmichael had had the foresight to bring in a couple of shovels the evening before, when it looked like the snow was setting in, and these sat waiting for them in the kitchen. As the two men wrapped themselves up against the cold to shovel a pathway through the snow to the church, Carmichael had to reassure his stepsons that they would definitely open the presents under the tree when they got back from recording the scene of the crime. They carried on jumping up and down, however, their hands pressed against their mouths to suppress what they might let slip, and pointing at Falconer, until their stepfather finally got the message.

'Of course!' he said, giving them a fond look. 'Sir, the boys have got a special present for you, and I think you'll need it for your time outside.' So saying, he leaned down and picked up a soft parcel from the front of the tree and handed it to Falconer with the words, 'They bought this for you with their own pocket-money.'

The boys, both too young to be bothered with the protocol of job titles, shouted as one, 'Open it, Uncle Harry. Open it! We bought it 'specially for you.'

Falconer took the brightly wrapped parcel with a smile and pulled off the paper. The smile froze on his lips, as he attempted to keep it there, and gazed down at a chicken hat, identical to the one that Carmichael had previously worn to work. It was of the same multi-coloured knit, with a crest running from front to back, and earflaps with strings that did up under the chin.

'Daddy thinks his is ever so warm,' crowed Dean.

'And he thinks it's very pretty too, so we thought you'd like one as well.'

Falconer knew when he was beaten and pulled the hat over his head, taking care that he tied a smart bow under his chin. Stylish and elegant it wasn't, but it seemed eminently practical in these freezing conditions, and he said thank you very politely for his lovely Christmas gift. Carmichael beamed with pride at his stepsons' timely suggestion, as he donned the identical hat that the boys had bought for him some time ago.

71

Their first hurdle occurred earlier than either of them had anticipated, as Carmichael threw open the front door with his usual enthusiasm and the snow that had been piled up against it began to slither slowly into the house. Even Falconer had been distracted enough by the call from George Covington to have overlooked this obvious eventuality, and cursed mildly under his breath as they both set to with their shovels to remove the obstacle that now prevented the door from being closed and let the heat that had started to build up in the house to escape.

Outside the cottage the weather was Siberian, the temperature lowered considerably by the wind-chill from the flying snow, which in places had drifted to almost waist height, even on Carmichael. Each armed with a shovel, they began the gargantuan task of digging a path to the church, both secretly grateful that Jasmine Cottage wasn't at the other end of the village, or even of the terrace.

George Covington had remained at the church and heard the scrape of their shovels, and they could just make out his figure, silhouetted in the soft yellow light that shone out of the church doorway. He had lit every candle he could find when the electricity had cut off, to provide as much light as possible. 'Ahoy there!' he called, using his hands as an improvised megaphone. 'I'll dig from this end, and we can meet in the middle to save time.'

Apart from the slight moaning of the wind, his voice carried clearly to them in the frozen air, and they appreciated his offer, which would save them a considerable amount of effort. George Covington was built like a navvy and was as fit as a flea, to coin but two clichés, and would make short work of his end of the digging.

By the time the three men met in the middle, the sun, such as it was, was up, but still shrouded by a fair thickness of cloud which drooped down and threatening to unburden its fecund load anytime now. Without preamble, George explained, 'I sent the old vicar back to the pub. I reckoned a skinny old fellow like 'im would freeze to death in less than an hour. Let's get ourselves into the church and out of that lazy wind, and I'll explain everything to you.'

They entered the church with gratitude at the shelter it provided, and subsided into pews, while the pub landlord joked, 'If anyone hollers to us, I'll tell them there ain't no one in here 'cept us chickens,' his beady eye on their unusual headgear.

'Very funny, George,' commented Falconer, removing his hat due to the change in temperature. The church may be cold inside, but when measured against the biting freeze outside, it seemed warm in comparison. 'Come on, where's this body?'

'Right in front of your eyes. Just look down the front, and then into the left hand corner. That ain't no fancy Christmas decoration over there. That's your corpse. Anyone'd think it was Easter instead of Christmas.' George was evidently employing graveyard humour to quell his horror.

Four eyes turned in the direction he had indicated. And there it was: or rather, there Digby Jeffries was, still in full seasonal fig, raised above floor level with his arms outstretched, his wire-framed specs awry on his face as if they had been replaced there after he had been crucified, and bathed in the softness of candle-light.

'That's absolutely grotesque!' exclaimed Falconer, feeling his stomach lurch, an alien experience after all the years he had spent in the army. Carmichael normally was the one with the dicky tummy. Tearing his eyes away from what lay before him he risked a glance at Carmichael, to see how he was coping with this grisly scenario.

Carmichael merely looked enraged, and said, 'What if we hadn't had all this snow? The little kiddies would've come in here this morning and found this. It's an absolute outrage, leaving this for little ones to see. Can you imagine their horror, when they saw Father Christmas murdered, and in their own village church, too?'

'It's not really him, Carmichael!' Falconer informed him. 'It's that bloke Jeffries who was always upsetting Kerry, and caused such a fuss in here at the crib service.'

'I know that, sir, but the kiddies wouldn't have done, would they?'

Carmichael had got him there with his childlike view on some aspects of life, and all he could say was, 'I suppose you're right. By the way, George, what have you done with the vicar? You said on the phone that he wanted to say morning prayers. Where is he now?'

'After he'd got over the shock of 'the obscene act that someone had committed in the house of God', as he put it, he just sat down and mumbled away until he got to the end of whatever he was doing, then I took him back to the pub. He was quite all right. Said he'd prayed for the soul of the dear departed – dear, my arse – and that he was in God's hands now, and there was nothing left that anyone could do for him on God's earth, except find his killer.

'The old chap had found another wrapped gift on one of the pews, and took it back with him to go with all the others he was given last night. People are really very kind, and he had quite a lot of presents to open. I was glad to get him back there, too, out in this temperature at his age. At least it's warm in the pub, and the wife's got all the oil lamps out; and opening his presents will keep him out of your way so that you can do whatever it is that has to be done at a crime scene.

'If I give you the key, you can get on with your job, and I can get back to my fireside. You know where I am if you need a hand with anything.'

George Covington shook hands with them both as a seasonal greeting, and made his way off down the passageway he had dug from the Fisherman's Flies, glad that he didn't have to spend any more time in the church's chilly interior.

Carmichael fetched the bag that he had dragged behind them every step of the way when they were shovelling a path to the church, and they began to record the scene of murder. As Falconer began to take photographs, and Carmichael began to film the position of the body and the wounds at its wrists and feet, Falconer commented, 'At least we know this wasn't a suicide.'

'How's that, sir?' asked Carmichael, focussing on the

victim's head.

'Because there's no way he could have nailed up that second hand, you twit.'

Ignoring this minor slur cast on his intellectual capabilities, Carmichael pointed out that, using the zoom lens, he could detect blood which seemed to have come from under the red hat. 'I think he was whacked first, sir, then put on the cross. And there seems to be a nail through his throat. How the heck didn't we hear all that hammering last night? It must've made one hell of a racket, putting in all those nails, and this cross is old. The wood would've been as hard as – well, nails.'

'I very much suspect that a nail gun was used, so that would've been – what? – five nails, five thunks, and the job would've been done. But it must've taken some muscle to lift both cross and Jeffries up and prop them up in that corner. Someone must've really hated him to do that to him.'

'Well, that leaves us with just about the entire population of Castle Farthing, sir.'

'So, we weed out those that would've been too weak to do all the humping around,' suggested Falconer, having finished his photography and putting away the camera. 'Now, what about the infamous blunt instrument, if he was whacked? I'll just take a look at the candlesticks. It's just a pity that Covington has collected them altogether and put them near the body. I've no idea where any of them came from. Aha!'

The church had become just a little bit darker, as Falconer had extinguished a candle, removed it from its holder, and now stood with the candlestick turned upside-down by a candle that was still glowing, examining its base. 'I think I've found the incriminating article. There are traces of blood, and a few hairs too, stuck to the base of this one. I think we can assume that this is what did the initial damage. I'll just get this into an evidence bag so I can get these latex gloves off and put my warm ones on. I can't feel my fingers any more.'

'Me neither,' agreed the sergeant, who had taken off his woollen ones to operate the video camera.

'If you'll just give me a hand to get this fellow and his cross into the vestry, I think we'd better be getting back to the cottage before we develop either frostbite or hypothermia. We can't just leave him there for anyone to see, even if it's fairly unlikely that anyone will come in here with the weather like this, but at least he won't go off in this temperature.'

As they exited the church they became aware of the sound of a vehicle and Carmichael explained that it was a local farmer with his snowplough. 'Kerry says he always comes out when there's a significant fall of snow. He only clears the village roads, but that's a huge help to the residents. We may not be able to get anywhere else, but at least we can get to each other, the shop and the pub.'

'Well, that's damned lucky for us then,' replied Falconer, 'otherwise we'd never be able to interview any of the possible suspects until the thaw. Let's get back to your place and make a list of anyone who had a bone to pick with that poor chap.'

'You'll need a very long piece of paper, then,' commented Carmichael, 'as I reckoned he'd ticked off just about everyone in the village.'

'Then we'll just have to do a lot of interviews, won't we?' were Falconer's final words on the matter, but not, apparently, Carmichael's.

'I hope Mrs Frazer can work out what we're doing,' he muttered, more to himself than to Falconer and, fortunately, the inspector didn't hear him, or he might have feared for the younger man's sanity.

Chapter Seven

Christmas Day – afternoon

Once back in the welcome warmth of Jasmine Cottage and salivating at all the wonderful smells coming from the kitchen, the boys were finally allowed to open their gifts from under the tree, a process which took longer than Falconer had anticipated, as everything had to be displayed to all present, so that thank you notes went to the right person for what they had kindly given them.

Kerry had tried to find out what they had discovered at the church and how they planned to deal with it, given the current weather conditions and the lack of any means of communication with the outside world, but Carmichael had told her not to ask him about it before the boys went to bed, as it was too disturbing to talk about with little ears pricked for anything they could pick up: and with this she had to be satisfied.

When the last present had been opened, however, Carmichael rose and announced that he had one final surprise for the family and, grabbing his shovel, went to the back door to dig a pathway to the shed. The poor chickens probably had frozen water, and would need food as well.

'What are you doing, Daddy?' asked Kyle, looking puzzled.

'You know what Daddy's like,' added Dean. 'He's probably bought a bull or something.'

'Don't be silly, boys,' Kerry admonished them, for although she wasn't in on the secret, she knew that even Carmichael couldn't be that reckless.

The two little dogs, one of them as round as a balloon, took one look out of the door, as did the cat, and all three returned to the warmth of the fireside. Mulligan, being of a rather larger stature, did just the opposite and leapt out into the whiteness, nearly disappearing in its depth, and surfaced every second or two as he attempted to bound through the snow.

This was a great relief to Falconer, who had had an ecstatic welcome when they returned from the church, which had included an embarrassingly intimate sniffing. The sooner its owners could get back and reclaim the animal, the better, he thought. Nothing could be worse than what he was going through with the Great Dane, although, he allowed, getting bitten or mauled by it would probably not be very pleasant either. At least it liked him!

Falconer, having accompanied his sergeant to the door and received a blast of icy air, went back inside with the other pets, sat down on the sofa, and tried to defrost his chilled limbs and body, while Kerry applied herself to the ingredients for the meal which they would eat early, for the sake of the boys. As he sat, he became aware that the radio was playing away to a totally unappreciative audience, and applied himself to listen to what was being broadcast, which seemed to be some sort of local news update:

If you've just tuned in, a very merry Christmas to you, and a white one at that. This is Steve Stuart from Radio Carsfold, bringing you up to date with the latest weather situation. I am a lone voice today, as no one else has yet been able to get to the radio station, so we'll probably spend the rest of the day together.

Power is out all across the region, as are telephone lines, and even mobile phones have been affected. If you have an elderly or vulnerable neighbour who lives alone, try to visit them to check that they're all right. The forecast doesn't look good, with more snow on the way over the next two days, so try to keep warm, get some hot food into yourselves if you can, and just treat it like winter Sundays used to be, long, long ago, before everyone had a television, central heating, or a telephone.

We've all been thrust back in time by this unusually severe weather, and we'll all have to make the effort to make the best of it. Get out those board games, jigsaw puzzles, and packs of playing cards, and pretend that it's so long ago that this is normal. I shall be with you throughout the day, playing all your favourite seasonal songs to keep your spirits up, and keeping you informed of any updates about the weather and the power and phone situation. Now, here's the incomparable Bing Crosby singing 'White Christmas' ...

Oh great! More snow on the way! When would he ever get out of this madhouse and back to his own home and his cats? He missed his solitude, but at least he knew his neighbour would feed his pets, and that they'd be warm, for he'd left the central heating on for them when he'd left. Oh, God! The central heating wouldn't work if there was no electricity, and he had visions of them all dying of hypothermia, when the jaunty voice of the radio presenter caught his attention again:

I'm interrupting this song to let you know that I've just had news that the power is on again in Market Darley, and so are the phones, but the relevant authorities say it will take them considerably longer to reinstate their services in the villages. Hang on in there, my lovely little villagers. Help will get to you. Don't forget to check out those neighbours, and look after anyone on their own at this difficult time. Snow ploughs are doing their best to clear the main roads, but it'll take some time to get to those outlying communities, so just be as patient as you can. And now we return to what has become a Christmas anthem, by Slade ...

Thank God for that! At least the cats would be fed *and* warm, even if they were a bit confused and lonely. They were his family, to all intents and purposes, and he couldn't bear to lose even one of them.

At that point, his thoughts were interrupted by the boys, who came rushing in, cheeks aglow, to announce with great excitement that Daddy had got them some chickens, and that they were to have freshly laid eggs for their breakfast every day if they wanted to. 'Daddy' also came in looking chilled to the bone, and warned them that it might not be every day. The chickens had to settle in first, and that they didn't lay so often in the winter when there was a severe shortage of daylight.

Mulligan also came in and made straight for his new 'bezzie mate', climbing up on the sofa and laying his head in Falconer's lap. It was like suddenly finding himself under an iceberg, and he shivered and gave a little moue of distaste. Why was he so attractive to the blasted animals, when he was a cat lover through and through?

Fortunately for him, his imprisonment under what he thought of as 'that wretched dog' was cut short by Kerry calling for assistance in the kitchen, as the food was ready to be served and she needed a hand to get everything through to the table.

Carmichael had insisted, after they had all eaten an excellent lunch, on crackers being pulled, all the jokes read out, and everyone donning paper hats. Falconer had a particular hatred for this sort of seasonal headgear, but was so moved by the pleas of the young Carmichaels that he eventually gave in and set one on the top of his head just to please them. He seemed to have no control over what happened to him in this household, and longed for when he could leave: not that they weren't a hospitable family, but because he was not used to company, his everyday home life being one of solitude and the time and space to think.

Feeling restless, he went over to the front window and took a peek outside, for no other reason than that he wouldn't have so many smiley, happy faces staring at him, as if expecting him to suddenly break out with a conjuring act, or perhaps juggle the uneaten sprouts for their entertainment.

For a moment his breath was taken away by the beauty of the snow. Snow wasn't white. It was a wide palette of blues and pinks and pale lilacs, and he just stared at it, marvelling at this display of colours and the diamonds that the weak sun sparked off its surface. Just for a moment, he could understand why some people wanted to be artists, and paint the miracles of nature in all their glory, and then his mind switched back to more prosaic matters.

'The Fisherman's Flies is blazing with lamplight,' he called over his shoulder. 'It's positively glowing yellow. I wonder what's going on over there.'

After a few moments for thought, it was Kerry who answered him. 'That'll be New Village,' she answered cryptically, then carried on to explain: 'All the older residents know the benefits of cooking by bottled gas and having wood for an open fire, even if they don't use it regularly. Those who've come to the village more recently or retired here from the towns and modernised their property have, in the main, installed electric cookers in the absence of mains gas, and the old fireplaces are either purely decorative now, with no wood to fuel them, or were blocked off.

'They'd have no way of keeping warm or of cooking their turkeys. I expect they took a quick look to see if the pub was open and, seeing light, made for there where it was warmer and might be able to provide a bite to eat.'

'In that case,' suggested Falconer, 'we'd better make our way over there and see who's in need of shelter. If we're lucky, there might be some who knew Digby Jeffries and had a bone to pick with him. We could get a whole run at interviews without having to visit them all in their own homes.'

'I'd rather we did that than sat with them in the dark, with no tea and biscuits and freezing our nuts off,' agreed Carmichael.

'Davey! Language!' his wife admonished him, only for her husband, not usually the quickest of thinkers, to come up with the excuse that he was referring to Christmas nuts and had said nothing whatsoever vulgar.

'And try to call in on Auntie Marian before you come back,' asked Kerry, looking anxious. You know she's been a bit off recently, and I'm worried about her. She won't talk about it, and Uncle Alan always says there's nothing wrong, but in my opinion she hasn't been herself since just before they retired from the post office.'

'Will do,' replied Carmichael. 'Provided that the road's been cleared up to Sheepwash Lane. I'm not doing any more digging today. I'm aching in places I didn't even know I had, and I never want to feel that cold again!'

The light was already fading when they left the house again, a couple of multi-coloured chickens out to peck around for crumbs of information. The walk to the pub was treacherous underfoot and both of them would have gone flying if it had not been for the one grabbing the other's arm.

Christmas carols flooded out of the pub, which did not boast double glazing, and on entering they stuffed their exotic headgear into their pockets before anyone saw what they had been wearing. They found half the village in the pub. The tables had all been pushed together to form one long dining area, and gathered around it were Cedric Malting, Henry Pistorius, Alice Diggory, and Robin De'ath.

Warren and Helena Stupple were also there with their brood, as was Rosemary Wilson, Kerry's aunt, who had been unfortunate enough to run out of gas on the one day of the year that she really needed it, having decided that she couldn't honour the invitation she had to lunch with the Warren-Brownes given the prevailing weather conditions.

The atmosphere was warm and convivial, although most of the conversation had been about the tragic event of the evening before, George Covington never being able to resist telling a good story. Paula Covington came through from the kitchen as they arrived, her face red and glistening with perspiration, and she informed them that she had half a dozen turkeys of various sizes in her ovens, and would they be joining them for a late lunch?

Falconer thanked her very prettily, explaining that they had already eaten, but would be grateful for the opportunity to speak to those present about the death that had occurred the previous night. He finished his little speech by enquiring, 'I thought you had the vicar staying with you. Is he not around? I can't see him in here.'

'Oh, I'd forgotten all about the poor old dear. George!' she shouted. 'Could you go upstairs and see what's happened to Rev. Searle. He's probably dropped off, poor old thing,' and George obediently went towards the door that led to the staircase, in search of the missing sheep from his flock for the day, but got waylaid by a group of customers at the bar, determined to be served. Well, it didn't matter too much. The old boy would come down when he was good and ready.

Banging on the table with a spoon, Paula asked for hush before explaining that Detective Inspector Falconer and Detective Sergeant Carmichael would like to have a private word with them all, and she'd be grateful if they'd move into the back parlour with them for this, as lunch wouldn't be ready yet for about another hour. Her announcement of such ranks being present in her pub made her feel, just for a moment, very important.

Falconer and Carmichael followed her out of the bar through another door, and she settled them at a table, promising to bring them hot coffee without further delay, and asking whom they would like her to send in first. Her face glowed with excitement at the unexpected turn of events since that morning. This wasn't the first time that death had stalked the village, and it wouldn't be the last, and she was just glad that it had been no one whom she considered 'nice' who had been eliminated.

'I think we'll have that Stupple chap in first, if you please.' He and his brood were certainly taking up a lot of space out there, he thought, although he couldn't see that the man would have anything against Jeffries. It would be an easy interview then, as the family probably had no reason ever to have spoken to the victim.

Warren Stupple arrived almost immediately and took a seat as requested. 'We're just speaking to everyone who attended church yesterday to ask them if they noticed anything unusual during the services concerning Mr Jeffries. We're also anxious to hear about anyone who had reason to dislike him. Do you have any information for me?' the inspector asked, not expecting to get anything positive, and was surprised when Stupple replied,

'Actually, my wife and I weren't too fond of him ourselves. We made sure that our children definitely went to the older Father Christmas at the Crib Service. Apart from the fact that the man made an embarrassing fuss by not giving way to the old gentleman who had played the part for years, I was not happy with his attitude towards my, or any other children.'

'What do you mean by that?' asked Falconer, definitely tantalised.

'He was far too physical with them. If he had an opportunity, he invaded their personal space, patting them on the arm or leg, and even, on one very uncomfortable occasion, actually picking up one of my daughters and hugging her. I felt he was far too tactile and familiar with them, and it made the whole family feel uncomfortable. We weren't averse to crossing the road to avoid him if we saw him first.'

'Oh!' This was something that neither Falconer nor Carmichael had heard anything about before.

'And he was far too eager to get access to the village children with his relentless pursuit of playing Father Christmas. If this hadn't happened, I'd probably have got in touch with you. Some of our Cubs and Brownies have had uncomfortable experiences with him too. It may all have been innocent, but I felt worried enough to consider alerting the police to his over-familiarity with the young in our community.'

'Really?'

'I saw nothing amiss at the church, but then I doubt he'd do anything in full view of the congregation. Although, for all I know, he might have fondled a leg or two under thick winter clothing while giving out the presents.'

'Thank you,' said Falconer, now thoroughly stunned. This was a line of enquiry that had never crossed his mind, and put all the parents of young children in the village in the frame. A parent would do anything to protect his or her child, and murder could not be ruled out if any sort of inappropriate behaviour had occurred.

'That will be all for now, Mr Stupple, and thank you very much for sparing the time to have a word with us. Don't send anyone else in for the moment. Detective Sergeant Carmichael will come through when we're ready to talk to the next person.'

When the man had left, considerately closing the door

behind him, Falconer looked at Carmichael and just exclaimed, 'Phew!'

'I know what you mean, sir,' replied Carmichael.

'That was all a bit unexpected, don't you think?'

'If he's laid one finger on my boys, I'll ...' the sergeant began, punching one fist into the palm of his other hand.

'You'll what, Carmichael? Kill him? Well, as you know, someone's beaten you to it. And maybe now we know why. As for your boys, you'll just have to ask them, and hope for the best,' replied Falconer pragmatically.

'Kerry'll go mad if she finds out he's 'been at' them.'

'Then ask them when she's not there. After this is all over, we'll get Social Services to have a quiet word with the Stupple kids, and let them take it from there if there's any evidence of deviant behaviour. Maybe he just loved children.'

'And maybe I'm a Dutchman, but I'm not wearing clogs and eating Edam. Who do you want in next, sir? I've got a list of names here.'

'Excellent work! Let me have a quick look ... I think we'll have Miss Diggory in. You've marked her down as a retired English teacher. Maybe she spotted something amiss in his attitude to children, being used to working with them.'

Alice Diggory was all of a flutter when she entered the room explaining before either detective could speak that she had never had any business with the police in her life before, and she was terribly upset about what was happening in Castle Farthing, which was such a quiet and peaceful place. She'd obviously moved here after Reginald Morley's untimely demise, and that of Mike Lowry, thought Falconer, looking back to the first case he and Carmichael had worked on together.

'Just sit down and try to keep calm,' Falconer advised her. 'We're only trying to find out if anything happened yesterday in the church that might have any bearing on this case. But we'd also like to know how Mr Jeffries got on with the other residents of the village.'

'I didn't notice anything untoward; well, with the exception of that disgraceful interlude when the two Father Christmases almost came to blows. I was so disgusted with grown men behaving like that in the hearing of innocent children that I left as soon as the last carol had been sung. I did manage to get to Midnight Mass, though, with the help of my neighbours.'

Alice Diggory lived in one of four new dwellings on the Carsfold Road, just south of the village green, her home bearing the name Hillview. On the same side of the road to her, but slightly to the south was The Nook, inhabited by Cedric Malting, on the other side of the road mirroring these two dwellings were Pastures New, the residence of Robin De'ath, and Michaelmas Cottage, the home of the late Digby Jeffries. The newness of the buildings was the main reason the residents had fled to The Fisherman's Flies, for there were no open fireplaces or bottled gas cookers to relieve their discomfort in such weather as this.

'Did you notice anything odd in that later part of the evening?' asked Falconer.

'Nothing other than that silly old man still dressed up in his red suit. In that weather! Why, he could have caught his death of cold! Oh!' she suddenly fell silent, as she remembered what had actually happened to the man in the red suit. 'I'm so sorry,' she apologised. 'I just wasn't thinking straight.'

'Don't apologise, Miss Diggory. It's quite understandable, in the circumstances. Now, can you tell us anything about Mr Jeffries' relations with other people in the village? Had he upset anyone? Made anyone angry with him?'

'I should have thought he'd upset just about every resident. Of course, it was all water off a duck's back to me.' Here she gave a little simper of superiority, then continued, 'But he really did upset poor Cedric Malting in particular. There was a little group of five of us. I have only ever worked in education, but the other four had all been in broadcasting – well, except for Cedric.

'But I'm not explaining things very well. Cedric was a playwright, but has never had a play put on by a professional company – only by amateurs. Robin De'ath worked for Channel 6 before he retired. Digby worked for BBC Television and, although Henry Pistorius had also worked for the BBC, it was in radio, not television.

'Digby looked down on us all and rather tried to be cock of the walk. Of course, he pointed out his superior position, but it was Cedric that he upset the most. He's been trying for years to get one of his plays accepted by anyone; radio, television, professional drama company, it didn't matter to him. He believed in his work, and was beginning to get a little interest in it.

'That dratted man, though, wouldn't leave him alone. Always calling him an amateur and a hack who ought to know when to throw in the towel. Well, you can understand how upset Cedric was by all this, but he'd never … Oh! I didn't mean to imply that Cedric killed him. I'm afraid I've let my mouth run away with itself again. Just ignore what I've said. I simply wasn't thinking.'

'Just one more question: did you ever have any uncomfortable feelings about his attitude towards children?'

This put her back into her previous flustered state, and she finally began to speak, her hands twisting together in her lap with anxiety. 'I really don't like to speak ill of the dead,' she began, conveniently forgetting all the other things she'd said about Jeffries, 'but I must admit that his behaviour was rather … over-familiar. I don't know how else to describe it, but I wouldn't have been happy to have him passing out presents in a school where I worked. There was just something about him that made me uneasy.'

Now she'd got this out of her system she relaxed again, and even managed a little smile of relief. Falconer dismissed her with a reassuring smile, but had been very interested in all the information she had given him: ever efficient, she was a teacher to the core. Carmichael had been sitting just out of view, and had got everything down in his notebook for later reference, then they'd decide how important what Alice Diggory had just told them was.

'With everyone in such a state, what with the murder and the weather, we might be lucky enough to get a good chorus of 'Grass thy Neighbour' in the first round of interviews,' declared Falconer, feeling pretty pleased with what had been imparted to them so far. When people were out of their comfort zone they said things they would never have considered saying, simply because they were in a state of heightened emotion and anxiety.

He was just choosing his next victim when they became aware of a woman screaming, and both men shot out of their seats and through the door back into the bar. Paula Covington was standing just inside the door from the stairs, yelling her head off. 'He's dead!' she screamed. 'The vicar's dead! Someone's killed him! Murder! Help!'

George rushed to her aid, taking her in his arms and holding her to his body to calm her, and Falconer and Carmichael rushed across the distance that separated them from this highly distressed woman as fast as they could, as the babble of voices that had filled the air a few seconds before withered and died as the import of Paula's announcement sunk in.

'What is it, Paula, love? Are you sure 'e wasn't just asleep?' asked her husband quietly. Every ear in the pub was pricked with interest.

'He was dead, George! He'd slid to the floor from his chair, and he wasn't breathing! Dead! Dead! And who did it? That's what I want to know.'

Chapter Eight

Christmas Day – later that afternoon

Falconer and Carmichael left the now-sobbing woman in her husband's arms and headed off up the staircase in search of Rev. Searle's room, leaving a room full of stunned people who were only now recovering their voices and beginning to communicate again, but in whispers.

Presuming correctly that it was the room with the door left wide open that they sought, the two policemen headed straight for it. Inside the room they found that Rev. Searle was, indeed, dead, and had slipped down from the old-fashioned armchair in which he had been sitting and now lay slumped on the floor.

Falconer approached the old man's body, taking care where he put his feet in case he disturbed something that would be useful as evidence, and bent down, putting his face as close to the victim's as he could. 'Bitter almonds!' he declared. 'The old man's been poisoned, if I'm not mistaken. Come over here – *very carefully*, Carmichael – and see if you agree with me.'

Carmichael did, and was the first to notice a hip flask that lay beside the chair. Neither of them went anywhere when working without a pair of latex gloves, and Carmichael slipped his on now and retrieved the discarded flask. 'This is where it came from,' he told Falconer. I can smell it in the flask, and there's a little cardboard label attached to the neck. Let me see … Amaretto di Saronno! That's that Italian liqueur, isn't it?'

'Dead on, Carmichael, and what an ingenious way to disguise the taste of the poison,' exclaimed Falconer, reluctantly admiring the cunning of whoever had given the old man the flask. 'Have you got any bags on you?'

'Of course I have, sir. Never go anywhere without them,' replied Carmichael, slipping an evidence bag from one of his many pockets and sliding the flask into it. 'What do we do now?'

'I think the only sensible thing to do is to go downstairs and get on with the interviews. This chap isn't going anywhere, and we can easily get the key and lock the door so that no one can attempt to enter and disturb the crime scene. We'll get back to this later.'

This taken care of and the keys – both the guest's and the pass key – were in Falconer's pocket when they settled, once again, in the downstairs sitting room and asked for Mr Robin De'ath to be shown in to them. Falconer asked the new interviewee to take a seat as soon as he entered the room, and enquired about the correct pronunciation of his surname. No one likes to have their name mispronounced.

'Deeth,' replied the rather superior man that Robin De'ath turned out to be. He was probably in his late sixties, and obviously dyed his hair black. A supercilious smile twitched at the sides of his mouth.

'Can you tell me if you noticed anything odd during the Crib Service and Midnight Mass yesterday? Anything at all, no matter how insignificant it appeared to you, that concerned Mr Jeffries?' asked the inspector.

'Apart from the disgraceful behaviour of old Digby, nothing whatsoever, Inspector,' replied De'ath with a superior look. 'He was never the most sensitive of men.'

'Do you know of anyone who has recently fallen out with Mr Jeffries?' asked Falconer, watching the man's face very carefully then, as he went to voice his denial, added, 'with the exception, of course, of yourself, sir, whom we already know about.'

De'ath looked stunned. 'I don't know what you're talking about.'

'Oh, come on, Mr De'ath. He was always having a go at you, wasn't he? Trumping your work at Channel 6 with his own BBC work. He really got to you, didn't he? He made you feel like you were always the best man and never the groom. If you could get him out of the picture you'd be top dog in your little gang.

'After all, Mr Pistorius only worked in radio, Mr Malting was, as he would no doubt express it, an "undiscovered" playwright, and Miss Diggory had only been a teacher. Those who can, do. Those who can't, teach. He had you all over a barrel, didn't he: top dog, and no way out of it, unless something was done about him.'

'That is not so. That is totally incorrect!' Robin De'ath's careful Received Pronunciation had slipped, and he made his denial in what was presumably his native Welsh accent. Falconer had rattled him. He knew by the glitter in the man's eyes and the fine dew of sweat that had broken out on his forehead. He was definitely on the run.

'I have never been so insulted in all my life. And let me tell you, bach, his top dog status was about to crumble. George Covington let it slip last night – accidentally-on-purpose, of course – that Digby had only ever been a floor manager. I, at least, was a producer.

'That nugget of information broke up our cosy little group like a bomb going off, and Digby scuttled off, saying he'd left his glasses in the church. He was unsettled and no mistake.'

'When was this?' asked Falconer, his ears pricked up. Even Carmichael's head had shot up from his notebook, and he now sat like a pointer dog that has spotted its prey.

'After Midnight Mass. George was feeling so convivial that he opened the pub for an hour or so: just so that people could have a bit of an internal warmer before they went home.'

'Nobody's mentioned this,' said Falconer, thoroughly thrown by this information. This shone a whole new light on things.

'Well, you ask George. Most of the others in the bar were here. Ask them. Given the circumstances, they probably won't volunteer the information. As I have done,' he added, now becoming more sure of his position, and losing the lilt of the Valleys.

'I most certainly will ask Mr Covington. Will you leave us now, and I'll send my sergeant to fetch the next person for interview.' Falconer was flabbergasted. How come nobody had said a word about this extra opening session? And then he answered his own question: because George didn't have permission to open after Midnight Mass, and was keeping it quiet in case he got in trouble with the licensing authorities. And, of course, not knowing about it himself, he had not known to ask Alice Diggory or Warren Stupple if they had attended this very late carousal session.

As Robin De'ath closed the door behind him, Carmichael gave a low whistle. 'We're doing well today, sir,' he commented. 'Another murder victim and a pub opening without permission. George still hasn't signed up for the all-day opening, so he's supposed to stick to regular hours. No wonder he hasn't said a dicky bird.'

'That puts a whole new light on things. Not only do we have to find out who else was out and about at such an ungodly hour, but anyone could have slipped out, if George was having a bit of a 'do' in the pub. I think we'll have to carry on with these initial interviews, and have a bit of a brainstorming session when we get back to your place. We'll follow up on the other things we've just learnt tomorrow, when we've had time to reflect on things.

'And I don't know who to have in next. I'm spoilt for choice. Shall we try Cedric Malting, Castle Farthing's own budding Shakespeare?'

'I'll fetch him, sir,' offered Carmichael, and went in search of their next victim.

Cedric Malting entered the room with a sort of sliding sideways movement, as if he were having trouble choosing between fight or flight, and flight was definitely fighting the hardest for supremacy.

'Do sit down, Mr Malting. We'd just like to ask you a few questions about whether you noticed anything out of kilter in the church yesterday, and how you got on with Digby Jeffries.'

Although Cedric knew why he had been summoned, his face still drained of colour. He was usually a mild man, and the only thing that had really made him angry since he had moved into his new house was the cruel teasing of his neighbour about his playwriting. How was he going to explain how he felt without positively incriminating himself?

'I didn't notice anything out of the ordinary in the church, apart from that disgraceful falling out over who was to play Father Christmas, and I didn't exactly see that, as it happened in the vestry,' he offered, hoping that they wouldn't delve too deeply about the run-ins he'd had with Digby. But his hope was to die immediately.

'We've heard that Mr Jeffries used to tease you about your writing. Would you like to tell us a bit about that, Mr Malting?'

And he felt the old fury rise in him, as he remembered some of the things that the man lately in the red suit had said to him. There was no way he could quell his ire, and the words burst from his mouth like machine gun fire.

'He used to ridicule my efforts. He said I was living in Cloud Cuckoo Land if I thought any of my puerile scribblings would ever attract a professional company. He said I'd be spending my time better if I took up something more appropriate to my intellect, like basket-weaving. He used to lord it over us all, putting us down and playing the part of our superior, and then we find out last night that he was only a floor manager.

'George Covington told us after Midnight Mass. I saw red and don't know how I stayed in my seat, I was so furious. All that superiority, you'd have thought he was something really high up, and it turns out he was just a *floor manager*!' Cedric almost spat the last two words. 'Well, if he'd lived, he'd have had the rough side of not just my tongue, but of all the others he has treated as inferiors since he came here.'

'What did Mr Jeffries do when Mr Covington let out his little secret?' asked Falconer, wondering how the great pretender had coped with this unmasking.

'He suddenly remembered he'd left his glasses in the

church – you know, his real ones, not those fake things he wore with his red suit – and he mumbled a bit in embarrassment, then said he was off to the church, as he knew it wasn't locked, and he needed his glasses for the Christmas telly.'

'And how did you feel when he left?' Falconer wasn't letting this fish off the hook so lightly.

Cedric sat for a moment or two in silence, deciding what to disclose, then said, 'I was just relieved that he could never look down on us again: that he wasn't something high-powered at all – just a floor manager with delusions of grandeur. Oh, he handled it quite well, in retrospect, even stopping at the bar to have a drink with someone else, but he made sure that Paula served him, and not George. There's going to be trouble there, I thought at the time.'

Neat! thought Falconer, deflecting suspicion away from himself, and trying to incriminate someone else. Maybe the man did have some talent, spinning fiction.

'Would you be so kind as to send in,' Falconer consulted his list, 'Mr Henry Pistorius, please. And thank you for your time, Mr Malting.' Might as well keep it civilised.

Henry Pistorius entered the room promptly, a gale of a man who radiated energy, wished them a booming 'Merry Christmas', and subsided into a chair like the aftermath of a storm. He was almost, but not quite, as tall as Carmichael, of a large loose build, his hair thin on top, and with what seemed the energy of a much younger man.

'I know what you want to know about,' he said in his deep resonant voice. 'You want me to tell you about anything I noticed in the church, and how I got on with that old devil Jeffries, don't you?'

'And a Merry Christmas to you too, Mr Pistorius,' replied Falconer politely. 'And, yes, you're quite right about the enquiries we have for you. Would you care to tell us?'

'Couldn't be more happy to. Apart from the obvious, it's come to my notice that there was something not quite kosher – if you know what I mean – about Jeffries' attitude to and

94

behaviour around children. It's a thought that's been slowly gelling in my mind for some time, but he always made me feel uncomfortable, even about the way he spoke about them.

'Yesterday, I was particularly on watch, for I would hate to be wrong about something like that and, in my opinion, I considered that Jeffries was rather too tactile with the kiddies he gave presents to, and it just confirmed what I'd already noticed – that he couldn't seem to keep his hands off very young 'uns skin.

'Oh, I've never known him do anything really out of order, but he did have this habit of stroking their arms and legs, which I found over-familiar. I doubt whether the man went any further than that. I never spoke to him about it: it would have been too distasteful, especially if I'd proved to be wrong.

'As for how we got on, well now, that man was a real tease. He used to rib me mercilessly about only having been involved in radio broadcasting, but I didn't let him get to me. He obviously suffered from some kind of inferiority complex, the way he treated everyone, he wasn't a happy man, and I felt sorry for him in a way. His ascendancy over us four – that's Miss Diggory, Mr Malting, Mr De'ath, and myself – was one of the ways he coped with feeling inferior, and if he had a thing about kiddies, that must have made him very uneasy, possibly making him feel guilty a lot of the time.

'He wasn't the nicest of men, and he upset a lot of people, but nobody deserves to die like he did. That was blasphemous and sacrilegious, and whoever did it had a lot of hatred in their heart: that, or they were out of their mind. Jeffries may have needed to be taken down a peg or two, but not to die like that. Nobody deserves to have that happen to them.'

'Can you tell me how he teased Alice Diggory?' asked Falconer, aware that there was a gap in his knowledge of the little media gang.

'He teased her mercilessly about the state of the English language today, which could only be down to the teachers they had been taught by during their schooldays. He even bought her a dictionary and a book on English grammar for her birthday, and I don't think I've seen the woman more embarrassed. And the biggest offender of them all, strangling the grammar of the language, was Digby himself, but he just couldn't – or wouldn't – see that.

'But that was just him. He had the sensitivity of a breeze block, and he behaved like a playground bully a lot of the time. Me, I've never had any trouble with bullies, so I just ignored him when I could. That's not to say he couldn't get my goat, but in the main I just took it as a demonstration of his own inadequacy.'

'Thank you for your honesty, Mr Pistorius. Can you remember who else was in the bar after Midnight Mass, by any chance?' Best to get a list of names, thought Falconer, as they hadn't known a thing about this little hoolie at the beginning of their interviews.

'There was that Stupple chap – the one who does the Cubs, and the couple that I believe used to run the post office, but they didn't stay very long. You must've made a run for it straight after the service if you didn't see us lot heading for the pub. There were also a few people that I didn't recognise, but that's probably because they're not regulars and only came along because of the novelty of the situation.'

Then, before the man could leave, he froze halfway out of his chair and exclaimed, 'Hey, before I go, I've got something highly coincidental to tell you.' Falconer pricked up his ears at this statement.

'Do go on, sir.'

'It must have been in the early sixties, and I think it was Reuters that reported it. There was to be the first Christmas display in a big department store in … Tokyo it was, I think; somewhere in Japan, anyway. The window display was kept under wraps until the press had all arrived, and then, when it was unveiled, there was this huge Father Christmas nailed to a cross. Unbelievable that that scene's been re-enacted in Castle Farthing, but with a real body. Who'd have believed it of a sleepy little place like this?'

'Extraordinary!' replied Falconer, for once completely taken by surprised, but keeping his reaction to himself. 'You've been very helpful, Mr Pistorius ...'

'Call me Henry, please.'

'Henry, did you notice if the Warren-Brownes were in the bar before you came in here? That's the couple who used to run the post office.'

'They weren't, no. That Warren-Browne woman always looks ill to me: very delicate, in my opinion. I understand she suffers from attacks of migraine. Shall I just go back to the bar, now?'

'No,' said Falconer, thinking. 'Ask Mrs Covington to come through, just for a minute. I know she's got a whole host of lunches to get served and she's had a huge shock this afternoon, so tell her I won't keep her long.'

Paula Covington swept in with a frown on her face. 'Do you know how much I've got to do?' she asked in an irritated voice before she'd even sat down, but it was easy to discern that the frown was only for show and that, underneath, she was severely affected by what she had found upstairs in one of the pub's guest rooms.

'Yes, and that's why I won't keep you long. Just a few questions. How long has your husband known about Jeffries' real job at the BBC? Who was here after Midnight Mass? And in what order did they arrive and leave?'

'Well, I can answer the first one straight off. He's known for a few months now, but he's managed to keep it under his hat until last night. I think he'd had enough of Mr Know-It-All Jeffries, hinting that our spirits were watered down and the beer not well kept. We never liked the way he was always having a go at that nice group of retired people, but the man's behaviour yesterday was just the last straw for George. He wanted the wind taken out of that man's sails, and to see how he liked it, being ridiculed.

'He wasn't at all sorry afterwards. He said that if the man never set foot in his pub again, it would be too soon. Oh, God! I didn't mean that! George wouldn't hurt a fly. He'd never have

done that to him! You surely can't think it was George that ...'
Her voice trailed off into a horrified silence.

'Of course I don't, Mrs Covington. I just want an accurate picture of what happened yesterday. Now, about the other two questions.'

'I can't possibly answer those off the top of my head. You'll have to give me time to consult with George. He's got a much better memory than me, and I can't think straight the way things have turned out today. And I must get off now, or I'll burn the turkeys.'

Paula Covington swept out of the room, her mind now totally distracted from the two murders, her thoughts all on the number of meals she had to serve up to the hungry customers in the bar. It was, after all, Christmas Day.

'Well, I think that about wraps it up for now, although we'll have to find out who else had fallen out with the man and if they came here for a drink last night. On the other hand, we promised to go and see Marian Warren-Browne. What do you think about all that stuff from Stupple then? I shall want another word with him, if it was his kids getting felt up. And his wife!'

'Would she have been strong enough, sir?' asked Carmichael.

'A mother in defence of her children can have the strength of ten,' Falconer replied.

'I can understand that, but how would she have known he'd gone back to the church if she wasn't at the service?'

'Her husband could've told her when he got back.'

'OK,' agreed Carmichael, reluctantly, 'but with all the Cubs and Brownies they look after, I'd thought that either of them would've thought it was a matter for the police.'

'Not in righteous anger, they wouldn't. Come on, let's get wrapped up, and get this afternoon done and dusted. I feel in need of your fireside at the moment, and I won't rest until I get there.'

Before he could get into his coat, however, Paula Covington put her head round the door and announced that Rosemary Wilson who ran the village shop had just not been interviewed yet, and did they want a word with her, too? With a sigh, Falconer hung up his coat again, and nodded his acquiescence. How could they have forgotten to speak to Kerry's aunt?

Rosemary Wilson, Kerry Carmichael's aunt, ran the shop that sold just about everything, which had the appropriate name of Allsorts. If you needed a new bucket, or mousetraps, Rosemary stocked them. If you needed a length of washing line, or some clothes pegs, you'd find them on her shelves. If you hankered after a new stepladder, or a pasting tray for decorating, these she had, too. Her shop was like an Aladdin's Cave, with almost anything you could think of on the shelves, hanging from the ceiling, or in the back of the shop in the stockroom.

As the plump woman bustled in and took a seat, she exclaimed, 'I never thought I'd see myself seeking sustenance here, today, but I'd only half-cooked the turkey when I ran out of gas. I was a right fool not to check it in good time. What a love Paula is, cooking for us all. It's just our good luck that's she's got a proper professional kitchen out the back, and can cook so many birds simultaneously.

'I'm not the only fluffy-head today, though. Mrs Stupple found herself out of gas too when she went to put her turkey in the oven, so they popped it on the kids' sledge and pulled it down here in the hope that Paula could help them out. She said she couldn't see them eating sandwiches on Christmas Day. And now I gather that you forgot all about me when you were speaking to everyone else.'

'Hello, Rosemary. Sorry. Our Christmas Day's not exactly going to plan, either,' Carmichael greeted her, a smile of welcome on his face. 'The inspector's just got a few questions for you, if you don't mind.'

Falconer cleared his throat, to remind Carmichael just who was in charge, and let him know that this was still a formal interview. He'd be calling her 'Auntie' next, and then where would their authority be?

Like the others, she had noticed nothing awry, apart from the obvious, at the services the day before, but she did make some comment about wandering hands where the youngsters were concerned. This information was coming out of the woodwork from all sides now, and yet no one had ever breathed a whisper of it before, not even on the village grapevine, which was considered to be all-knowing and all-seeing.

'I've seen it in my shop,' she declared. 'While mummy or daddy was looking for what they wanted, he'd sidle up to them, and just put a hand on their arm or tousle their hair, and ask if they'd like any sweeties.

'I've taken him to task for it on many an occasion when I've seen him at it, but I'd be willing to bet that there were a lot of times he made sure I couldn't see what he was up to.'

'So you fell out with him, did you?'

'I certainly did. I said only a few days ago that if I caught him at it again on my premises, I'd bar him and I'd seriously consider calling the police.'

'And what did he say to that?' This was getting very interesting.

'Made out he didn't know what I was talking about. Called me a dirty-minded old gossip, and stalked out of the shop. I was relieved, I can tell you. The thought of him taking umbrage and not coming in any more just about made my day.'

'Can you remember which children you caught him acting inappropriately with?'

'Not off-hand, but I could think about it and make you a list, if you want me to.'

'That would be fantastic, Mrs Wilson,' agreed Falconer with enthusiasm. They could really be onto something here, although it would take a lot of investigating by Social Services, even after this case was all finished and tidied away. And the perpetrator could never even be punished, because he was dead.

'Is anyone going to call on Alan and Marian today, do you know?' she asked. 'Marian's not been out and about much lately and I'm just a bit worried about her. She seems to be getting more and more headaches, and sometimes, she's – well, to be brutally honest about it, she's rather muddled and forgetful.'

'We'll be calling in ourselves after we've finished here,' volunteered Carmichael. 'Kerry's orders.'

'That puts my mind at rest. All things being normal, I would have gone up to hers today, but I don't really feel up to struggling through this weather. Let me know how she is, won't you?'

'Will do, Auntie Rosemary,' replied Carmichael, making Falconer wince with embarrassment. No detective sergeant worth his salt should refer to someone under police interview as 'Auntie' anything. He'd have to have a word with him, and get him to remember that he was a representative of law and order, not some schoolboy talking to a relative.

He finally decided not to chide Carmichael, today being the day it was, and merely asked him to make a note of the fact that they'd need to call on the old man whom he referred to as 'Father Christmas Two' and his nephew, to find out where they were in the early hours of the morning. Murder had been done before over somebody stealing someone else's prize position in the community.

Back out into the cold once more, they donned their non-uniform headgear and headed off past the village green for Sheepwash Lane, where they would call first at The Beehive before scuttling back to Jasmine Cottage. Sheepwash Lane had been cleared even before the roads round the village green as this was the route from the farm, so they knew that they weren't wasting their time.

It was Alan Warren-Browne who opened the door to them, letting out a shout of laughter as he looked at what they had on their heads. They had been so warm that they had forgotten they were wearing the monstrosities, and snatched them off simultaneously as he asked, 'Is this part of the new winter uniform, or is it only for plain clothes chickens?' And he stood, silhouetted against the lamplight from the interior and chuckled to himself, before asking them in and calling upstairs, 'Marian, we've got a couple of 'fowl' police officers come to visit. Are you coming down?'

When they sat down in the sitting room, even in the dimness of the lamplight, they could see that Alan Warren-Browne had a glorious black eye. 'How did you get that?' asked Carmichael, studying the other man's face minutely.

'Slipped coming home from the pub after Midnight Mass,' Alan Warren-Browne said, and his hand went unthinkingly to his bruised face. 'Silly really. I should know better at my age to try to hurry when conditions are so treacherous underfoot,' he further explained, but he met no one's eye when he said it, which Falconer took to mean that his attention was all on the shuffling they could hear, as of someone coming down the stairs very slowly. Marian was on her way.

Alan leapt to his feet and went to guide his wife in, explaining that she'd had 'one of her heads' come on in the pub after Midnight Mass, and had gone to bed as soon as they had got home and hadn't been up yet today, which was witnessed by the pile of unwrapped presents under the unlit Christmas tree.

Marian was wearing only a nightdress, a dressing gown, and a pair of slippers, and made straight for a chair in front of the log fire as the two detectives looked at her in concern. 'Has she seen a doctor, Alan?' asked Carmichael.

'She's got an appointment in the New Year. Don't worry: she's often like this after one of her headaches.

'This bad?' asked Falconer, looking carefully at the strained face and hands twisting unconsciously in her lap.

'She'll be all right, won't you, my girl?' said Alan with a note of false cheerfulness in his voice, at the sound of which Marian raised her head and seemed to notice for the first time that they had visitors.

'Hello,' she greeted them. 'Do I know you?'

'It's me, Auntie Marian: Kerry's husband,' replied Carmichael as both he and Falconer looked on, aghast.

'Kerry … Kerry,' the woman muttered quietly, then her face brightened, and she announced, 'I've got a baby goddaughter called Kerry. Do you know her?'

Alan Warren-Browne rose swiftly from his chair and made

to usher them out of the house. 'She sometimes gets confused when she's had a really bad migraine. If you could come back some other time, I'd be most grateful.'

'Did you know that both Digby Jeffries and Rev. Searle are both dead?' Falconer asked, determined not to leave with nothing.

'How dreadful,' Warren-Browne responded, but there was no concern in his voice for the departed. 'I must get back to Marian. You can see yourselves out, can't you?'

'I need to know what you did after Midnight Mass, sir,' Falconer challenged him.

With a sigh of exasperation, the man replied, 'We went to the pub for a drink, but Marian said she wasn't feeling very well, so we came home. Satisfied?'

'Straight home?'

'And straight to bed, where my wife has been ever since, so if you would excuse me, I need to go and see how she's feeling. What are you doing there, darling?' he asked, as Marian joined them in the hall.

'Saying goodbye to your friends,' she replied, as both policemen donned their multi-coloured hats. She pointed at them and laughed with the glee and unselfconsciousness of an amused child, and that was the last they saw of her that day.

The door slammed in their faces and they adjusted their chicken disguises against the knives of the bitter wind. That woman's lost the plot, thought Falconer. She's completely away with the fairies.

Chapter Nine

Christmas Day – evening

The light had totally gone by now, and Carmichael produced a torch to light their way along Sheepwash Lane back to Jasmine Cottage, both perplexed and concerned at what they had just witnessed.

It had been a day of unpleasant surprises: from the finding of the body of Digby Jeffries in such bizarre circumstances first thing that morning, then had followed the surprise of the old clergyman's unnatural death and the allegations against Jeffries of paedophilic tendencies. Finally, they had found Marian Warren-Browne in a state of great confusion, not recognising either of them, and believing that Kerry was still a baby. Maybe she was having some sort of a breakdown.

'What am I going to tell Kerry, sir?' asked Carmichael, in turmoil after their unsettling visit to his wife's godparents. 'If I tell her the truth, she'll want to go straight round there, and I can't have her going out in weather like this. She'll fall over and hurt herself and the baby.'

'I think telling her about Marian's condition can wait until there's been a thaw, then you can run her there in the car. And Alan said she had a doctor's appointment in the New Year. It can't do her any good to know what a state her godmother's in: it might even trigger early labour, and there's no way we can get her to the hospital in these conditions.'

Falconer was quite right, and Carmichael knew it. He'd just have to keep this to himself until such times as it was more sensible to bring up the subject.

To lighten matters, Falconer said, 'I'm really glad you

thought to bring a torch. It hadn't crossed my mind that the Christmas tree lights would be out as well as the street lights. I guess I wasn't thinking straight. Good work, man.'

'Thank you, sir,' replied Carmichael, but he didn't seem any the more cheerful.

Kerry welcomed them back to the cottage as if they had been gone days, for it felt like that to her on such a special day. This was the first Christmas they'd been married, and this wasn't what they'd planned at all. She'd even had reservations when Davey said he'd invited his boss, but she'd had no idea the day itself would end up the way it had.

As they entered the cottage Mulligan fell on Falconer as if he were a long-lost friend he hadn't seen for years and gave him a damned good sniffing-over, licking his face until the inspector called for help. The boys were also over-excited because they'd been out in the back garden, where Carmichael had dug a path to the garden shed, and had had a very boisterous snowball fight until their mother had called them in before they got frostbite.

Kerry's first words were not about their visit to the Warren-Brownes, however. She had other things on her mind. 'It's Mistress Fang,' she opened the conversation. 'She's been whining now for about an hour, and I think she's about to whelp. What on earth are we going to do? There's no way we can get in touch with a vet.'

Falconer took one look at Carmichael's stricken and helpless countenance and said, 'Get some clean towels, and boil some water. We may need to sterilise a pair of scissors, but first, let's get her up on the table where we can get at her easily. You'll have to help, Kerry, because I don't think your husband's going to be much good to us. Carmichael, go and get a big bowl.'

'What for, sir?'

'For you to be sick in, of course. I've been a victim of your dicky tummy before, and I have no intention whatsoever of giving you the opportunity to vomit all over me on Christmas Day.'

'Yes, sir.' Carmichael's face was already turning green as he looked at the little dog lying on the table, whimpering and whining. Sir was right: he did need a bowl.

When Kerry arrived back with the towels, had got out a pair of scissors, and put some water on to boil, Falconer explained to her, 'She should be able to manage perfectly well on her own. Animals have still got instincts about this sort of thing. We're only here to make sure that things go all right. Now, as each new pup is born, she'll probably give it a good licking to get it ticking, and she should deal with the umbilical cord on her own.

'If, however, any of them are reluctant to breathe, we should give it a good rub with a towel to stimulate it to take its first breath. Now, do you feel up to this?'

'No problem,' Kerry replied, stoically. I'm just glad it's not me in labour while we're snowed in.'

From the kitchen came the sound of vomiting.

By half-past ten it was all over, and Mistress Fang lay happily suckling the three minuscule puppies she had just ushered into this world. Falconer was having a celebratory glass of wine while Kerry joined him in some sparkling grape juice. Carmichael sat miserably in an armchair looking decidedly nauseous and – if it may be dared – hang-dog.

'Nothing to it!' declared the inspector, raising his glass to the new mum and her pups. He'd been in a complete panic when he realised he was going to have to assist at the birth of the puppies. He had covered it well, and Carmichael's sickly turn had deflected any suspicion away from him, but he wouldn't like to have to do it again. He'd only ever seen anything like that done on television before, but he'd kept his calm, and now he was the hero of the hour. He had no quarrel with that.

As Carmichael was still slumped in his chair, Falconer suggested that Kerry get herself off to bed. The boys had already gone up, exhausted from their early start to the day, the excitement of all the presents they had received, and the energy they had expended throwing snowballs at each other. 'We've got a lot to sort out today from the evidence we've gathered today, and we've still got to look at the video footage and the stills from the church. We'll be going over to the vicar's room again tomorrow morning.'

'Why?' asked Kerry, wondering if he was intending to join some sort of church group.

Good God! They hadn't told her about the murder of the clergyman with everything else that was going on. 'Look, I'm sorry to have to tell you that there's been another murder. I don't want you to get upset about it, but Rev. Searle is also dead. It seems that someone gave him a hip flask with poisoned spirits in it. Just don't dwell on it, and try to get some sleep. I'll send your husband up when we've finished.'

Kerry's face had looked anguished when she'd received the news of this further death, but she bore it stoically, not wanting to precipitate the end of her pregnancy before its time, and promised to do her best to put it out of her head for, as she honestly stated, she hadn't actually known him well, although she felt sorry for any family he left behind.

When she'd gone upstairs, Carmichael refreshed himself with a can of chilled lager, and Falconer asked him where his laptop was, so that they could view what they had captured earlier that day, and saw his sergeant's shoulders slump. 'I've only gone and left it in the office,' he replied, looking sheepish.

'What on earth did you take it into the office for?' Falconer asked, horrified that even this should be denied them.

'It was playing up a bit, so I was going to take it in to the shop to get them to have a look at it, but I left it too late, so I thought I'd leave it there to remind me when I went back in. After all, I thought, we've got the main computer at home but, of course, now we haven't got any power to run it.'

'Great!' Falconer, like both Carmichael and Queen Victoria before him, was not amused. 'So now we'll have to take it in turns to squint into the video recorder to review what was filmed, and fight for space to look at the back of the camera to see what that captured. And then they'll both run out of battery power, and we'll be completely wiped out. Great!'

'Sorry, sir!'

'Arse!' said Falconer, but he said it under his breath. He didn't usually swear or cuss, but he just couldn't help himself, at this latest blow. The only tool they had left, he'd believed, was the laptop, with its limited battery life, and now they didn't even have that. 'Arse and double arse!'

Left to their own devices, they made themselves some turkey and stuffing sandwiches and a pot of tea, and sat down at the dining table to rationalise what they had learnt that day, and where the greatest suspicion lay.

'We've got the paedophile angle,' spluttered Carmichael through a mouthful of bread. 'That was a bit of a facer, wasn't it, sir?'

'You can say that again. It seems that adults aren't the only local residents that Jeffries has been disturbing. I'm surprised that Kerry didn't pick up anything on the grapevine. I'm surprised, too, that she didn't know about the state her godmother's in.'

'She has been worried about her, you know, but she hasn't been going out much the last month or so. I told you how she tried to avoid that old fiend. It would seem, from what her aunt said, that neither has Marian Warren-Browne. So Kerry not only hasn't had the opportunity to plug into the local gossip, she hasn't seen much of Marian for some time. I dread to think what's she's going to say when she finds out. What the hell was all that when we were there earlier?'

'Don't think about it now. Let's get on and make some lists. Who have we got for the paedophile angle?'

'Well, given the timing, I'd have said it was definitely someone who'd been at Midnight Mass, and then to the pub.'

'Good thinking, Sergeant! And here was me thinking we'd have to get Social Services out to interview all the families with children in the village.' There was a pause. 'Which we probably will have to do when we can get in touch with them, but for us now it will only be those families who went on to the pub, or maybe someone who'd come back later perhaps because one of their children said something after the crib service.

'It would be quite cunning not to go to Midnight Mass, then

catch the dirty old devil on his way out of the bar. What do you think of that one, then, Carmichael?'

'I think we'll still have to get Social Services out, as you said, just to make sure that the village kids are OK after what Auntie Rosemary said.'

'True! But who can we put on our list that we definitely know about. I've got no idea who all the Brownies and Cubs were, so we're stymied there, but to go back to the crib service, who was there who had children, apart from just about everybody. Who do we know for definite?'

'Apart from the Stupples, you mean?'

'Yes.'

'Well, there's me for a start, sir. I was there with the boys.'

'And you think nobody would have noticed if you'd gone out in the night and done that? You haven't got the stomach for it. You proved that earlier. And don't tell me Kerry just conjured up the rumours about him from the ether, because not only is it impossible, so is what was done in that church for someone in her condition.'

'I was only being fair, sir. Actually, the only other kiddie I can think of is Tristram Rollason. I saw him there with his parents, and they're hopelessly devoted to their little darling: always have been since he was born. But I don't really know any of the other kids, as I seem to spend most of my time at work. Like today, for instance. Sometimes I wish I had a nice nine-to-five job like everyone else.'

'Carmichael, you're surely not thinking of leaving the Force?' Falconer was horrified at this prospect.

'Of course not, sir. It's just that sometimes I wish I had more time to spend with Kerry and the boys, especially with another kiddie on the way.'

'Hang on in there, Carmichael. You're an excellent detective, and it would be the Force's loss if you left.'

There was a moment of silence as both of them acknowledged how far their partnership had come. Carmichael felt that Falconer was becoming like a real fiend to him. (He also knew, in the back of his mind, that the missing 'r' didn't matter, because he understood that Mrs Frazer was a somewhat cavalier typist and a rather hit-and-miss proofreader, and her little error wouldn't be catastrophic.)[4] Shaking himself out of his reverie, he said, 'Right, sir; so that's the Stupples on the list, and the Rollasons, until we can get a bit more mobile after the thaw.'

'I'm afraid that's all we've got to go on at the moment. But we've always got the adults he fell out with, and, no, I won't put Kerry at the top of the list. We'll start with Robin De'ath and Cedric ... Oh, God! What's his name?'

'Malting,' replied Carmichael, referring to his notes, 'and don't forget Alice Diggory and Henry Pistorius. It doesn't matter how rational people appear after the event. They may have done something dreadful in a moment of madness.

'I don't suppose the oldies could have got together and got rid of the biggest pest in their lives as a group? What do you think, sir?'

'You mean it wouldn't need one really strong person, rather three or four weaker ones working together. What about the nail gun, though?' Falconer was intrigued by this idea.

'Who's to say it wasn't wrapped up in Christmas paper and in a bag that one of them carried, just looking like another innocent present if anyone managed to catch a glimpse of it.' Carmichael was rather pleased with his suggestion. It certainly put a new light on matters, if more than one person had conspired to do away with the old devil.

'And none of them would be any stranger to putting on an act, considering what they used to do for a living. Malting's always writing dialogue to suit the mood of his plays, Diggory would have had to do a lot of acting, dealing with her classes, for you can't let pupils see who you really are.'

'And Pistorius was used to delivering lines; De'ath, no doubt, mixing with actors and the like all the time,' Carmichael finished.

'Very true, and this person had already arranged a little gift

---

[4] Read your Edmund Crispin!

for Rev. Searle, which could also just have sat in a bag until it was time to plant it on one of the deserted pews, but we'll go into that later. It's certainly not impossible that this crime was carried out by more than one person, one of them even being a woman if she had some help.'

Abandoning that highly interesting line of thinking and moving on, Carmichael suggested, 'In that case, you'd better add Rosemary Wilson to your list, and both the Covingtons. Jeffries had, after all, been casting aspersions on their honesty with regard to the drinks they served.'

'Very true. What a large suspect pool we have. That's what you get when someone very unpopular comes to a sticky end. Now, that leaves us photos and videoing at the pub to get through tomorrow. We'll have to move the vicar's body down to the cellar, too. We don't want it going off like an out-of-date Christmas turkey, and it should be nice and cool down there.

'Then we've got to re-interview the Stupples, Pistorius, Diggory, Malting, and De'ath, not forgetting a more satisfying interview with the Warren-Brownes – perhaps Marian will be feeling a little better tomorrow – and the Rollasons, which was a brainwave of yours. Oh God! And Mrs Wilson and the Covingtons. So much for a peaceful Yuletide. We'll still be on this case come Easter if we don't get an early break.

'We'd better have a look at what we filmed today as well, before we go up.' Falconer now had his head in his hands as he surveyed the amount of work they had to do on the morrow. 'You take the video camera, and I'll take the camera, then we'll swap, then I think we'd better go to bed before we meet ourselves on the stairs getting up tomorrow morning.'

When Falconer finally reached his room he found that Mulligan had managed to wriggle his way under the duvet and was snoring loudly and contentedly with his head on the pillows. 'Move over, you great lug, and let me share the bed. You might not be my bedfellow of choice, but at least you're warm. And absolutely no farting! Do you understand? Not even one little toot on the bum-trumpet. I don't want to suffocate in the night.'

112

As he got ready for bed, he could hear the wind begin to howl again and, taking a quick look out of the window, he realised with a sinking heart that the blizzard was back. They'd no doubt have to dig their way out again in the morning, and his shoulders and back still ached from all the shovelling they'd done only that morning.

During the night the snow began to lie again, making short work of the pathways that had been sliced through them with both shovels and tractor. The weather hadn't done with Castle Farthing yet. It still had plenty more to offer, to test both the patience and the ingenuity of its residents.

No soft yellow lamplight spilled out of the houses now. Everyone was in bed with hot water bottles if they had them, trying to keep warm and to forget the severe trials of the worst Christmas Day any of them could remember. The village was clothed in a darkness so complete that Castle Farthing might not even exist outside its residents' dreams. The only evidence that it did was in the shapes that resisted the urgent fall of the snow, and there wasn't a soul that did or could see this passive but solid resistance.

The wind drove the whirling storm of flakes in avalanches of snow and howled mercilessly in the eaves and chimneys, master of this little world, for the moment.

Chapter Ten

Boxing Day – morning

In the intense cold caused by the snow lying outside, Falconer had decided, even wrapped as he was in winter flannelette pyjamas, to lose his inhibitions a bit and, when he woke up the next morning with his arms round Mulligan's thick neck, he didn't turn a hair. The dog was warm and, in consequence, so was he, and he closed his eyes to go back to sleep, as it was much too early to get up yet, given the time he'd got to bed.

But he hadn't considered that there were young children in this house so, no sooner had he snuggled down under the duvet for another hour or so of repose, he heard the bedroom door open and two joyous voices welcome him to another day in the Carmichael household. Rudely pulling the duvet away from both him and his bedfellow, the boys informed him that it had snowed again in the night, and all their hard work in creating paths the day before was once more under a thick blanket of snow. At their tender years, they were thrilled, but the information left Falconer decidedly unimpressed.

A tired voice from the next bedroom told them to leave Uncle Harry alone to get a bit more sleep, but it was too late now. Falconer was wide awake, and would only court sleep in vain if he settled down in the bed again. Besides, it sounded as if the whole household was getting up. He heard the sounds of little feet padding down the stairs, followed by the heavier ones of Kerry moving as fast as her swollen bulk would allow, and the sound of Carmichael's razor could be heard from the bathroom.

Dressing as quickly as he could, he decided he'd try to get sole tenancy of the bathroom a bit later, as the pipes for the downstairs shower room had frozen, and went down to see what help he could provide in getting the fire going again and lighting the lamps. His first action was to fling open the curtains. There might not be much light outside, but any there was would reflect on the snow and make some inroads into the dark house.

Outside, their energetically dug paths from the previous day had disappeared under the fresh fall in the overnight blizzard, but he could already hear the sound of the farmer's tractor, clearing a path once more so that the residents wouldn't be trapped in their homes. That at least meant that Carmichael and he could get on with making a list of tasks for the day, get to The Fisherman's Flies to get the photographic evidence they needed, move the body, and visit people in their own homes to interview them in more depth.

Carmichael made his way downstairs about twenty minutes later, pink and fresh from the shower and Kerry immediately shooed the boys upstairs to clean their teeth and have a wash. The master of the house headed straight for the fire and Falconer left him to it. He knew nothing about keeping a fire in all night and resurrecting it again the next morning. Kerry was busy lighting the lamps and candles, having already put a kettle on a gas ring to boil water for tea, so he went over to the basket that had been placed to the side of the fire to see how mother and pups were doing this morning.

Mistress Fang lay on her side, the three pups suckling happily, and Mr Knuckles had curled himself up round her back, so a very happy doggy basket indeed met Falconer's eyes. He was still amazed at how he had coped with the pups' arrival into this cold and inhospitable world, working purely from instinct and common sense, and having inconveniently forgotten all the television programmes he had watched showing the birth of animals. He still felt like a hero though, and decided to enjoy it. It didn't happen often, and should be revelled in.

The boys tripped back downstairs, but so involved had he become in watching the pups that Kerry beat him to the bathroom, and he went disconsolately into the kitchen to see if he could give Carmichael a hand preparing breakfast. He *would* get a shower this morning. Thank God that the Carmichaels had one that was run on bottled gas and didn't rely on a tank of heated water. Otherwise, by the end of his imprisonment at *chez Carmichael* they'd all reek to high heaven. Sending up a silent prayer that the people they were going to interview today were equally blessed with this system, he put toast under the grill and watched it intently.

Carmichael meanwhile, had gone outside to give the chickens some unfrozen water and feed them, and returned to make the scrambled eggs, huffing and puffing with cold. 'Poor little things,' he remarked. 'I don't know how they stand it out there in that shed, but they seem perfectly happy, and it felt quite warm in there.' But Falconer wasn't listening. He'd just heard Kerry coming out of the bathroom, and he was already halfway up the stairs before Carmichael noticed that he was talking to thin air.

When breakfast was cleared away, Falconer returned to the table to work out their schedule for the day while Carmichael dealt with the washing-up. Kerry was exhausted from all the disruption and extra cooking the day before, and had slumped into an armchair, looking as if she could sleep for a fortnight, and had only made one comment with animation since she had got up. She had declared that she had names for the puppies, and that they were to be called Little Dream, Fantasy, and Cloud. That way, it didn't matter whether they turned out to be boys or girls.

As she dozed and Carmichael clattered dishes around in the kitchen, Falconer looked at all the appointments he intended them to make that day with a jaundiced eye, and felt a deep longing for the services of PCs Merv Green and 'Twinkle' Starr – and even work-shy, lazy PC Proudfoot. Never had he appreciated all the foot-slogging they did on their door-to-door enquiries for him, and he wished mightily that they could be transported here to help out. They were going to be rushed off their feet, but there was no point in making any bones about it.

It had to be done, no matter how long it took.

When Carmichael appeared at the kitchen door with a cloth across one shoulder, to see if there was any more washing-up, he asked him, 'Where do the old man and his nephew live? That old chap who turned up in his Father Christmas costume?'

'You mean John and old Albert Carpenter,' replied Carmichael. 'They live at the other end of this terrace, in Woodbine Cottage.'

Falconer returned to his list, and when Carmichael finally came in from the kitchen he indicated for him to join him at the table. 'I've planned that we go down to those new houses where Jeffries lived and have a word with the three stooges first, then I thought we'd better check out that place you told me about, that's taken over what was the vicarage.'

'That's Dr Griddle's lot. It's called Blue Sky now. I must admit, I haven't seen any of the residents out and about for some time, but I think I got a glimpse of Hector Griddle at the back of the church at Midnight Mass.'

'Right: we definitely need to check that lot out then. What did you say the place was?'

'It's a sort of halfway house for people who've been coming off drink and drugs. It's not been open a year yet, and there was some trouble when it first opened. Some of the patients there seemed to think they could sneak off to the pub without anyone noticing, but Dr Griddle soon sorted that out. He gave George Covington snapshots of everyone who was in residence so that he could eject any of them trying to sneak a crafty drink. They soon caught on that there was no use in even making the attempt, because if they were caught, they lost privileges.'

'Well, it's a damned nuisance having it on our doorstep when we're cut off like this, and with a double murder on our hands. If there's any likelihood that it was one of them, we're going to run into a mountain of bureaucracy just to get a peek at their records.'

'Where to after that, sir?' asked Carmichael, not so much concerned with as yet un-encountered bureaucracy as to where else they might be headed.

'I thought that might be about lunchtime, then I thought we could look at the upper village; start off with the pub – we really do have to do something about that body, and we can talk to the Covingtons at the same time – then call in on Rosemary Wilson, up and across to Woodbine Cottage, then we can call in on the Stupples and Henry Pistorius in The Old School House.'

'What about the Warren-Brownes?' asked Carmichael.

'I thought we might leave them for today, what with Mrs Warren-Browne having been in such a state yesterday. I think we ought to give her a day to recover before we call round again.'

'That's very considerate of you. Thank you, sir, but maybe we'll decide nearer to the time. I'm sure Kerry'll want us to call in, even if we haven't told her what we found yesterday. Right, let's make like chickens again and get on out there. There's only a bit of digging to do to join us up to where the farmer went through.'

Looking with loathing at the shovels that stood ready by the front door, Falconer gave a deep sigh of resignation, started to pull on his coat which was barely dry from the night before, and thought, here we go again!

Although the fire had only just got going, the cold air outside hit them with an icy blast which produced a gasp of shock from them both. Today wasn't going to be an easy day, Falconer thought, as they started to move the snow that had accumulated during the previous night. Although the front path was short, with muscles already aching from the unexpected exercise of the previous day, it seemed a lot longer than it actually was.

The sky was a clear bright blue, and the sun was creeping up over the horizon so there was no need for a torch, although both men now had one about their person as it was highly unlikely that they would finish their visits before dusk.

The snow-plough-scraped ground was slippery under their feet, and they walked warily down to the end of the village green before crossing the road to the first homes on their list. As they approached Alice Diggory's house at Hillview, Falconer noticed the absence of lamplight from Michaelmas Cottage where Digby Jeffries had lived, and determined that one of the first things he would do when they were reunited with the rest of the world was to trace the man's next of kin. They had to be informed, and without too much delay. It would be a disaster if the media somehow got hold of the story and they learnt about it that way.

The thought of gifts waiting pointlessly under a tree that would never light up the room again with its coloured lights sent a wave of sadness through him. No matter what the man had done, and they hadn't proved anything yet, he was still loved or cared for by somebody, and those somebodies had carefully chosen, paid for, wrapped, and delivered presents for him, which he would never have the pleasure of opening now: would never see, use, or enjoy.

At Hillview, Alice Diggory invited them in and informed them that Cedric Malting and Robin De'ath were visiting as she had a mobile gas fire, and neither of them had such a facility. They were keeping warm together, she explained, and keeping each other company at the same time. It made sense, as there were no telephones, no mobiles, and no televisions to entertain them. They might as well be together, as spread across three separate households, two of them bitterly cold. Quite right! Thought Falconer, and it saved them two more visits too, with exactly the same questions as he would ask on this one. That should save some time.

They found the two men in armchairs, huddled round the mobile gas heater, their hands held out towards it for warmth. When Alice joined them she invited the new arrivals to sit down on the sofa, apologising that she could not offer them any tea or coffee because she only had an electric kettle. Apart from yesterday's lunch, the three of them were sustaining themselves with sandwiches made from the sliced cold turkey that Paula Covington had shared out before they left the pub the day before.

'I understand that the pub will be opening for hot drinks and food later, and Mrs Covington said she'd call round to The

Rookery to see if she could persuade the Rollasons to open up their tea shop, too. Even if it's only a drink, people need something hot inside them, don't you think?'

Both men nodded in agreement and took a seat on the sofa. Fortunately it was a three-seater, for Alice had to squeeze on to it too to be near enough the fire to keep warm. 'We haven't resorted to sleeping together yet, but it might be on the cards if there's no break in this weather,' said Robin De'ath with a teasing tone in his voice.

'Robin!' exclaimed Cedric Malting, shocked to his conservative roots, and Alice Diggory's face turned an unlovely red with embarrassment. 'That's quite enough of that, Robin, dear,' she told him. 'Any more of that and I shall have to send you home.' This was a threat that he had to take seriously, and he subsided back into his chair, any signs of amusement wiped away by the thought of spending the rest of the day with no real source of heat.

Carmichael, perched on the end of the sofa, got out his notebook and tried his best to appear invisible, while Falconer started the questioning. 'I'd like you to tell me everything you know about the late Mr Jeffries, and don't hold back anything. You can't do him any harm now, and we do need to find his killer. No matter how much he's got under your skins, you wouldn't want to deny him justice, I'm sure.'

'He was a terror for finding somebody's weak spot and played on it mercilessly,' offered Robin De'ath.

'Robin!' interrupted Alice. 'One shouldn't speak ill of the dead.'

'But we should speak the truth, otherwise whoever did away with him will get away with it. I'm sure he had no illusions about himself, and he'd rather we helped the police with their enquiries honestly than hold back information and scupper the investigation.'

'I'm sorry. I wasn't thinking straight,' Alice apologised, then handed the baton back to Robin, who was obviously bursting to have a good bitch about his late 'friend'.

'But we told you all this, yesterday,' protested De'ath.

'Then we'd like you to tell us again, please,' requested Falconer. 'You might have remembered something overnight that you forgot to share with us yesterday.'

'Very well,' he began with a sigh, 'He used to like playing 'king of the shit heap' with us three,' he said, with a bitchy gleam in his eye. 'And Henry, too, of course. He saw himself as superior as he'd worked for the British Broadcasting Corporation; blessed be its name. We all knew that Henry did too – Pistorius,' he elucidated pompously, for the benefit of the two policemen, 'but Henry only worked in radio, which Digby considered a very inferior arm of the corporation. I must say, Henry gave a very good showing of taking it all in good part, but underneath, I could see that he was seething when it was his turn in the barrel. I presume you'll be calling on him later.'

When Falconer had confirmed this with a nod, he went on, 'Me, he despised because I worked for Channel 6, which, as you might know, is a minority channel which doesn't have much of a reputation at the moment. On the other hand, it doesn't have the benefit of the licence payers' money, which the BBC has, and I think it does a jolly good job on a fraction of the budget that other channels enjoy. Especially the BBC! Not difficult to produce lavish programmes when you've got all that public loot at your disposal, is it?'

Cedric Malting now took up the conversational reins. 'He was always teasing me about my plays because they'd only ever been performed by amateur groups, but it's not easy to get established as a playwright. I thought I'd found someone to give me a bit of a step up when I met him, but he refused point-blank, saying that my work should shine through on its own merit if it was any good.

'I explained to him that it wouldn't have a chance to shine unless someone actually read it, but he wouldn't yield to my pleas.'

'Well, you know why that was, don't you?' interrupted Robin. 'He made us think he was in a position of power when he had only been a lowly floor manager, and there we were, all either being jealous or looking up to him, when he was an absolute nothing.'

'That's a bit strong, isn't it, Robin?' asked Alice.

'Absolutely not!' he replied. 'The police are here to hear the unvarnished truth, and that's exactly what I'm telling them. What about the things he said to you? I don't know how you didn't give him a good slapping.'

'I wouldn't stoop so low as to behave like that Robin, but he said some very cruel things to me.'

'Like what?' asked Falconer, suddenly ceasing to sit statue-still and joining in.

With a slight grimace as she gathered her thoughts, Alice began her tale of how she had suffered under the tongue of the late, and presumably unmissed, Digby Jeffries. 'He kept on at me about how English teachers were responsible for the lack of correct grammar, spelling and pronunciation in English today. He used to suddenly start quizzing me on obscure points of the language, and if he flustered me with the unexpectedness of his questions, he informed me that I didn't know my subject well enough to have been a teacher, and should have done something useful with my life, and maybe worked in a factory. A factory! I ask you!'

Taking a moment or two to regain her calm, she continued, 'He used to upset me a great deal, as I was always graded as an excellent teacher, and worked at schools which had *marvellous* reports from Ofsted. And when I pointed this out to him, along with the pronunciation and grammatical errors that most of those currently working for the BBC made, he used to push it back in my direction, saying it was because they'd been educated by low-grade teachers like me.'

'It's a wonder you ever socialised with him at all,' interjected Falconer.

'Who else do I know in this little village, except for old codgers like us and Henry?' she retorted.

'Why did you move here in the first place?' asked Falconer, as the wind suddenly howled round the building, causing him to add, 'I'd have thought these places would've had double glazing, given how recently they were built.'

'Thrown up, you mean,' said Robin De'ath, re-joining the conversation. 'Every short cut taken and every corner cut with these places.'

'I wouldn't have come here at all, if it hadn't been for the low price,' Alice explained. 'As you know, I never married, and you don't get a lot of 'bang for your bucks' on a teacher's pension. When I retired I had to sell my old place just to give me some capital to help me live comfortably. It's not easy, not being part of a marriage or a partnership, and I should have hated to throw my lot in with a friend or relative and not have my independence any more.'

Carmichael looked up in astonishment at her phraseology. She had kept up with her subject, even though she was retired now. 'Bang for your bucks'! Way to go, lady!

'And if you really know why we associated with him, Inspector, it was because we were all newcomers and close neighbours as well, and it would have looked a bit off if we'd excluded him from our little group when Henry Pistorius was part of it, and he lives all the way up Sheepwash Lane. We were just too well-brought up to ostracise him, and that's the bottom line.'

This explanation from Robin De'ath did indeed have the ring of truth about it, and Falconer decided that they'd learnt as much as they could from them about their relationships with the dead man, but there still remained the actual events of what happened on Christmas Eve: what they may have noticed that other people had missed or forborne to mention. And whether they had all got together to rid the village of a thoroughly unpleasant old man.

'I wonder if you could tell me about what happened on the twenty-fourth: the Crib Service, Midnight Mass, and afterwards, in the pub.'

'We didn't go to the pub after the Crib Service like a lot of people did because the place would have been full of children,' Alice explained, just so that they should understand they had only made one visit to The Fisherman's Flies.

'I couldn't believe the sheer brass neck of the man,' said the quiet voice of Cedric Malting. 'Just swanning in like that and taking over. I mean, I know he had permission from the locum vicar, but I thought he would have stepped down when the old man showed up. That's when he should have disappeared out of the back of the vestry, and not challenged the belief of the younger children by them having to see two Father Christmases at the same time.' This was an unusually bold speech for Cedric, and Falconer thought that maybe the man only found his voice through writing his plays.

'Discretion never was the better part of valour in Digby's opinion. He had the hide of a rhinoceros and the stubbornness of a mule. He'd not have yielded his role if a whole coach-load of red-suited gentlemen had turned up,' agreed Robin.

'Hear hear, Cedric!' added Alice. 'It was absolutely disgraceful! He should have been ashamed of himself, and then to turn up to Midnight Mass in the same costume. I would have died of embarrassment if I'd done something like that. He was completely insensitive to the feelings of others, and just liked showing off in my opinion.'

'Did you notice his behaviour with the children to whom he handed out presents?' asked Falconer, which elicited a delighted comment from Alice.

'Lovely grammar, Inspector. There's not much of it about these days, so well done. Well done indeed!'

'Thank you very much, Miss Diggory. I take that as a real compliment, coming from an English teacher,' replied Falconer, his manners, as usual, impeccable.

'And as for turning up at the pub in that ghastly costume, he really was the biggest show-off I know,' said Robin De'ath sourly.

'Yes, but he didn't stay till closing time, did he?'

Pricking up his ears, Falconer asked, 'When did he leave?' hoping to get a bit more information on this little incident in relation to his group of oldies.

'When he discovered he'd left his real glasses in the church. He must have taken them off after having to read the words of the carols, and put his silly wire-framed ones on so that he could be the complete Father Christmas in the pub,' Cedric informed him.

'Even then he couldn't resist standing at the bar and chatting for another half an hour before he actually left the place. He just couldn't resist attention.' Alice had a very disapproving look on her face.

'Did anyone else leave during that time?' Maybe they were getting somewhere at last.

'That woman with the headaches. She doesn't socialise much and always looks ill. I think she used to run the post office. Warren-Browne, that's her name. Marian, I think. They left, but then there was a bit of an exodus, and there were so many people drifting away that I couldn't really identify anyone else with any accuracy,' added Alice, thinking that they must have covered everything by now.

'And you three left when?'

'About the same time as everyone started to go,' replied Alice. It was late, and there was no point in staying when everyone else was off home.'

'Now, one last question,' stated Falconer, making them all sigh. Would these accursed policemen never go and leave them in peace again?

'Did you, and this may sound an odd question, ever notice the way he behaved around children? I know we touched on this subject yesterday, but I wonder if you've had the chance to remember anything else on the subject.' Cunning Falconer!

There was a stunned silence. The question had really been a curved ball for them, and they looked as if they were all waiting for someone else to speak first. It was Alice Diggory who blinked first. 'In what way, Inspector?' she asked.

'Did you ever see him with young children and feel uncomfortable?' Falconer wasn't going to waste time beating about the bush.

Again, there was a silence which seemed to stretch out into infinity, which Alice again broke, looking anywhere but at Falconer. 'I always thought that I wouldn't have been happy with him having contact with any of my pupils, but then I've

126

already told you that,' she stated, flushing again and wondering if the others might follow this lead.

'I saw him in the tea shop once,' Cedric Malting piped up. 'It was a day when little Tristram was running round the place because there was no playgroup.' He stopped for a while to muster his thoughts, before continuing. 'I'd just dropped in for a coffee and didn't see Digby until he called the little chap over. When he'd toddled up to the table, Digby picked him up and swung him high in the air, then sat him on his lap.

'It all looked perfectly normal till then, but while the little boy was on his lap he kept running his hands over his arms and legs, and it made me feel a bit creeped out.' Here, indeed, was new evidence of Jeffries' inappropriate behaviour.

'Now, I'm not saying there was anything wrong, just that it made me feel very uncomfortable, and when his mother saw what was happening she very quickly came and took him away, saying that if he should come out of the back room again would someone call her immediately, as she was worried that he might get outside. Get outside, my foot! She just didn't like the thought of him being fondled by Digby, or at least that's what I thought when I got home and mulled it over in my mind.'

'I can't remember a specific incident, but I know that something left alarm bells ringing in my mind about him.' Robin De'ath didn't like being left out, and volunteered this even if he couldn't readily call anything to mind. 'I do remember that Stupple chap being a bit concerned, though. I overheard him in the pub, talking about his own kids and the Cubs and Brownies. Obviously his wife shared his concern.'

Isn't it funny, thought Falconer, that no one ever says anything about things like this until someone's dead or moved away. Everyone has concerns, but no one's willing to be the first to air them; then, after something like this, it all comes pouring out. It was too late now! If only someone had spoken up sooner they could have got him, but now they'd just have to leave it to Social Services to pick up the pieces after the event. Damned nuisance, and no mistake!

'Well, thank you all for your time. We'll be on our way now, and leave you good folks in peace,' he said, rising and nodding to Carmichael to indicate that they were leaving.

'I hated him! Really hated him! He did everything he could to make me feel small and insignificant, and I'm glad someone's finally nailed the bastard!' Cedric Malting was seething with emotion as he said this, only to be answered by the other two.

'Oh, really bad joke, Ced! 'Nailed' him'. Bad, bad taste,' said Robin De'ath.

'We all hated him, but I don't think you ought to go around saying things like that, Cedric; at least not before they've caught whoever's done this awful thing,' Alice added, getting her two-penn'orth in as well.

Falconer stared at them all after this little outburst, then bade them the compliments of the season and led Carmichael outside into the fresh air once more.

'I'm glad to get out of there,' he said, once the door had been closed on them.

'Me too,' agreed Carmichael. 'You could feel the build-up of hatred, couldn't you?'

'Definitely. So, this little visit hasn't crossed anyone off our list of suspects. And Jeffries announced to anyone within earshot that he was going back to the church, then delayed his departure. If anyone had the slightest notion of doing him harm, that gave them the ideal opportunity to slip home for a weapon of sorts, brass candlesticks aside, even if they hadn't already had the foresight to bring along a nail gun to aid their carol singing.

'Just about the same as yesterday, then – everybody hated him, but nobody had anything to do with his murder.'

'SOS,' sir,' replied Carmichael.

'Pardon?'

'Same old shit, sir,' the sergeant enlightened his superior, with a little grin.

Their next call was at Blue Sky, the halfway house for recovering alcoholics and drug addicts, and neither of them was relishing what lay ahead of them: Carmichael, because he thought the very existence of such a place in a small village was asking for trouble, and Falconer just because he was a fastidious man himself who never over-indulged in anything, and found it hard to sympathise with others who had done so to the detriment of their way of life.

His years at prep and senior school, followed by university and the army had left him self-reliant and sober: a man very much in charge of his own destiny, and he couldn't understand how others could follow such a highway to hell with apparent disregard for the consequences. One of the reasons that he had joined the police force was because he wanted to be a part of ensuring that people lived honest and respectable lives, and were protected from those who didn't. On this subject, he was a hard and unforgiving man.

Carmichael, on the other hand, never having gone away to school, and receiving his education at the comprehensive school in Market Darley, was more of a realist, and was of the opinion, given the choices he could have made, that 'there, but for the grace of God, go I'. He knew that some people couldn't resist temptation, especially if they didn't have much of a home life, and would succumb out as somewhere to hide from the harsh realities of their lives, or even out of boredom. Maybe, between the two detectives, there was a well-balanced outlook on life.

Dr Hector Griddle had to stifle a look of pure alarm as he surveyed their warrant cards, and his thoughts immediately went into overdrive. Surely one of his patients hadn't committed some offence? They had all seemed so well-readjusted to life, and were almost ready to return to the community.

He led the two policemen to his office and bade them take a seat, asking, 'How can I help you, officers?' He was aware of how squeaky and nervous his voice sounded, but there was nothing he could do about it. He was riddled with anxiety that there should be a blot on the copy book of his establishment when it was so close to closing down.

'We're making enquiries into the death of one of the

residents of the village, and of the visiting clergyman, and would like to know where your patients were after Midnight Mass on Christmas Eve. I know that they attended, and I want to know exactly what they did and where they went directly after the service.'

'They all came back here,' answered Griddle, a sheen of sweat visible on his upper lip. 'I supervised them myself, then locked the establishment for the night. I assure you that none of them could have gone wandering after that. They also wear tags, so if they achieved the impossible and managed to get out, an alarm would have gone off, and I would have responded immediately.'

It had cost Falconer a lot to use the word 'patients', and now he was stunned by the sheer defensiveness of the man. Could anywhere be as secure as he claimed Blue Sky was? Even Alcatraz had had at least one escapee, and Colditz had had its fair share of absconders, too.

His cynical expression had evidently been noted by Griddle, because he suddenly broke into speech again. 'The patients under my care here are on the last leg of their journey back into society and, in fact, we have only six residents at the moment. The charity only took a twelve-month lease on this property, and will not be renewing it. Donations are right down, due to the financial downturn, and this place will have to close. These are hard times, Inspector, for everyone, and charitable donations are nowhere as near as high as they once were.

'The last six people left here will be back in the community within the next three months, and I can hardly see any of them jeopardising the chance of getting on with their lives by doing something stupid so close to them leaving here.'

'Is it possible that I could speak to them individually?' This wasn't something that Falconer relished, and he was rather glad when Dr Griddle replied,

'I really wouldn't advise it at the moment. I can assure you that all of them were safely behind these doors only a few minutes after the service ended, and if you could bring yourself to exhaust every other avenue before unsettling them with an enquiry like this, I should be forever grateful.'

The inspector saw the bait and took it with relief. 'We'll take your word for that at the moment, but if my enquiries don't throw up anything else, I shall return, and I shall expect to interview each and every one of them. Do I make myself clear?'

'As crystal,' replied Griddle, a wave of relief washing over him. He just wanted to get to the end of his time at this establishment and look for a job with prospects, instead of hanging around here in the middle of nowhere looking after people who were already cured. This time! He had known that Blue Sky was small potatoes when he'd taken the job, and although it was preferable to be in work than out of it, he'd be relieved when he could get back to a town or city and look for something with more of a challenge to it.

As he saw them off the premises, Falconer sighed with relief then remembered that they still had to go over to the pub and sort out the body of Rev. Searle. 'Have you got the photographic equipment?' he asked, and Carmichael indicated the rucksack on his back which had accompanied him all morning without attracting comment.

'Sure thing, sir,' he replied. 'I wondered when you were going to remember that we hadn't been there yet,' but he said it with a smile. There was no chance that the body had 'turned' in the temperatures they were experiencing.

'I wondered when you'd notice that,' commented Falconer, with a twinkle in his eye. Still, he was so relieved to have got the visit to Blue Sky out of the way that he didn't think it mattered too much that he'd had a little lapse of memory. And it was probably the thought of having to go to that establishment which had made him temporarily forget about The Fisherman's Flies, and what awaited them there. And he'd had Allsorts on his list for the morning, so it was just as well that he'd managed to get three of his suspects together in the same room at Hillview.

George Covington was just opening the pub doors when they arrived and had put a chalked board outside in the snow which advertised hot drinks, sandwiches, and soup for anyone who visited during the lunchtime opening hours. Normal menu would be resumed this evening.

'I've still got that there dead cleric upstairs!' he called, as Falconer and Carmichael came into view. 'Oh, bugger!' he suddenly exclaimed. 'And I've only forgotten to turn off the radiator in there. We're going to need to get him somewhere cool before he starts to go off. The smell of a corpse isn't going to do anything for my trade, you know.'

'Just about to get underway,' Falconer hailed him, then, drawing closer, he explained that they would do all the photographic work necessary, take measurements, and collect any evidence they could find and perhaps after that, George would be kind enough to give them a hand moving the body down to the cellar.

'It is probably the coldest place in the pub. You're right about that, but I don't know what Paula's going to say about it. She's got a thing about death.'

Haven't we all! thought the inspector, especially if it concerns our own. 'I don't want to move him to the church, which *is* possibly colder, George. But it wouldn't be seemly to be seen moving a body around, even if there aren't many people about.'

'OK, but if he's still here in a couple of days' time, I'm going to have to insist that he's taken off the premises. It's not exactly compliant with food hygiene regulations to have a corpse installed in the cellar, which is where our food freezers are.'

'Perfectly understandable. We'll just go on up then, shall we?'

'You help yourselves. I wouldn't go into that room again if you paid me. Gives me the willies, that does, him just lying there as if he were asleep, and I can't say as I'll relish going down to the cellar when he's in residence, either.'

The room struck warm as they entered it, and when Falconer checked the body, he was dismayed to discover that rigor mortis had not yet worn off and the limbs were frozen in a position that would give them some considerable trouble transferring him down to the cellar. If only there had been no heating in the room, he would have been as floppy as a rag doll. And now he wasn't. Just their luck!

'Right, Carmichael, you do the videoing again and I'll take care of the photography, then we can draw a plan of the scene and put in some measurements. We'll have to bag up all the crumpled wrapping paper as well, for fingerprints. Let's get this scene recorded as quickly as possible, so that we can get on with the job of finding out who killed them both, although I can't think of a motive for anyone wanting to do away with a locum clergyman, can you?'

'Seems daft to me. I don't think he knew anybody in the village, so why murder him?'

'My thoughts exactly.'

As they talked, they worked, and it wasn't too long before Falconer yelled downstairs for George to come to their aid in getting the mortal remains of Rev. Searle down to the cellar.

When George arrived, he took one look at the position of the body and declared, 'I hope he's not still stiff, for if he is, I don't see how we're going to get him through the doors and down the stairs with his legs flopped apart like that.'

'Stiff as a board, I'm afraid, George. You really ought to have turned off that radiator,' Falconer informed the publican bluntly.

'I can't be expected to think of everything round here,' George retorted, a grim expression eclipsing his normal happy 'mine host' face.

The three men stood contemplating the body, and a grimace of distaste washed over Falconer's face, a greenish tinge, over Carmichael's. 'We'll just have to see how we can manage, before doing *anything drastic*,' Falconer advised, emphasising the last two words for all they implied, and the three of them went over to see which part of the deceased vicar they would each be holding, as they took him to his next, but not last, resting place.

As it worked out, George took the body by the shoulders,

Falconer and Carmichael being left with a leg each. 'Up with him!' ordered the inspector, which was easier said than done. He might have been a frail figure of a man but in death he seemed to have put on an awful lot of weight.

Their first attempt to get him to leave the room feet first didn't work, as the two policeman were standing one either side of their load. 'Do it the other way round,' advised George Covington. 'If I get 'is head out first, you can support 'im from behind his feet, that way you won't be either side of 'im, and 'e should just about fit through.'

George was correct and, with a little local difficulty, they were able to get the body out of the room and onto the landing. The stairs proved a most awkward obstacle to overcome, and Carmichael nearly lost the leg he was holding as he followed the body down the stairs. 'Hold fast, there, Sergeant. 'E might be dead, but we don't want to break 'is bloody neck, do we?' yelled George, struggling not to lose his hold as Carmichael recovered his grip.

The entrance to the cellar was from the actual barroom itself, so they had two doorways to negotiate before they could get him down the cellar steps and put him down. George knew that the cellar door was wide, but he expressed doubts about the width of the door to the bar as they reached the foot of the stairs.

They approached the opening with caution as Paula Covington came to see what all the noise and shouting was about. Her unexpected exclamation of, 'Oh, my God!' nearly unsettled them sufficiently to let go of their load, but George saved the day by shoving a knee into the old man's back while his two companions got a firmer hold of his ankles.

'Come on, let's see if he'll fit,' said George, anxious to get back to his bar.

He didn't fit! They stood there for more than a minute contemplating the problem. Falconer knew that if the worst came to the worst they could always break the resistance in his thighs by cracking the joints, but he wouldn't be responsible for his own stomach, let alone Carmichael's, if they had to do this.

As he was contemplating this grisly plan, Paula suggested, 'Why don't you just turn him sideways? That way, you should be able to get him through.' And she was right, although as they turned him as directed, a plethora of small objects and coins fell from the man's trouser pockets and showered their feet with debris.

'It looks like you've hit the jackpot, Inspector,' commented George. 'I've never seen such an exotic slot machine before in all my life.'

Falconer smiled at this graveyard humour. Carmichael began to laugh, then to choke, and Paula rushed from the scene calling, 'I'll get you a bucket from the kitchen, love.' The sergeant put down his portion of their burden, and the other two leaned the unbending old man against the doorframe as Carmichael ran after Paula before he threw up over the corpse.

'That young man all right?' queried George, looking after Carmichael's retreating back when there was a sliding noise and the mortal remains of Rev. Searle, losing their precarious balance against the doorframe, went bowling down the flight of stairs, becoming more pliant after every step it hit.

'Fine!' replied Falconer. 'He's just got a bit of a dicky tummy. He'll be as right as nine-pence once he's had a good boke. Now, I suppose we'd better go down and see what state that body's in. Bloody careless of us, that was.' He was amazed at how calm he felt after such a calamity. Maybe he'd just tipped himself over the edge.

George, too, was unexpectedly insouciant. 'Good: I'm glad 'e's down there, because I don't want to be seen by my customers moving dead bodies around as if I were Sweeny Todd. I'd be out of business in a week if that happened. Thank God there's no one in yet to see what we're up to.'

'That's not quite the point, though, is it?' queried Falconer. 'We've just let a corpse – evidence of extreme importance in a case of murder – fall down a flight of stairs into a pub cellar, doing God knows what damage to it on the way down.'

'Damned lucky that 'e was dead, then, and couldn't feel a thing, isn't it?' commented George Covington, not worried a jot

135

about what the powers that be would say about such a calamity.

Carmichael returned looking rather shamefaced, and they trooped down the steps to make sure that the rest of Rev. Searle's trip to its resting place down below went without hitch. From the deep, Carmichael's voice echoed hollowly upwards. 'Oh my God, sir! Look at the angle of his head! He looks just like that kid from *The Exorcist*. Should we try to make him look a bit less ... broken?'

There was a pause. 'And where the hell have his teeth disappeared to? They must be down here somewhere.'

'Don't move another step, Carmichael!' yelled Falconer. If his jumbo-sized sergeant managed to do the fandango on them, they'd be reduced to dust!

At this point, Paula Covington closed the door at the top of the staircase, and this was just as well, as the first customers of the day were making their way into the bar in search of warmth and hot drinks, and wouldn't have been very impressed if they could see the contortions that were going on under their very feet.

Paula had already returned to scoop up the flotsam and jetsam that had issued from the body's pockets before it took a tumble, and had it all gathered in a crumpled moneybag for Falconer when they all came back into the bar. 'There you go, Inspector. All tidied up and ready for your inspection,' she said, as she handed it to him.

'Thanks for all your cooperation and patience,' he said, putting the bag into one of the capacious pockets in his coat. 'We'll leave you in peace now, although we'll have to have another word with you sometime. I'd thought we could do that this morning, but I hadn't counted on the little local difficulty we encountered moving the 'you-know-what'. Come along Carmichael.'

Once outside, he enquired after his sergeant's well-being. 'I'm fine, sir. It was the thought that we might have to break some of his joints to get him through that really got to me.'

'Me too, although I didn't think you'd be so imaginative, so I didn't actually vocalise the thought, when it went through my mind,' retorted Falconer, but he smiled as he said it. He hadn't fancied the possibility of them having to do that any more than Carmichael had. He just had slightly better control of his stomach.

Rosemary Wilson had opened her shop, knowing that people wouldn't be able to cook, and might want to stock up on things that they could eat without having to heat. She'd also done so in order to catch up on the gossip, but wild horses wouldn't have dragged that particular information out of her.

The place was full of people, either fighting over the last tin of peaches or the last hot water bottle and box of candles, but when Rosemary spied their faces through the throng she gave an enormous smile of welcome, thinking that here at last would be news, and grist for the gossip mill. 'Love the hats!' she shouted over the heads of her customers.

Falconer put his hand to his head and heaved another great sigh of failure. They'd been very good so far today at whipping off their downright weird headgear, but their entrance to the shop after what had just happened had left them off their guard, and the damned chicken monstrosities were still on both their heads. Well, there was no point in being coy about them any more. They might as well wear them and be damned, he thought, as some of the people now staring at them started to cluck and crow at the sight of them thus attired.

Rosemary, however, had nothing to add to their knowledge so far, and was more concerned with asking if they'd visited Marian Warren-Browne. 'I'm worried about her,' she confided in them. 'Some days she looks like death. And she's started saying some very strange things. I've had a word with Alan, but he just keeps saying there's nothing to worry about and that it's all in hand.'

She had nothing to add to what they already knew about Jeffries' behaviour in her establishment, and they left shortly afterwards and headed back to Jasmine Cottage for something hot to eat and drink. 'I hope you can eat fast,' said Falconer, thinking of all the visits they had to make that afternoon.

'Oh, I can get it down almost as fast as I can get it up,' replied Carmichael, and then descended into a pensive silence, as he realised what he had just said, and fought the nausea that washed over him again as he remembered the rapid loss of what had remained of his breakfast back in the pub.

Chapter Eleven

Boxing Day – afternoon

Kerry had a huge spread of cold meats, mashed potatoes, salad, and pickles waiting for them, as well as a pot of tea, and for just over an hour, they ate, drank, and basked in the warmth of the house, but it was soon time to get their outdoor gear on and get back on the job. Carmichael was glad he could discard the rucksack of photographic equipment, and went upstairs to get a different coat for their afternoon out in the bitter weather.

Hurtling downstairs again, ready for the off, Falconer caught sight of him wearing what he'd gone to fetch, and shouted, 'No! You're surely not going out in that thing? You know how I feel about it.'

'I don't really think it matters what you feel about it,' replied Carmichael rebelliously, pulling up the collar of the ancient, moth-eaten (and huge!) fur coat he had worn once before, to the office. 'It's me who's wearing it, and it's the warmest thing I've got.'

'But people will see me with you,' the inspector spat back.

'Then let them. I live here, and they know my ways, and they'll not think the less of you because you've let me wear my warmest coat in the coldest weather we've had for years.'

'He's right, you know,' chimed in Kerry, and Falconer had to admit defeat on this occasion. Carmichael was Carmichael, and nothing he could say or do would ever alter the man's basic character.

Their first visit was to old Albert Carpenter and his great-nephew, John, at the north end of the terrace in which Carmichael's home was situated. There had been plenty of ill-feeling from both of them over Albert's well-established role as Father Christmas being usurped.

Falconer's first impression of the interior of the little cottage was that John Carpenter must have moved in with his great-uncle. The furniture was certainly of the right period, and the large television stuck out like a sore thumb in the tiny parlour. The little Christmas tree was real, the decorations on it, as with the ones strung from the ceiling, very old and well-used, most of them being of paper and carved wood rather than the plastic and tinsel decorations that have taken over from traditional ones.

The old man had been listening to the radio when they entered the room, but soon became garrulous when they mentioned the inclement weather. 'This ain't nothin' to what we 'ad in 1962-63. Nigh on buried the 'ouses, that did. The sea and everythin' froze. I got some pictures somewhere of my niece and nephew when they was young, a-standin' on the waves down on the coast. 'Tis true. The sea itself froze over, and people could walk on it like they was doin' a miracle. Ice stayed around till Easter, too. Don't get winters like that no more. Everyone's too namby-pamby to cope with weather like that these days. 'Why, some folks even chopped up their banisters and shelves because they ran out of things to burn to keep warm, and we 'ad to 'ave food parcels dropped to us by 'elicopter because there was no way for deliveries to get through for weeks. We 'ad 'ard times that winter. Never seen anythin' like it before,' he informed them, then added, 'Exceptin' for '47 and '48, a course. That were even worse!'

When Albert had completed his tale of times gone by, they announced their business there, and John turned off the radio as his elderly relative's voice raised in indignation and fury. ''E 'ad no business bein' there in that there red suit. Father Christmas I be in this village, and 'ave been for donkey's years. ''E 'ad no right to try and take my place. I'm not dead yet, even if that old bugger is. I 'ope 'is soul rots in 'ell, puttin' 'is nose in where it 'ad no right nor business to be.'

By the time Albert had finished this heartfelt speech, he had risen from his chair and was shaking his fist in the air. John moved over to get him back down again and apologised for his great-uncle's behaviour. 'He's been really worked up about all the upset, and it took me till yesterday evening to get him calmed down, and then you come round and start him off all over again; but he shouldn't have spoken like that in front of you.'

He eventually took them into the kitchen where they could sit at the wooden table after he had put the radio back on for Albert, which settled the old man back into silence so that they could leave him in peace.

'Your great-uncle really had his nose put out by Mr Jeffries, didn't he?' Falconer opened. 'Had you not thought to contact the locum vicar and tell him that he played the part by dint of long tradition?'

'Didn't know how to,' replied the younger man, looking somewhat sulky at this intrusion upon his private life. 'Anyhow, if no one says anything to him, he'll just forget about it now, so least said, soonest mended, as far as he's concerned.'

'But he was furious right up to last night?' Falconer made this a question.

'That he were. He was ranting and raving all over the house after that nasty business at the church, and he still wouldn't let it go yesterday, either.'

'Did either of you leave the house after you got home from church?'

'We haven't gone out since the crib service. There's no way I was going to have to haul the old man down there again, what with the snow and everything. It was hard enough to pull him through it for the crib service, let alone do it again at that time of night in the dark.'

Well, that was a point-blank denial, and there didn't seem any point in prolonging their time here. The old man wouldn't have been strong enough to do what was done, and his great-nephew wasn't giving anything away for now. And they had other fish to fry. Standing up, they took their leave of John Carpenter, not bothering to disturb old Albert again in case he worked himself up into another fury, had a heart attack, and left them with another seasonal corpse on their hands: one for which they were personally responsible!

It was Nicholas Rollason who answered their knock at the door of The Rookery, explaining that they'd just missed Rebecca as she'd gone to open up the Tea Shop for cold folks to drop in for tea, coffee, or hot chocolate. She knew she didn't have enough bread for sandwiches until she'd had another delivery, but she had plenty of tins of home-made biscuits she could offer them.

He invited them into the sitting room where a delighted Tristram, now a rumbustious three-year-old, was playing with his new toys. They had heard news of the deaths, as Nicholas had gone into Allsorts earlier on, to get another box of candles, as they had no paraffin lamps, and they had both been shocked that such violence could occur again in such a peaceful village.

'It was really Mr Jeffries that I wanted to speak to you about,' Falconer said, as they sipped a very naughty and very much on-duty sherry – just to keep out the cold, you understand.

'I'd have been having words with him at the crib service if he hadn't been there in that ridiculous outfit,' Nicholas said with anger in his voice.

'Why's that, Mr Rollason?' So they had noticed the kind of man that so many others thought he was!

'Not all that long ago he was too bloody familiar with our Tristram, and I wanted to have it out with him. Rebecca told me about him, with his hands all over the poor little soul's arms and legs, and I didn't like the sound of that one bloody bit. I'd have sorted it out there and then, but there's a lot going on at the farm where I work – a lot more than usual for this time of year, and I just hadn't got round to it.

'And now it seems as though someone else had a much bigger beef with him than I did. I'd just have blacked his eye for him, but someone else had a big enough grudge to kill him. Any further forward with the investigation, Inspector?'

'We have a few ideas we're working on,' fenced Falconer,

unwilling to let him know that so many people had an axe to grind with the man that they were spoilt for choice as far as suspects went, and that the man they were talking to was one of them.

'Was it common knowledge, what you thought of him?' he asked, to distract him from enquiring any further into their investigation.

'No one ever said anything. I did ask Rebecca if she could be mistaken, but she gave me that look that women give you: the one that says you're an out-and-out fool, so I just crumbled and felt sure that she knew what she was talking about.'

'Has she mentioned any further similar incidents to you?'

'No, but then she's made sure that she has someone to look after Tristram when she's working and there's no playgroup. That was the last time he was in the tea shop running free, as it were. Why don't you go down to the teashop and have a word with her?'

'She'll probably be run off her feet, but we may call back again at a more convenient time if we think a word with her could prove helpful. Thank you for your time.'

Once outside again chicken hats were donned as they headed for the Stupple residence at Pilgrim's Rest.

The household was in uproar when they arrived, the four children zooming around with their new playthings like turbo-charged pixies. In the grate a fire was roaring, and Warren Stupple explained that it was usually empty with just a screen in front of it, but because of the emergency caused by the weather he had gone outside to collect as much wood as he could and chopped it up for them to burn. There were six of them after all, and they had to keep warm somehow.

Both Falconer and Carmichael agreed with him, and sat down in front of his fire with relish. They were chilled to the very marrow. 'Have you ever had occasion to observe anything to his detriment about Mr Jeffries' behaviour towards young children?' Falconer thought that this was the best approach to get the man talking.

143

'Yes, I damned well have,' replied Stupple, with vehemence. 'And I was going to do something about it as soon as this damned snow thawed. I was disgusted with his behaviour on several occasions, and the way he unnecessarily touched the children at the crib service just about made me sick. Of course, it was expertly done, and no one who wasn't looking out for it would have noticed anything untoward, but I knew what the man was like, and watched him like a hawk.'

'Has anyone else, to your knowledge, noticed anything out of order?' This was an important question, as everyone else seemed to have kept their doubts about Jeffries' integrity to themselves.

'I've heard talk between the mothers at Cubs, as has Helena, my wife, between the Brownies' mothers, but nobody has spoken directly to us. I was so concerned at him playing Father Christmas that I'd determined to report his behaviour to your lot as soon as was humanly possible. But it looks like someone got there before me, doesn't it?'

'It certainly does, Mr Stupple. Is your wife around, by any chance, so that we can have a word with her about what she heard, too?'

'She's in the kitchen hand-washing some socks and underwear for the kids. Do you want to go through?' They did.

But Helena could only confirm what her husband had already said, and it added up to some very overt and inappropriate behaviour with young children, when he didn't think anyone was looking his way. 'I don't know why no one ever spoke out before,' Helena stated.

'Because no one wanted to be first,' replied her husband. 'After all, we've never said anything to anyone official, so we're just as bad as everyone else.'

'But we would have done in the New Year,' Helena countered.

'So may a lot of others have determined so to do, but someone else felt much stronger than the rest of us, and actually murdered him.' Warren had a very old-fashioned turn of phrase sometimes.

'Warren!'

'Well, it's true, and it's impossible to hide from the fact that now *two* people have been killed in the village, and these two gentlemen here are obviously doing their level best to find out whodunit, and in such atrocious conditions, too.'

'I realise that. I'm sorry for the old clergyman, but Jeffries is no loss to this world. It'll be a much better place without him, and I know you feel just the same as I do.'

As they trudged off to their next call, the light almost gone, Carmichael gasped so loudly that Falconer stopped to ask him what the matter was. 'What if he touched my kids, too?' he asked, his face ashen. Although this had been touched on before, it was evident that Carmichael had only just intellectualised the possibility.

'There's no point in worrying about that now, Carmichael. Wait till we get back, and maybe you can have a discreet word with them, to see if they've been upset by him. Just try to put it out of your mind until we get back. I'll tell you what; we'll give the Warren-Brownes a miss today, make them more of a social call tomorrow, and just call in on Mr Pistorius now in The Old School House. That way you'll be back sooner to have a word with the boys and put your mind at rest.'

'We can't do that, sir. There's no way out of going there. I promised Kerry we'd call in to see how Auntie Marian was. I should have said something before, when you said we could give it a miss, but she's dead worried about her, so I can't not go, can I? I'll just have to wait a little longer to have a word with the boys.'

'We'll go there last, then, as it's more of a social call,' agreed Falconer, more depressed than he would have thought at the sudden urgency of a visit he thought he could avoid, at the end of what was proving to be a long day.

Henry Pistorius had bought The Old School House from the late Martha Cadogan's estate: an elderly lady who had made sure that her house still contained an open fireplace and had cooked

145

with bottled gas. These facts alone made the detectives anxious to reach the property, for they were assured at least of a warm house and a hot drink, things that had been sorely missed on their trudge round the houses, although they had noticed the sound of dripping, and that the ice that had made walking outside such a hazard was slowly turning into slush. Maybe a thaw was on the way.

Henry Pistorius answered his door, looking the perfect country gent relaxing at home. He wore a cream-coloured Guernsey sweater over a checked shirt and brown cord trousers. The only incongruous area of his person was his feet, which were shoved into what are usually referred to as 'granddad' slippers with a zip up the front and a pom-pom at the top of the zip, and these gave him a friendly approachable air. They added a slightly zany note to his appearance, as he could seem a formidable man even in his later years, being almost as tall and as broad as Carmichael.

'Do come in,' he bade them. 'I'll just slip off and make some tea. You must be frozen. Away with you and get yourselves warm.'

The inside of the house, although much changed since Martha Cadogan's tenure, was furnished in the perfect country cottage style, any ornaments and paintings being of high quality and in good taste, and Falconer immediately felt at home.

'What a lovely home you've made here,' he commented, looking around him with appreciation as Pistorius came in from the kitchen with a tray laden with tea things and a plate of what looked very much like home-made Christmas cake. 'And may I compliment you on your taste in interior design.' This last remark wasn't at all professional, and he didn't realise he was going to say it until it was out of his mouth.

Henry Pistorius took full advantage of his air of embarrassment and said, with a twinkle in his eye, 'I didn't realise I was expecting a call from *Country House* magazine. Would you like me to show you around?'

'I'm sorry, sir, it just slipped out. I didn't mean to sound as if I was valuing the place.'

'Don't think anything of it. I'm just glad someone else likes it as much as I do. It's the perfect little retirement home for me, now I'm on my own,' Henry replied with a disarming smile, and ushered them to chairs before the blazing grate. 'Now, how else can I help you?'

He answered their questions thoughtfully. 'You know, I spend so much time on my own that when something out of the normal run of events occurs, sometimes I don't know whether it's real or I dreamt it, but I can assure you that I haven't set foot outside my own door since I got back here after Christmas lunch at the pub.

'I know that farmer chappie came round and ploughed the roads, but I didn't want to take a second risk of falling and breaking something at my age, and I have everything I need in the house. It was just Christmas lunch that I couldn't provide for, and I didn't want to miss out and have to eat cold food on such a day,' he explained.

'I can quite understand your apprehension at risking an accident a second time,' Falconer agreed. 'Just to summarise, then, and I'm sorry to sound like a looped tape, but we do have to go over things again and again to get at the truth: Mr Digby Jeffries, a friend of yours, I believe, was murdered in the early hours of Christmas morning in the church, and Rev. Searle, who was staying at The Fisherman's Flies, was found dead in his room on Christmas Day, and that is the reason I'm here now: to see if you may have heard or seen anything which will help us with those enquiries. Maybe you've remembered something that hadn't come back to you when we last spoke.'

'I don't think so, but I must say this all seems more like a bad dream, considering I saw old Digby at Midnight Mass – and the vicar, too. It doesn't seem possible that they can both be gone, even though I know it without a shadow of a doubt. And why kill a vicar? He wasn't even the incumbent of St Cuthbert's, I understood; only standing in as locum so that Castle Farthing could have some Christmas services for a change. There haven't been any since I've moved here.'

'That's what we're trying to find out.'

'Two symbols of Christmas murdered: both pagan and Christian. Doesn't that strike you as just a little bit odd?' he asked. 'Have you looked into the idea that it may be someone – maybe someone of a different faith – that's trying to strike a blow against Christian festivals?'

'I can't say we have, sir,' replied Falconer; and he hadn't even thought of this view of events, let alone considered it.

'Well, I should look into it if I were you. There're all sorts of violent acts of intolerance in the world today, and this could be one of them.'

'I'll give it some thought,' replied Falconer, without the least intention of doing so, and glared at Carmichael who was looking puzzled, and appeared to be about to speak. Best to quell him before he plunged them into even deeper waters.

'So, let's get back to the late Mr Jeffries and his relations with other residents of the village, and also to try to track everyone's movements after Midnight Mass. I wonder if we could start with how you got on with him? I'm sorry to have to take you all through it again, sir.'

'No problem. What else would I be doing in such ghastly weather conditions, and I'm just grateful for some company. Right, Jeffries: fairly objectionable fellow, but mostly harmless. He never spared a thought for other people's feelings, and let his mouth run away with him without putting his brain into gear first. He was a terrible egotist, thinking himself superior to everyone else, and frequently voicing this opinion without a thought to how what he said would affect others.'

'You didn't get on with him, then?'

'I got on with him as well as I could, for the sake of peace. I quite like Alice Diggory and Cedric Malting, and can even put up with the snide and sarcastic comments of Robin De'ath, so I just ignored Digby in the main, for the sake of my friendship with the others.'

'Was he insulting to you, as well?' Falconer had no doubt that the man's answer would be in the affirmative.

'Of course he was. I was his main rival, having worked for the BBC myself, so he had to judge me inferior because I had worked for the radio branch of the corporation. Never mind that I wrote and produced my own programmes.

'To listen to him you'd have thought he'd run the corporation, and then we all found out he was only a floor manager. It's probably just as well that someone did away with him, for I don't think he could have lived with the embarrassment of his actual position coming out and being public knowledge.'

'So he didn't get under your skin at all?'

'Oh, sometimes he did, but I just used to think nice thoughts and ignore him. He really wasn't worth losing any sleep over; just a little man dealing with an inferiority complex the best way he knew how.'

'That's very candid of you, sir,' replied Falconer, thinking that it could also be a very cunning bluff, but he'd have to ascertain from the other members of the little gang whether Jeffries did manage to make him rise to the bait. 'Can you tell me now about Christmas Eve? You did go to the pub after the late service, didn't you?'

'I did. Both my children live abroad, so I try to acquire company as and when I can over the Christmas season. A little drink after church seemed like a good idea, as I wasn't likely to see anyone for the next few days, even without all this snow we've had, so I jumped at the opportunity.

'We'd already exchanged our little gifts earlier in the day, and I had my torch and stick with me, but I decided that if there was any more snow I shouldn't risk going out with it being so treacherous underfoot until after the thaw. And that can't come too soon for me, especially with the power and the phones being out as well.

'I want to get out and change my library books, and weather like this will keep the mobile service away. They're due round in a couple of days, so I'm hoping for a change in the wind direction, and for life to return to normal as soon as possible.'

'Quite. And what little gift did you give to Digby Jeffries? Was it by any chance a hip flask?' Falconer felt quite cunning, slipping that question in so innocently.

'No! He wasn't worth anything like that. I gave him a neck-tie. I got it myself last Christmas and didn't like it: it was too garish for me, so I passed it on to him. He wasn't worth spending real money on. On the other hand, he didn't deserve to die in such a bizarre and public way. Nobody does.' Henry was still shocked at the manner of his old sparring partner's demise.

Falconer added some details about the locum vicar's death which had not been bandied about the day before. 'The vicar was given a number of small wrapped gifts at Midnight Mass, and it would seem that one of these was a hip flask containing what the label attached to it identified as Amaretto di Saronno, but which had in fact been laced with poison. He was found dead in his room at The Fisherman's Flies, as you no doubt remember, by the landlady on Christmas Day afternoon, as I mentioned before.'

'Yes, by gad! What evil is nurtured in people's hearts we could never imagine. That makes me even more positive that it was a hate crime against either the Christian church, or Christmas. You're going to need the services of a psychiatrist for this one, Inspector. Take my word for it; that's what it'll take to solve this.'

'Changing the subject slightly, did you ever notice anything about the way Jeffries behaved around young children?' It was just as well to distract the old man, or they'd be here all day, although Falconer couldn't raise any objection to the opinion of a psychiatrist being sought. It would undoubtedly give him the opportunity to see Dr Honey Dubois again, and that was very much to his taste. In fact, he decided on the spot to make this one of his New Year's resolutions: to see Honey again and ask her out for a meal.

Henry's reply was par for the course. 'God, he was a terrible groper, wasn't he? I thought on more than one occasion that if he didn't watch himself somebody would report him to the authorities, and where would that have left him? But there was no point in even mentioning it to him. In his opinion he could do no wrong. Far too touchy-feely for comfort, though, to my mind.'

'That's very honest of you, sir, and now we'll leave you in peace. Thank you for your time.'

'Finish your tea before you go. It's brass monkeys out there. Do you know the story about why we use the expression 'cold enough to freeze the balls off a brass monkey'?

'I always thought it was something rude,' said Carmichael through a mouthful of cake.

'No, not at all, young man. It comes from the days of cannon balls, when they needed to be stacked into a sort of pyramid. But, being round, they wouldn't stack easily, so they made this kind of brass frame which they put between the layers of balls to keep them from slipping. In very cold weather, the brass used to shrink, and the balls would all fall off, and the contrivance they had invented was called a monkey: hence, in very cold weather, it froze the balls – cannon balls: off a brass monkey – a thing made to keep them in place.'

'That's a very interesting story, Mr Pistorius,' said Falconer, charmed by the little tale.

'So, it's not at all rude then,' commented Carmichael. How differently the minds of men work, one from the other.

They took their leave of Henry shortly after that, leaving the cosy interior of his home reluctantly to face dark and the snow for the penultimate time that day.

Their final call was just next door at The Beehive. A promise to Carmichael's wife wasn't to be broken lightly. Tall and broad as he was, Kerry could wrap Carmichael round her little finger when she wanted to, and he was unlikely to want to arrive back home without having checked on the Warren-Brownes.

Alan Warren-Browne answered the door with his finger to his lips so that they wouldn't speak too loudly. 'Marian's asleep,' he informed them, 'and I think it would be better for her if she got all the rest she can, the way she's feeling at the moment.'

'That bad, is she?' asked Falconer.

'Well, you know how ill she can be when she gets one of her attacks,' he explained, but he said no more on the subject, and showed them into the sitting room. 'Can I get you a brandy or something, to chase away the cold?' asked Warren-Browne, and Falconer saw that their host had a nearly empty spirit glass beside his armchair.

'Maybe just this once,' he replied. 'What about you, Carmichael?'

'Not for me. I've already got acid from that sherry we had earlier,' came the reply, and Alan Warren-Browne immediately seized on this comment, to add, 'Aha! Drinking on duty, are we? That won't go down well with your superintendent, will it?'

'He'd have to prove it first.' Falconer refused to take a threat like that sitting down.

Carmichael asked if he could have a glass of milk, and Alan went off to get a brandy for Falconer and a glass of cow juice for his sergeant. When he got back with a tray he gave a huge sigh as he sunk back into his chair, his own glass refreshed as well: in fact more than refreshed; what was in it must have been drowned in fresh spirit, as the brandy glass was nearly half full.

'Having a bad time?' asked Falconer, eyeing the huge measure the man had poured for himself.

'Not so good. I've never known Marian this bad, before,' he answered, but he didn't look the inspector in the eye as he said it. 'Anyway, update me on how your investigations are going. There hasn't been so much happening in Castle Farthing since that old git Reg Morley was done away with, and the weather's certainly kept any sniff of it getting to the media.'

'That's certainly true,' agreed Falconer, now thoroughly distracted by the change of subject, and told the man what they had learnt so far. After all, Kerry's godparents were hardly likely to be responsible for two such bizarre murders in this little community. They had lived a very quiet life since they retired, keeping themselves to themselves, mainly due to the fact that they were fairly self-sufficient, but also because of Marian's frequent and severe migraines. Or maybe they were just sick and tired of other people, having spent so many years attending to their needs running the village post office.

When the conversation had petered out, Falconer asked if he could use their lavatory, as the cold outside would turn the slight reminder that he hadn't 'been', since they'd left Carmichael's house after lunch into an urgency that he didn't want to have to address out in the open. Carmichael also confirmed that he needed to 'go' too, so Falconer volunteered to go upstairs as what he now also needed to do was something of which he wouldn't like to leave lingering evidence in the downstairs cloakroom.

At the top of the stairs he became aware of a shadowy figure in the gloom at the other end of the landing, and realised that Marian was awake and out of bed.

'What are you doing up here, wandering in the corridor? I don't know you. You're not staying here,' she said in a husky voice, startling Falconer into a state of speechlessness. Whatever was she talking about? 'There's a man downstairs,' she continued, 'in the residents' lounge, who keeps coming into my room. I don't know how he gets hold of a key.'

And suddenly it clicked in the inspector's mind. Marian was so confused that she thought she was in an hotel, and didn't even recognise her own husband. This was much more serious than he had thought, but Alan must realise how bad she was, and he had told them he would seek help as soon as the atrocious weather abated.

'I've just booked in,' he told her, hoping that going along with her illusion would reassure her.

'Well, you just watch out that that man doesn't start walking into your room without an invitation,' she warned him, and floated off back into her bedroom, a sad little ghost who didn't even recognise the place she was haunting. This was a terrible situation, and Alan must be worried sick. No wonder he'd had so much brandy in his glass.

Just before they left, Falconer advised him to get a doctor to see Marian, as her condition seemed to be worsening, and the man agreed with him, stating that he would phone her doctor as soon as the snow had thawed.

'I don't think that'll be very long, either,' prophesied

Falconer. 'It doesn't feel quite so cold out here now.'

Once more out in the dark, their torches lighting their precarious way back to Jasmine Cottage, Carmichael's mind returned to the unpleasant task that lay ahead of him: that of questioning his children about whether they had been the victims of any inappropriate behaviour at the hands – literally the hands, and wandering hands, at that – of Digby Jeffries.

Falconer was more interested in what the light from his torch was revealing and, as an experiment, he took off his hat. 'I do believe that the wind's turned, and we're getting the beginnings of a thaw,' he said optimistically.

'Wossat?' asked Carmichael, sunk in misery as he imagined what lay ahead of him.

'Don't dwell on it, Carmichael,' advised the inspector. 'We'll be back there soon enough, and I'm sure one of them would have said something to you if he's been trying to feel them up.'

'People like that always have a very imaginative threat as to why they mustn't say anything to a grown-up about what's happened. You know that, as well as I do, sir.'

'I do, but I've got a feeling he hadn't got round to actual sexual assault yet, otherwise I'm sure someone would have let the cat out of the bag. There's no way it could all have been suppressed if he'd gone that far. I think he was feeling his way – if you'll pardon the atrocious pun – to taking it a bit further, but hadn't got to that yet.

'The only way we'll find out, apart from questioning all the local children, is to go through his past with a fine-toothed comb and see if there's anything murky lurking in there. He's not lived here very long, and he might not have plucked up the courage to go any further until he had the children's trust.'

'Well, I wouldn't have trusted him as far as I could throw a tractor,' growled Carmichael, his face a mask of tragedy.

'Come on, Sergeant. Cheer up! I'll bet there's absolutely nothing in your suspicions and, remember, in a couple of weeks you'll be a real father with a child of your own. I know you love the boys to bits, but this one will be the one that unites you and Kerry in flesh and blood.' Lord, he was getting poetic, thought Falconer, but he couldn't stand to see his sergeant so down-hearted and worried.

Kerry was delighted to see them back, but Carmichael waylaid her and took her into the kitchen, closing the door behind them, and Falconer sat down by the fireside, being joined instantly by Mulligan, who saw it as his duty to keep as close to this nice man as possible, so that he shouldn't come to any harm.

Mr Knuckles sat at his feet, having exhausted the opportunity of finding anything interesting to do with the new arrivals, and chewed meditatively on a trouser leg. Uncle Tasty-Trousers could be a great comfort in confusing times, and Knuckles was sore-pressed to work out where the three tiny dogs now in the basket had come from, and why his playmate Mistress Fang seemed so inordinately fond of them.

After a few minutes where the buzz of urgent conversation had been just discernible through the door, Carmichael and Kerry came back into the room and called the boys to come downstairs for a few minutes.

Falconer, feeling unbelievably embarrassed, decided to take this opportunity of having a shower. He had no wish to listen into what had or hadn't happened to Dean and Kyle. These people were his friends, and he'd been asked to act as godfather for the two lads once Carmichael got round to organising the christening.

He didn't come back downstairs again until he heard the clatter of four young feet scrambling up the stairs, and when he got back to the living room Carmichael had a broad grin splashed across his face.

'Everything OK, then?' he asked, noticing how happy his sergeant looked.

'You'll never believe this, sir, but when I asked them about it Kyle said that when he saw Father Christmas – and he actually winked at me as he said the name – putting his hand on Dean's face, he stamped hard on his foot, and the old sod soon took his hand away. They're not the little boys I think they are. They're growing up, and I think they're just about finished with the Father Christmas thing.

'Still, we'll be able to keep the dream alive when the little one arrives. I'm sure they'll go along with it for his or her sake,' then he added, 'I've been worried sick, and they'd sorted things out in their own way. God! It's hard trying to be a good parent!'

'And you're doing a fantastic job of it. Well done!' Falconer complimented him sincerely. He'd have loved a father like his sergeant. He would be a totally different man, had his father been like Carmichael.

Chapter Twelve

Boxing Day – evening

Although no one noticed it, the weather vane on the top of St Cuthbert's had swung round from the north-east to the south-west, heralding in a band of slightly warmer weather and winds, and the white blanket that had covered the little world of Castle Farthing would soon melt away into nothingness, with only a bit of extra muddiness to mark that it had ever been there in the first place.

Kerry took herself off to bed as soon as the boys had gone up. She cited exhaustion as her reason, but also complained that her back had been aching all afternoon. This she put down to hauling enormous lumps of meat around over the last couple of days, as well as her grossly swollen body, and said she'd leave them to it to talk over the case so far to their hearts' content.

Falconer said nothing of his encounter with Marian Warren-Browne on her landing, hoping that medical help could be got to her as soon as possible, to relieve her husband of the appalling stress he must be suffering.

Carmichael went round to the area on the other side of the double-sided fireplace and began to type up the day's notes on an old manual typewriter he had rescued from the shed. He had been doing this before the boys went to bed, while they were having their bath, but all three members of his family had gone up early tonight, and Falconer sat just the other side of the fire, listening to him clack away on the ancient machine which fortunately still had a ribbon that worked.

Clack clack clack clack, ting, whizz. Clack clack clack.
'Damn!'
Clack clack clack clack.

157

'Bum!'

Clack clack clack clack clack.

'Arse! Bugger! Poo! Sorry, sir!'

Clack clack clack clack clack clack clack, ting, whizz. Clack clack clack.

'Oh God!'

Clack clack clack clack clack clack clack.

'Shite!' (Sound of pen being thrown against wall.)

Clack clack clack clack.

'You sodding machine!'

Clack clack clack clack, ting, whizz, clack clack clack.

'Bugger it!' *Thump*! 'Stuff it!' (Sound of paper being ripped from behind the platen in a rage, screwed into a ball, then a quiet 'pock' as it, too, hit the wall.)

The last sound, a metallic thump, indicated that the user had had enough of his machine, and had resorted to punching it in fury. For Carmichael, who never used bad language if it could be avoided, this had been an absolute cuss-fest.

He reappeared looking both frustrated and embarrassed. 'Not going very well tonight?' asked Falconer, with a perfectly straight face, although it cost him a great deal of effort to retain his serious expression.

'I just can't concentrate,' Carmichael explained, 'what with all this stuff about interfering with kids and Auntie Marian seeming to have bats in the belfry. And this weather's not helping. No power, no phones, no computer. How are we supposed to work with none of the stuff we're used to?'

'You don't remember the days when typists had to type with nothing other than a typewriter rubber to help them, with two carbons to cope with as well: all that masking to do if you had to rub something out. They also had to type waxed stencils, which had to be thrown away if even one mistake was made. We've got photocopiers these days, but back then, they had to type on these waxed sheets, then they were put on to something called a Roneo machine which inked the stencil, and produced copies when a handle was turned.

'And I hope you understand that this was long before my

time, too. I sometimes had to spend time in my parents' offices, and I used to pass the time … OK, *flirt* with their secretaries, who would respond by showing me everything they had to do. I suppose it kept me out of their hair, and let them get on with their job with the least possible disruption.'

'Good grief! That sounds like the Dark Ages. I don't think I could have coped with that,' exclaimed Carmichael, not understanding all the technicalities. 'Didn't they even have Tippex?'

'Absolutely not! It had barely been invented back then. You don't know you're born now. Actually, neither do I. As I said, this was all well before my time too, but we do take technology for granted, and sometimes it's good for us to do without. Shows we've still got resourceful brains and can improvise.'

'But we've got no fingerprints, no forensics, no nothing' countered Carmichael.

'We just have to do it like they did when none of those things existed. Sit down and calm down, Carmichael, and we'll throw around what we've got from your notes, and chew it over together. Maybe the power will come back later, but for now we've just got to manage completely on our own. Now, what have we got in your notes? Let's look at everyone, one at a time, and see what sort of case we can make against them. You never know, we might both come out with a favourite.'

'But, where shall we start, sir? We just seem to keep going round in circles, saying the same old things – the same old information from the same old people. It's hopeless, trying to do this by ourselves. We haven't even got access to CRO to see if anyone's got previous. Just like last year, but even worse.'

'At least last year we didn't have to dig our way to the crime scene,' commented Falconer sourly.

'And now, it's like we're prisoners.'

'It's just claustrophobia, Carmichael. Just rest easy that we're not the only rural officers trying to do an almost impossible job in the areas affected by this atrocious weather.'

'If you say so, sir. And was that really true, what you told me about those stencil thingies?'

'Sure was. Now, I suggest we start with our first interviewee and work our way through from there,' said Falconer, pleased that he had dispelled Carmichael's mood with his little tangent into office practice history. 'I propose right at the beginning that we discount Blue Sky. There doesn't seem to be anything there, and I doubt its residents knew anyone in the village well enough to hate them. They might have popped into the shop to get something, but they were banned from the pub because of the reason they were staying there in the first place.'

'I agree, sir. So, we start with those three from the new houses, then?'

'That's right. What are your thoughts there? There was obviously a lot of animosity.'

'I agree, sir,' said Carmichael, nodding his head sagely. 'I'd say they were all pretty insecure. That De'ath character was acting very arrogantly, but underneath I don't think he had a lot of self-confidence. The arrogant manner was just a front to make people think that he had a good self-image.'

'Well analysed, Sergeant. I totally agree with you. But, do you think there could have been a case there of 'the straw that broke the camel's back'?'

'It's a possibility. The worm might finally have turned. There's definitely motive there, though. Here they are, in search of a happy and peaceful retirement, then along comes Mr Mighty Mouth, braying about how second-rate they are compared to him.'

'They could all be in it together, Carmichael. A sort of pensioners' outing, to get rid of the greatest fly in all their ointments,' suggested Falconer with a grin. '*We* said earlier that we'd consider the idea, so I don't see why we should abandon it as ridiculous just because they're all old.'

'Stranger things have happened, sir,' replied Carmichael, and wiped the smile right off his face. 'Between the three of them, they could have managed it easier, and who's going to suspect a bunch of pensioners of doing something like that? Except, perhaps, for us two.'

'I see what you mean, but that doesn't get us any further

with why the old vicar was killed. We don't seem to have got any leads on that one. Who on earth could have had it in for him here? Now, what about George at the pub? We know Jeffries had been telling people that he watered down his drinks. A rumour like that could've put them out of business.'

'It's more likely that George would have settled Jeffries' hash with his fists if he was really worried. I don't think he'd go so far as to murder him: just rough him up a bit as a warning.'

'True, true,' said Falconer, as both of them gazed at the fire, and silence fell, except for the hiss of the flaming logs and the drip, drip from the guttering.

'What do you think of the old fellow and his great-nephew?' asked Falconer, finally breaking the hush that had settled on the room.

'Don't know, sir. I suppose the younger one could've done it, but I don't see the old man having anything to do with it. He's much too frail,' said Carmichael, rising to fetch them a can of shandy each.

'He could have egged his great-nephew on. Used emotional blackmail to get him to do his bidding,' Falconer suggested, unwilling to give up the bizarre idea of Father Christmas crucifying Father Christmas.

'And the vicar? Because he let Jeffries play the part?' said Carmichael, handing a chilled can to the inspector.

'At last! A hint of a motive for killing the vicar. Well done, Carmichael! That'll give us something to work on, although I'd like to carry on going through the suspects. Let's look at Rosemary Wilson. I know she's Kerry aunt, but we can't just ignore her because of that. Come to think of it, if everything were up and running, you'd be taken off the case because of personal involvement. After all, Jeffries did put the wind up Kerry and upset her at every opportunity he got, didn't he?

'Maybe you slipped out when everyone was asleep and did the dirty deed, and had slipped the parcel for the vicar in the church at Midnight Mass, so that he'd die as well and muddy the waters.'

Carmichael had never been so insulted in his life, and had a little rant just to prove it.

It took some time to cool down the sergeant, and Falconer diplomatically didn't mention anything about Carmichael or Rosemary Wilson being suspects again. The latter was unlikely. The former was impossible, but it seemed that his sergeant didn't have a sense of humour about the suggestion that he might have done away with the two victims. It hadn't really been very funny, and Falconer could see this now. Hindsight is all-seeing: if only we could enjoy its benefits before the event!

'Let's move on to the Stupples,' he suggested, when Carmichael was once more in his seat and sucking consolingly at his tin of fizzy drink. 'Those two have quite a gang of children of their own, and their activities allow them to mix with a lot more. Could one of them have got so incensed that he or she couldn't bear to see any more children upset, and just lost their rag?'

'Where's the motive for the vicar, then?' Carmichael was still not in the best of moods.

'For giving Jeffries the opportunity for such close contact with so many of them at the crib service,' replied Falconer, grabbing at the only reason he could think of on the spur of the moment.

'I'd like to take a look at Henry Pistorius. He was rather a superior old smoothie, wasn't he? But I suppose he lives so far away from the church ... and he said he came straight home.'

'Yes, Carmichael, but he didn't produce any witnesses, did he? He could have lurked around somewhere, waiting for Jeffries to leave the pub, and got him then,' Falconer suggested.

'And where precisely would he lurk in these sub-zero temperatures, sir?' asked Carmichael, sounding huffy still, and rather rebellious.

'Why, in the church, of course. Everyone knew it was going to be left open all night. It would be the perfect place to take shelter if he knew Jeffries was going to go back looking for his glasses. I think you're onto something here, Carmichael. He could easily have gone back there and waited in ambush for him.'

'And the vicar?'

'Oh, who knows? That could just have been a blind, or he could have known the vicar before, and Rev. Searle knew something to his detriment. It could've been anything. We can research stuff like that when we get all our resources back. I'm definitely putting my money on Henry. He lived further away than the others, so therefore nobody walked all the way home with him.

'What if he started going off in the right direction, then doubled back round the other side of the village green? That would take him right up to the church. Nothing easier for him than to slip inside, unnoticed, then wait for his victim to come to him. I know he said he let all Jeffries' cutting little remarks wash over him, but that could just have been bluff on his part.'

'I think you're onto something there, sir. I'd never have thought of him, really. I only suggested him because you seemed to like him and his olde-worlde house.'

'Well, in that case, you're a genius, Carmichael. We'll get up there again first thing tomorrow morning, and have it out with him.'

'Time we were getting off to bed, sir. You go on up and I'll stoke up the fire, put the guards up, and extinguish all the lamps. Got your chamber stick?'

'Got it,' confirmed Falconer, picking it up from the mantelpiece. At this movement, Mulligan, who had been happily asleep at his feet, raised his head, then got to his feet, ready to accompany this kind man back to their 'basket' for the third night in a row.

Outside, the thaw continued to gather pace, and away from Castle Farthing telephone and electricity maintenance workers continued to try to reconnect the villages who had been out of contact for so long. The internet server was soon to be restored, and the problem with the mobile phone mast was nearly solved. Falconer and Carmichael were about to be catapulted back into the twenty-first century, and all the facilities and resources it could offer them.

Chapter Thirteen

Monday 27th December (Bank Holiday)

It was the sound of the telephone that woke Falconer the next morning, although his brain didn't immediately compute that this was anything unusual. It just informed him that he wasn't at home and, therefore, didn't have to rush to answer it.

He opened bleary eyes to their now familiar view of Mulligan's thick neck, his muzzle drooling enthusiastically on to his head. This was the strangest bed-fellow he could ever have imagined, and wondered what other people would say if he said he'd met a right dog over Christmas, and they had shared a bed all over the festive period.

Best not! Apart from it sounding too male chauvinist pig, Mulligan was male, and all sorts of thoughts shot through his mind. Would his colleagues think he'd picked up an old slapper? Would they think he was into bestiality? Would they think he batted for the other side, sleeping with a male for nights in a row; one that was probably the same weight as him, and was definitely taller on his hind legs?

As he tried to banish such upsetting scenarios from his mind, he heard Carmichael's voice calling up the stairs. 'I've just had Chivers on the phone, and he wants you to call him back as soon as possible to explain why we seem to have gone AWOL over Christmas.'

Superintendent 'Jelly' Chivers was their superior at the station, which he ruled with a rod of iron and a voice that could break glass at a hundred paces and cause dogs in neighbouring towns to howl in distress (or, at least, it certainly felt that way). He lived just outside Market Darley, and would have had no trouble getting into the station. His power and telephone had probably been restored long ago, and he was no doubt wondering why his DI and DS appeared to be skiving off.

Pulling on some clothes as rapidly as he could, and just making a lightning trip to the bathroom to relieve his necessity, Falconer went down to the telephone, rang the station, and asked to be put through to Superintendent Chivers with a heavy heart. How was he going to explain away what had been going on, while they had been incommunicado?

There were no polite greeting or seasonal wishes, and after announcing that they were investigating a double murder, Falconer held the phone away from his ear before his ear-drums exploded.

'That's right, sir. Two murders.'

'^&&^%@%$')(*@&&^^**@*!' Chivers was not best pleased.

'But we were completely snowed in, sir. There was no way we could communic –'

'**@%$£$|*&^@%%$!' Chivers never accepted excuses.

'Now look here, sir; with the greatest respect, we've had no power, no telephone, no mobile service, no intern –'

'@&%$%£*&@£%$&!' Chivers expected miracles throughout the year, and not just at Christmas.

'Well, it's not my bloody fault! The snow ploughs simply couldn't get out this far. We've been working our socks off interviewing anybody who might be involved, we've got the bodies in cool places, and we've filmed, photographed, and measured everything, as well as collecting what evidence we could. Carmichael has notes of everything we've done, and every interview we've conducted.' (Pause.)

'Yes, I should be very grateful if you would send out Dr Christmas and a couple of PCs to help. We'll also need a vehicle to transport the bodies and I'd be obliged if you could be just a little more sympathe … Hello? Hello?' But Chivers had hung up. Like all bullies, he didn't like his word challenged, and had cut the call before it became too hot for him to handle.

'What did he say, sir? – Hurray!' crowed Carmichael: this

last, because the electricity had just come back on, and the Christmas tree now blazed with colour. 'I can put my notes on the computer now, if the server's back up and the power back on.'

'To answer your question, I think I just bawled out the super, and I just hope he doesn't hold a grudge. I was just so furious at how hard we'd been working with no outside help or modern technology, and he just went off on one. So I did, too. I couldn't help myself.'

'Good for you, sir. Now for these case notes.'

'You read the notes and I'll type,' offered the inspector who, being the sort of man he was – the sort that some may describe as having a stick up his bum – had done a course in touch typing and had reached an impressive speed that helped him no end with his office paperwork. 'The server's back up. Let's get those dawgies rollin', Sergeant,' he instructed, already sat at the computer and ready to go.

Not long after, Kerry brought them coffee, wincing as she set down the cups. 'What's up, love?' asked Carmichael, noticing her expression of pain.

'Just a bit of backache. I thought it'd go off if I went to bed early last night, but it doesn't seem to have worked. Never mind. I'm the size of a whale now: I shouldn't expect to be perfectly comfortable.'

The telephone rang and disturbed this little discussion and Kerry went to answer it. She was back in less than a minute, and looking utterly distraught. 'I think something awful is happening up at The Beehive! That was Uncle Alan. He just managed to say, "Can you get Davey up here, because …", then there was this awful yell and a load of thuds, and the line went dead. I think you'd better get up there as quickly as possible. I think someone must've broken in and is attacking them.'

Carmichael ran to get his coat while Falconer complained, 'How come Castle Farthing's suddenly become the crime capital of the county?' And how long had he, himself, got to live? he thought, now that he'd lost his rag with old Jelly?

So effective had the overnight thaw been that it was just

about safe to take the car. Falconer knew that anyone sent out to the village to assist them would go first to Jasmine Cottage, and Kerry would redirect them to their present destination. If Doc Christmas were to arrive, she could also tell him where the bodies were hidden!

The Beehive was in complete darkness, in contrast to all the other properties they had passed, which had blazed with light, as it was such a dark, sullen day and the miracle of electricity had been restored. As they stood outside, knocking and ringing urgently at the front door, Carmichael leaned towards the obscured-glass panel in the top of it, and cupped his hands round his face, in an attempt to see in.

'I'm sure there's someone there, sir, but they're not making any attempt to answer the door. 'Alan! Marian!' he shouted through the letter box, but still there was no reply; no attempt to open the door.

'Round the back! Now!' Falconer breathed in his ear. 'If there's someone in there who didn't ought to be, perhaps we can get in round the back and surprise them. Come on, man!' Putting his own mouth to the letterbox, he called, 'We'll come back later,' a bizarre bit of play-acting that failed to convince even him.

Signalling for Carmichael to follow him, he led the way as they began to ease their way round to the back of the house, in the hope that they could gain access via the back door. It was, of course, locked, and, after a brief and whispered discussion about what to do, Falconer decided that they had sufficient suspicions of the presence of an intruder to gain access by force: in this case, *police* force, and he ordered Carmichael to put his mighty shoulder to the door so that they could get in and find out what was going on.

As the door gave way there was a huge clatter, and they saw that a large kitchen refuse bin had, for some reason, been the victim of this irruptive entry, and its contents were now scattered across the floor. At the sudden noise both of them froze, hardly daring to breathe in case someone was waiting for them. Falconer got his torch out of his pocket after Carmichael had tried the light switch and nothing had happened.

Either the mains had tripped, or someone had turned the electricity off for their own nefarious devices. They couldn't be sure which of these alternatives was the correct one, so they would have to proceed with extreme caution. Anyone could be waiting to ambush them in the silent and gloomy house.

There had been the sound as of a glass container rolling across the floor when the bin had fallen, and in the torch's beam was revealed, from the detritus now scattered everywhere, was an empty Amaretto di Saronno bottle, which gave them much pause for thought. 'I don't have the faintest idea what's going on here, Carmichael, but our first priority is the safety of the Warren-Brownes.'

'I'll have a look at the consumer unit,' offered Carmichael. 'Maybe it just tripped at the power outage.'

'Well, go as quietly as you can. If there's someone in here, we don't want to be either tackled or attacked. Keep your torch at the ready: it makes a very handy improvised weapon. I'll go through to the hall and see what it was you saw through the letterbox,' Falconer volunteered, so they went their separate ways, Falconer with his torch now firmly clutched in one hand, but switched off. He didn't want its light to advertise his presence, any more than he wanted his approach to, and he took extra care to walk very lightly.

The presence of the bottle in the bin probably meant nothing. A lot of people liked amaretto, especially at Christmas. He'd put money on there being at least half a dozen bottles of the stuff in houses around the village at this time of year.

In the hall he almost tripped over the prone figure of Alan Warren-Browne, head and shoulders on the hall floor, his body and legs lying pointing upwards on the bottom steps. He wasn't moving, and after checking that he was still alive Falconer decided against his better judgment to put him into a more comfortable position; although he may have suffered a trauma, he was likely to freeze to death where he was.

As he moved him, he heard a sighing breath, and knew that the man was only injured and unconscious, but he had no idea what whoever had done this would have done to Marian. He had to find her, given vulnerable she was at the moment. She could be lying injured or dead upstairs, and he had to locate such a vulnerable woman with as little delay as possible.

Slowly he crept up the stairs, his hand on the torch now in his pocket: such a handy weapon should he find he had to defend himself from intruders. At the top of the stairs all was in gloom, and he was just wondering whether to go along the landing towards the back or the front of the house when several things seemed to happen simultaneously.

The lights came back on with a glare that almost blinded him, he was aware of a screech of brakes from the road outside, and he heard Carmichael's voice roar out one word, 'Duck!' His reaction was instinctive, and his body moved without his conscious brain having time to catch up with what was actually happening. A split-second later, something whooshed past his head, narrowly missing him, and he heard footsteps thundering up the stairs.

Carmichael arrived on the landing and made a grab for something or somebody Falconer couldn't see, and there were more footsteps heading up the staircase. 'Got her, sir!' exclaimed Carmichael with a note of triumph in his voice, and the inspector turned round to see his sergeant restraining Marian Warren-Browne by the simple but effective method of wrapping his arms round her from behind and clasping his hands in front of her body, thus not only confining her but keeping her arms captured as well.

Other bodies arrived on the landing, making quite a crowd, and escorted Marian down the stairs and into the waiting police car outside, as Falconer fought to work out exactly what had happened in that whirlwind of time since he had reached the first floor of the house.

Turning to the now free Carmichael, he said, 'Thanks for the warning to duck. If you hadn't called out, she'd have hit me.'

'I wasn't warning you, sir,' Carmichael replied with a slight flush of embarrassment. 'I just shouted out what she was holding. I saw it silhouetted in the light from outside. It was that

170

plaster duck that always stands near the top of the stairs, and I knew it was heavy. There wasn't time to shout, "Look out for the duck!" so I just shouted "Duck!"'

'!' Falconer was speechless, but nonetheless grateful that it hadn't been a vase or a figurine. A yell of 'vase' or 'figurine' would have produced no reaction from him whatsoever, and he thanked God that Marian had picked up what she had, or he would at this very moment have been spark out, having measured his length on the floor after being brained with a miscellaneous decorative household item.

'She must have thought you were the intruder, sir,' explained Carmichael, as if to a five-year-old. 'Anyway, I handed her over to Green and Starr, and they're taking her to the hospital to be checked over. Alan's being taken off in an ambulance. The paramedics don't think he'll be unconscious for long, so we can go and talk to him when they've got his injuries sorted out and got him settled.'

'So, the whole team was alerted in the nick of time,' sighed Falconer in relief, having worked out why the house had been so suddenly full of other people. 'Good old Kerry. We were in a bit of a jam, weren't we? But what the hell has been going on in this house?'

'No idea at the moment,' replied Carmichael. 'Merv Green said a SOCO team was on its way, and so was Doc Christmas, so I suggest we follow the ambulance to the hospital and wait to find out how they are. We can go into the office later to debrief with Chivers. Come on: we'll go in my car as that's the one we've come up here in. You can come back and collect yours later.'

'Oh my God! Chivers!' moaned Falconer. 'He'll have my guts for garters after that bollocking I gave him this morning. He'll have me right on the carpet for the way I spoke to him.'

'Never mind,' Carmichael comforted him. 'It'll make a change from Mulligan, won't it?'

PC John Proudfoot was on duty outside the front door, standing there in the cold with his usual phlegmatic stolidity. 'Has anyone secured the back door?' asked Falconer, as they left the house. 'Only we had to break it to gain access, and I'd hate to think someone could just slip in and help themselves to anything they fancied while you were standing here guarding an open Aladdin's cave.'

'I'll see to that right away, Inspector, sir. Nobody said nothin' to me about an open back door.'

'Best get on with it then, man. Chop chop!'

Carmichael drove carefully to the hospital in Market Darley, while Falconer sat in the passenger seat and calmed down after nearly being assaulted by an elderly woman in the lawful pursuit of his duty.

They asked first to speak to Marian, to see if she could remember exactly what had happened, although Falconer thought they had about as little chance of that as a snowflake's chance in a microwave, and he proved to be right. All she seemed to be able to say was, 'There was a man. There was a man. He was outside my room.'

When she saw Falconer, she changed this slightly to, 'Was it that man from the resident's lounge? Did you see him too? I nearly got him, you know.' Then she just relapsed back into 'There was a man.'

One of the duty doctors came and spoke to them, and informed them that they had summoned someone with psychiatric experience and, as there were rather complicated circumstances – whatever that may mean – they had called in Dr Dubois. Did Falconer, by any chance, know her?

'!' Speechless again.

Alan Warren-Browne was being kept in overnight, just as a precaution because he had a head injury, but other than a fair amount of bruising where he had tumbled down the stairs he was not seriously injured, and they could see him now if they wanted to. They did. He at least may be able to explain what the dickens had been going on in that house when they arrived, and exactly why he had made his call for help in the first place.

They found him lying against propped pillows in a general ward, and immediately drew the curtains round his bed so that

172

he could speak to them without an audience. 'What, in the name of all that's holy, happened today at your place?' asked Falconer, sitting gingerly on the edge of the bed, while Carmichael took the metal and plastic visitor's chair so that he could take notes.

'It was all Marian,' he said.

'Marian?' chorused both detectives.

'We thought you were in the process of being burgled,' said Falconer with surprise.

'We thought you'd been attacked when you surprised them, and that Marian was in danger – or even worse,' added Carmichael, vocalising his original fears when they had broken in and found Alan unconscious.

'No, it was just Marian. Just! – what a stupid word in the circumstances. I've tried to keep the lid on things until I could get her to the doctor when the roads were cleared, but I just couldn't cope any more. It was getting beyond me, and I was desperate for some professional help. Dear God! What have we done? What have I done?'

'We don't know, Alan. Why don't you tell us, but start at the very beginning, please, so that we don't get even more confused than we already are.'

'Confused? There's a word I *never* want to hear again.'

'Take it slowly, and explain in your own time,' Falconer advised, and sat back while the man gathered his thoughts together.

After a monumental sigh, Alan began his long tale. 'It all started before we left the post office,' he said, with another sigh. 'That's why we gave it up, really. She was getting forgetful and muddled – only now and again, mind – and what with her headaches as well, it seemed best to get her as far away as possible from any source of stress, so we bought The Beehive, which was much quieter than being behind a post office counter and living in the middle of the village.

'After we moved, she didn't go out very much, and she was only occasionally getting muddled. She had Kerry and the boys round to visit at first, letting them play in the garden and the building that used to be a studio at the bottom of the garden. We did have some ideas and actually kitted that out as a playhouse for them so that they could stay over and feel that they were having an adventure.

'Then she started asking me who those two little boys were after they'd gone home, and, a couple of times, when Kerry's been round with them, she told me that she didn't know who that young woman was either, but that she wished she could see her baby goddaughter, as she hadn't seen her for ages.

'I managed to get her to the doctor, and he diagnosed an early-onset type of dementia; maybe even some sort of damage caused by the prolonged nature and severity of her headaches. He gave her some tablets to take and, for a while, they seemed to help a bit. Then she started going downhill again, and by the time Christmas was approaching I didn't know what she was going to do next.

'I found her once in full make-up and evening dress at three o'clock in the morning, apparently waiting for a taxi to take her on a date with me. She started getting argumentative, too. She blacked my eye recently. No doubt you just took my story that I'd slipped over in the snow at face value, but the truth is, she thumped me one when she couldn't get her own way.'

'How on earth have you coped with all this on your own?' asked Carmichael.

'I haven't really. I've just tried to contain it and keep a lid on it. This weather's really been the straw that broke the camel's back, imprisoning us both in the house without any chance of summoning outside medical or psychiatric help.

'I even found her in the church one day giving that Jeffries chap what for. Of course, I apologised and got her away, and when I asked what it was all about she was all muddled up with Kerry having a baby, and Kerry's mother expecting Kerry. She didn't seem to know whom she was defending; whether it was Kerry, or whether the poor man had been upsetting the girl's mother sometime in the past.

'I know I'm not explaining this very well, but she'd also seen that old creep feeling up some kids one day when we were in the shop, and everything got muddled in her head. That's what I'm trying to tell you. It was Marian who was responsible for those two deaths over Christmas.'

'She couldn't have done it!' exclaimed Falconer, aghast. 'She's nowhere near strong enough to have done what was done in that church. She would've needed considerable help. And why kill the vicar?'

'That's what I'm trying to explain to you. She did have some help. *Me*!'

'*You*? Alan! You don't know what you're saying. This all sounds so impossible. Wait until you're feeling better. You're probably all confused from the knock on the head.' Falconer was shocked to his roots and assumed that the man was rambling due to his fall.

'I'm perfectly lucid: if you would just listen to me. I'll tell it from where things got really serious, and I didn't know what to do for the best any more,' he said, his face a mask of misery.

'When we went to church on Christmas Eve – the crib service – Marian kept muttering about Jeffries (God rest his soul) and what she called his "perverted tendencies", complaining that the vicar should never have let him anywhere near children. I tried to hush her up as best as I could, but she started again during Midnight Mass. Trust him to be daft enough to wear the costume to that service as well.

'When he came into the pub wearing it and sat at the table next to us, I thought she was going to blow a fuse. Then the vicar came downstairs and joined us, calling out some sort of … Oh, I can't remember what he said, but he said something to Jeffries, and that was it for Marian. She was up and off home.

'I thought I'd got her settled down for the night, but something – I've no idea what – woke me about half an hour after I'd got off to sleep, and Marian wasn't in bed. In fact, she wasn't anywhere in the house, but the door to the garage was wide open. That's when I really started to worry.

'I got a torch and looked outside the front door, and there were footprints leading down to and out of the gate. That's when I realised she'd gone wandering, and I was worried sick about where she might have gone. I donned my outdoor gear and headed for the village centre. I didn't dare call on anyone at that time of night, and the only light shining anywhere was from the church.

'I went in to see if she was in there, and that's when I realised what she was up to. I found her in the vestry. She'd managed to drag that big wooden cross from Stoney Cross away from the wall and get it flat on the ground. She must have been in such a rage that she didn't know her own strength.

'When I went in there she had Jeffries, already dead, and was using my cordless nail gun to fix him to the cross. It looked like she'd shot him in the head, then dragged him in there to crucify him, and her only reaction when I spoke was, 'Give me a hand, darling. I've got to get him propped up against the wall in the church so that everyone can see that he won't be a problem any more.'

'What could I do? By the time I'd got her home and settled, and waited for her to fall asleep, there was no way of contacting anyone. Everything was down. It'd taken hours, and I was in a complete panic. In the end, I actually slipped her a couple of pills to get her off. All I could think of doing was containing her until I could call for outside help. What else was there to do? I had to help her, or she'd probably have started on me; which she did the next day, but that's further on in the story.

'I got her unconscious as best as I could, and simply put the nail gun back in the garage. Once the tablets started to kick in, she went to sleep like a lamb, and so pleased with ridding the world of someone she considered didn't deserve to live.

'When I got back downstairs again and began to gather my wits about me, I decided that I needed a stiff drink, and went to the sideboard where we keep the bottles. That's when I noticed that the amaretto bottle was empty, and it was over half-full only a couple of days ago. I thought Marian had drunk it, but when she woke up I asked her, she denied it vehemently, and that's when she thumped me one.

'When I'd recovered from the shock, I put the bottle in the bin and decided that I needed a snifter even more, so I went

176

back to the sideboard and found that my hip flask had gone, too. Again, I asked her if she'd moved it, and she started to laugh like a maniac. When I'd calmed her down, she started to look sly and cunning with a little hint of amusement. I couldn't work out what she'd done. Then she told me.

'She'd decided at the crib service that that old vicar – I can't even remember the poor old chap's name – would have to go too, because of the licence he'd given Jeffries to touch children, so she'd put what was left of the amaretto in the hip flask, and topped it up with something she'd come across in the garage from the boxes of junk that were left behind when we moved in. I've searched it out, and it was poison all right. It's all there waiting for the police.

'She said she'd made up a little parcel for the vicar that he wouldn't forget in a hurry, and he'd have no more opportunity to do anything so irresponsible ever again. That's when I realised that if the weather conditions didn't improve soon, that I'd be as mad as she was when it all cleared up.

'I was scared stiff from that moment onwards. I watched her like a hawk, and I slipped her more Valium and sleeping tablets to try to keep her sedated until I could get a doctor or the police to her. She woke up once, when you two called round, and I thought she'd mouth off about how clever she'd been, but I think she'd forgotten she'd done it by then.

'Then this morning, when the phones came back, I rang you at Jasmine Cottage, trying to summon help to get her restrained. I'd checked that she was asleep, but she must have been pretending, because I made the call, and the next thing I knew, she'd pushed me down the stairs. I remember how much it hurt, bouncing all the way down the flight, and then I don't remember another thing till I came round in the ambulance.

'I've had hardly any sleep since Christmas Eve. I was too scared to do anything more than doze in case she came for me with a hammer or something ghastly like that. She had no idea who I was and seemed to think she was staying in a hotel. I was at my wits' end.'

'Good God, man. You've had a real time of it, haven't you?'

murmured Falconer, stunned by what he'd just heard.

'It was a nightmare. And I didn't dare leave her to get help. There's no telling what she might have done if I'd left her on her own, and what could anyone else have done? Locked her in a coal shed? We don't have a police station in the village, and we were totally cut off from the outside world. I've never been so frightened in my life. And this is all my fault, you see.'

'How on earth do you make that out, Alan?' asked Falconer, shocked by this final sentence.

'It was all my doing. Because I used to be a church warden, Jeffries got the contact details of the locum vicar from me. And everything stemmed from that. If I'd given him the brush-off, which I felt like doing, but didn't want to seem ill-mannered, then none of this would have ever happened: so you see, it really *is* all my fault!

'Calm down, Alan! The man would no doubt have badgered the information out of someone else. He'd have found out whatever. He was that sort of man,' Falconer comforted the distraught man.

'What am I going to tell Kerry?' asked Carmichael, his face ashen at how his wife would react to the news that her godmother was a double murderess and her godfather thought that it was all his fault.

'You'll just have to tell her the truth. It's better she hears it from you than from the television or a newspaper. Just tell her I'm sorry there was nothing else I could do, and that her godmother loved her very much. It's just that the Marian we all knew and loved isn't here any more. She's long gone, and I miss her. God! She went downhill so fast, and they'd warned me she could get sneaky, or even violent, but it wasn't supposed to come on this quickly.'

'I'll speak to Superintendent Chivers when I get back to the office and see what he thinks. I would suspect that only a very hard-hearted judge would deem you responsible for any of this. Yes, you helped her, but that was really an act of self-defence. If you hadn't have done, she would probably have turned on you, and you'd be dead, too.' This was all Falconer could think

178

of saying, and he believed it, but couldn't even imagine how the man in the hospital bed was feeling, after all that had happened to him in the last few days.

When they left Alan, now dozing lightly, they returned to see how Marian was getting on, only for Falconer to spot a familiar and very welcome sight just outside the ward doors. Talking to the doctor who had been assigned the case and PC Starr, was the dark-skinned figure of Dr Honey Dubois.

Falconer felt his insides jiggle around as if he were on a rollercoaster, and a sweat of fear and longing break out all the way down his back. He'd need to apprise her of what he had just learnt, before she could make any assessment. He wanted to do it on his own. Now. Immediately. It couldn't wait!

Dispatching Carmichael to get himself something to eat in the hospital cafeteria, he tried to swagger up to her, but realised he must have looked more like an eager puppy desperate to have his tummy tickled, as he, with a mouth as dry as the Sahara, muttered, 'Hello, Dr Dubois. I believe we have some consultation to carry out over a new case which involves both of us?'

'Oh, Harry, don't be so dry and dusty. I thought you were calling me Honey now. Relax!' Her voice was like rich chocolaty velvet, and her eyes ... That was enough of that! Taking his courage in both hands, he managed to squeak, 'Nothing to do with work, but would you consider having dinner with me some time?'

'You know I'd love to, Harry. Let's get something down in our diaries before we get down to the nitty-gritty of what you've got for me here ...'

Chapter Fourteen

Monday 27th December (Bank Holiday) – later

Falconer travelled back to Castle Farthing in Carmichael's car, as his Boxster was still outside Jasmine Cottage, but it was not a convivial journey, both men sunk in shock and deep misery for the man they had left to face his future in the light of what he had gone through recently. And all this in conflict, in Falconer's mind, about his meeting with Honey, and the thought that he would soon be taking her out for a meal *a deux*.

When they arrived, Carmichael had determined that he would send the boys upstairs so that he could explain to Kerry the dreadful events in which her godparents had been swept up. Falconer went up to what had been his bedroom since Christmas Eve to pack his clothes and accoutrements, and determined to stay up there until Carmichael called him down.

He found Mulligan dozing on the duvet, and sat down beside him to give him a pat. He may not be a big fan of dogs, but Mulligan had kept him warm in the coldest Christmas he had ever known, and he owed him some affection for that alone. And apart from that, part of his heart was singing with joy. There'd have to be meetings in the near future over this case, and he would be seeing a lot more of his current *objet d'amour* professionally, as well as, he prayed fervently, privately. He was like a smitten schoolboy.

His musings were interrupted by an almost animal cry from downstairs, and first he thought that that was the result of Carmichael reporting the dreadful news to Kerry, but the cry was followed by a mighty bellow from Carmichael. 'Come downstairs, sir. Now! Help!'

He clattered down the stairs as fast as he could and found Kerry, her hands on the back of the sofa, leaning against it and breathing as if she had been running. 'That backache I've been getting,' she panted. 'It must have been labour. I've never had it like that before. Davey's phoning for an ambulance, but I don't think I'm going to be able to wait for it.

'This baby wants to come out, and it wants to come out now. I want to push. Help me get out of my knickers, somebody. Please!'

Carmichael reappeared at this juncture, and delicately helped his wife with her underwear. 'Don't worry, sir. An ambulance is on its way: it shouldn't be long.'

'I haven't *got* long. It's coming *now*!' yelled Kerry, and her face went red as she strained, helpless against the urges of nature. 'You two are going to have to deliver this baby, and it's not going to be too long before it's out. Get this bloody thing out of my body. *Now*!'

'Transition, sir. They always get grumpy at some point in the labour process.'

'*Now,* you gibbering fool!' she screamed, going purple. It's coming out! *Right this minute*!'

'If it's a girl we'll call it Harriet, sir, as you're going to be in at the birth,' declared Carmichael cheerfully, and then reacted in exactly the same way as he had when informed that Kerry was expecting this, his first baby. He keeled over on to the settee, completely unconscious.

'For a big lad, he's not got a strong constitution,' grunted Kerry through gritted teeth, in mitigation of her husband's unconscious condition.

'Would you like to lie down?' asked Falconer, knowing that this was what usually happened if there were a scene like this on television – that was normally his cue to go to the kitchen to put on the kettle. He'd always preferred to remain in ignorance of exactly what happened next.

'*No*!' she yelled. 'Got to squat. Use gravity to help,' she ground out, and assumed the position while Falconer thanked his lucky stars that she'd hadn't taken his suggestion at face value, for if she had he'd never be able to look her in the face again; or anywhere else for that matter. This was one view of his sergeant's wife that he never, ever wanted to become acquainted with.

Kerry began to make some very strange whimpering noises, and Falconer got down on his hands and knees and removed his jumper to put underneath her for when the inevitable happened, noting with sorrow that what he had grabbed to put on that morning had been the pale pink cashmere jumper that his mother had sent him for Christmas. Placing it just below the bit of Kerry's body that he didn't want to think about, he prayed that the ambulance would arrive before this went much further.

Kerry Carmichael was delivered of a baby girl who was, indeed, named Harriet. The ambulance arrived just as Carmichael regained consciousness. Five minutes *after* her birth!

As the inspector finally decamped from the cottage that had given him such an exciting and unexpected Christmas, an elderly Jaguar drew up across the green outside The Fisherman's Flies and disgorged the figure of the Brigadier, who hadn't made an appearance since ... ooh, round about chapter two.

'Season's greetings, Inspector. Just arriving to set out my battle scene in the snooker room. Any chance of you coming? It'll be nice to get a bit of company again, after the isolation of the last few days? What? Hope you had a peaceful Christmas.' Was he in for a shock when he found out what he'd missed!

THE END

An excerpt from

Grave Stones

Book Nine in the Falconer Files

by

Andrea Frazer

PROLOGUE

Shepford St Bernard was another of the area's postcard-pretty villages, but with nothing to really attract tourists. It was a passing-through place, with very few houses, and could only be called a village rather than a hamlet because it had its own church.

As a passing-through place, however, it was ideal, and any trade it did pick up was probably due to the very few facilities that it boasted. It had a very picturesque pub, a garage with a mini-mart attached, a small independent shop, both ladies' and gentlemen's public conveniences, and a truly old-fashioned red phone box.

Thus, it was ideal for the motorists driving through, for they could fill up with petrol or diesel, stop into the pub for lunch or an evening meal or, if they had little time, grab a pasty or a sandwich from the general store, use the conveniences and, as there was a very erratic mobile phone signal in the village's environs, make any urgent phone calls that could not wait until they reached an area with better reception. There were even benches on the Green on which one could sit and eat a picnic lunch, if the weather was sufficiently clement.

The church, which was ancient, might have attracted some interest, had it not been located down a small lane, rendering it invisible from the main road, which was a pity, not just because it was a very pretty old church and eminently photogenic, but because it had probably the most esoteric name of any church in the area: St Bernard-in-the-Downs.

Shepford St Bernard was a quiet village with very few

commuters rushing to and fro to Market Darley every weekday. Only one of its houses had been a weekend bolt-hole, and even that now had a more or less permanent resident.

For the ladies of this tiny watering hole there was even a minute hairdressing salon that catered for the shampoo-and-set and blue-rinse brigades. All in all, it served admirably for both those who lived there, and those who only made its acquaintance on four wheels, and life ticked over there sleepily and peacefully.

Chapter One

Rev. Florence Feldman (Florrie to her friends) sang loudly and tunelessly as she prepared for the next day's Special Occasion, which definitely had initial capitals whenever she thought about it. 'All Things Bright and Beautiful' echoed tunelessly in her flat but surprisingly strong alto voice, as she beat the cake mixture for some of her offerings for the next day. The sound echoed mercilessly round the vast, high-ceilinged kitchen of The Rectory, but of this she was totally unaware as she worked. This was her first parish and, even a couple of months after her Induction she was engulfed in enthusiasm and joy for her new position.

Her appointment at St Bernard-in-the-Downs in Shepford St Bernard had been a shock for the parishioners, even those who did not attend services, and a few of the old guard had even had the brass neck to walk out of her Induction service, once they realised that the replacement for the seventy-eight-year-old male incumbent was a young(ish) woman.

Her first Sunday service had been sparsely attended, the majority of the regular congregation – not over-large in the first place – had deserted the church in protest at having a female vicar foisted on them. Rev. Florrie, however, just ignored the lack of communicants and started on a relentless round of parish visits to try to tempt back the regulars and bulk up the congregation with younger members.

Although she was unable to find many young residents in

the village, she worked with what she had and had increased attendance significantly; this being, in her opinion, for the village to have the opportunity either to blacken her name still further, or from sheer curiosity at how she would perform. Her visits carried on until she had more than doubled the attendance since she had arrived, and was still involved in a charm offensive on those she had not yet won over.

'All things wise and wonderful ...' she sang, as she shot two trays of fairy cakes into the oven and began to make the mixture for a chocolate sponge cake. She had always been an optimist, to the point that her glass was not merely half-full, but was brimming over with the intoxicating wine of enthusiasm and hope. She'd break them in the end, she just knew she would.

The next day would witness her first venture into a parish 'occasion', as she had decided that a parish party was the best way to get to know people better. It was much more efficient than visiting parishioners individually in their homes. Get them all together in one place, and she could make enormous inroads with enthusing them for her mission, as she too had been enthused, with the charming village and the pretty old church.

She had churned out over a hundred leaflets advertising the event on the old Roneo machine in the little office of the village hall, and personally put one through every letterbox in the vicinity. She had put one in the shop, the pub, the hairdresser's, and on the parish noticeboard, and exhorted all her regular worshippers to work on their friends and neighbours, particularly those who never came to the church, to meet the vicar and have a good time to boot.

Her leaflet had advertised it not just as an opportunity to meet their new incumbent, but as a 'Feed the Five Thousand' party, with a briefly worded explanation underneath, to advise people that it would not be fully catered, but that the intention was that everybody brought something to eat and drink with them, and so, between all of them, they would have a spectacular offering of refreshments.

'We plough the fields and scatter ...' she growled as she

removed the fairy cakes from the oven, shot in the two cake tins of chocolate sponge to replace them, then rinsed her bowl in preparation for making butter drop biscuits, simultaneously thinking it odd that she should have picked a harvest hymn when spring was in the air.

It must be the rural setting, she decided, as she put the butter on to melt and weighed the flour. She'd spent all her life, up till now, in an urban or semi-urban environment, and she was delighted to find herself deep in the countryside, and working with a completely new rhythm of life. How lucky could a person get? And tomorrow was party day!

She wasn't completely naïve, and had already obtained a special license to sell alcoholic drinks on the premises, the bar being run by the publican's wife. No party, in the circumstances, could go with a swing without a tot or two to get people relaxed and talking, and she'd also had an offer from the two sons of a parishioner to DJ for the event. She had even persuaded grim old Lettice Keighley-Armstrong to come along, provided Rev. Florrie picked her up in her ancient car and brought her home afterwards. Now that really was progress!

'All we like sheep, have gone astray-ay-ay-ay-ay-ay-ay-ay …' her tortured voice now offered to an audience of only her cat, a dumb creature with no cognizance of the fact that she had now shifted her performance to a snippet from the *Messiah*.

Becoming aware of what she was lustily roaring out made her think that it must be the rural situation of her new home that had brought that one to the surface. There were sheep everywhere surrounding the village, their lambs leaping and pirouetting in the sunshine, glad to be alive, and unaware of how short that life was going to be before they graced someone's Sunday dining table.

Out with the two halves of the chocolate sponge, and onto the cooling trays, then in with the biscuits. These offerings, along with a couple of bottles of sherry, one sweet and one dry, should be sufficient for her contribution to the party. Now, she'd have to see about putting up some bunting in the hall and inflating as many balloons as she could manage before running out of puff.

A quick glance in the mirror in the hall convinced her that she had need of a quick trip to the bathroom as she had chocolate sponge-mix stigmata on her chin and forehead, and she thundered joyously up the staircase, now whistling, in her enthusiasm for life.

She left The Rectory five minutes later, to make the short trip through the graveyard to the village hall, her short thick curls being tossed by the playful spring breeze. Rev. Florrie was of medium height and just a bit on the chubby side, but had a kind face and lively hazel eyes that held those of anyone who spoke to her, and somehow communicated her caring nature and genuine interest in others and their problems.

As she approached the hall, a stray gust of wind lifted her cassock and wrapped her head in the folds of its inky blackness, and she pulled it away from her face with a chuckle. She wore the ungainly garment with pride, and eschewed civvies whenever she could, so proud was she to have the right to be thus enrobed. She was going to enjoy decorating the hall for their forthcoming celebration, and the liveliness of the wind had merely put her in a more playful mood.

In Carpe Diem, Coopers Lane, Gwendolyn Galton was packing bibelots in newsprint in preparation for her Sunday foray into the antiques world. She was a dealer in small collectables, and made her way from fair to fair every weekend with her booty, spending her weekdays searching for new stock and cleaning and repairing her finds.

As she wrapped a particularly ugly but rare Toby jug, she sighed with pleasure, and decided that when she had filled the box she was currently working on, it would not be indecently early to stop for a cup of coffee.

Gwendolyn was a slim woman with long snow-white hair, passable features, and pale blue eyes. About fifty, she had never been married and never felt the need for a life companion. She was comfortable in her own company and only sought that of others if she was in one of her rare sociable moods. Her solitary existence bothered her not a whit, as her profession was all-consuming, and she loved what she did.

When she tripped off to the kitchen to put on the kettle, the reason for packing early recurred to her, and she decided that she really must make something for the party the following evening, immediately setting her mind to decide what would have the most impact, with the least effort.

Trifle! That was it; she'd make a trifle. Everyone loved it and, since the advent of tinned custard, its assembly couldn't have been easier. It was really only a case of waiting for the jelly to set before adding the other layers.

Placing a large glass bowl and a jug on her work surface, she reached into her food cupboard and extracted two sachets of strawberry jelly crystals and a tin of fruit cocktail. A quick look in her cake tin revealed the remains of an angel cake and a raspberry Swiss roll. They would do admirably, and that would leave only the custard and whipped cream to add, with a few hundreds and thousands sprinkled on at the last minute, so that the colour hadn't bled by the time she handed it over.

She could use the water from the kettle to melt the jellies, and it could boil again for her coffee, while she arranged slices of stale cake, covered them with drained fruit, added the syrup to the jelly mix, and poured it over, although it would have to be covered and put in the fridge out of harm's way. Although she lived alone, her ginger cat, Marmalade, had esoteric tastes, and she wouldn't put it past him to develop an over-riding passion for unset strawberry jelly.

Finally pouring water over a teaspoonful of coffee granules and adding a splash of milk, she returned to contemplate what other little trifles of the collectable kind she should include for her stall on Sunday. It would be an early start, so she wouldn't stay over-long at the party; just long enough to have a little chat with her friends and acquaintances, and then head off for an early night.

Tossing her snowy locks over her shoulders, she settled down, kneeling on the floor to survey her treasures, hoping that the weather would be as fair as today when she went out touting her wares. There really was nothing worse than paying what she considered a small fortune for a pitch at a big fair, then having the turnout ruined by torrential rain, high winds, or a combination of both.

In Sweet Dreams on The Green, Krystal Yaxley's fraternal twins, Kevin and Keith, entered the kitchen, to find that most of their view was taken up by their mother's wide buttocks sticking out of a cupboard door as she knelt on the floor rummaging in the back of the shelves. 'What the hell are you doing, Ma?' asked Kevin, the oldest by twenty-three minutes.

'You look like a hippo foraging in a skip,' added Keith, oblivious to how sensitive his mother was about how big she had got in the months since her husband had walked out on her.

'If you must know,' she replied, her voice muffled, as she made no effort to remove her head from the inside of the cupboard, 'I'm looking for something I can take along to that damned party without having to shell out for anything. I can't just be throwing money around, as well you know.'

'But we need some petrol money for the weekend,' Kevin informed her, a wheedling whine entering his voice.

'Look in the usual place then,' she suggested and, when Keith asked them where that might be, informed them that the best place was down the back of the sofa or the armchairs. 'Never know what treasure you're going to come up with down there,' she added, switching her attention back to what she had in her store cupboard that would not only solve the problem, but which might also be nearly out of date, thus using up something she might otherwise have to throw away if she didn't find it soon.

'Mother!' exclaimed Kevin with disgust. 'Don't you have any real money? I'm fed up going to the shop for a newspaper with a handful of coins from the small change jar.'

At this, another of life's little stings, Krystal swiftly removed her head from inside the cupboard, incautiously banging it in her haste, and raised her voice, to inform her two needy teenaged sons, 'I haven't had a penny from your father since he left. I'm well into my overdraft, even though it's only the beginning of the month, and I have no other means of getting my hands on hard cash. What do you want to do? Send me out onto the streets and pimp me?

'Why don't you get in touch with your father instead of whining at me, as if I were some sort of cash-point. I'm potless! Don't you understand the situation? He's done a bunk and taken his nice regular salary with him. Go and whinge at him, if you think it'll do you any good. If not, it's the sofa or nothing.

'And if you're bored, the lawns need mowing, the flower beds need weeding, and you could do a lot more around the house to help me, instead of just lying in bed half the day then playing your damned music for the rest of it while stuffing your faces as if you were constantly starving.'

'Bor-ing!' both lads chorused in unison.

'Boring it might be, but it's all got to be done, and I don't see why I should have to be the only one who does it when there are three of us living in this house. If you want money, go and see if you can get some bar work; wash cars, ask people if they want any gardening done. The Bank of Mum and Dad has closed down until further notice, and you'll just have to find a different source of cash. This cash-cow is milked dry. The end.'

Kevin and Keith slouched off back into the living room with sneers on their faces. So much for this being the house of their dreams: nightmares more like, the way things were going from bad to worse.

Krystal put her head back into the depths of the cupboard, thinking how spoilt the twins had been in the past. Ken had had a six-figure salary, and they'd never wanted for anything. Now he'd gone, she had no idea how on earth she was going to find the wherewithal just to keep the house going, never mind pay next term's tuition fees for them both. At least they'd be out of mischief tomorrow night DJ-ing the music for the parish party.

With a muffled yell of glee, she laid hands on two boxes of cake mix and a packet that promised a perfect lemon meringue pie; and both of them were nearly out of date. Perfect! Six months ago she could never have imagined that such meagre finds could instil her with so much triumph, but she was learning to adapt. She had no other choice.

For a few guilty seconds she remembered the appointment she had made with Wanda Warwick for the next day, and what that would cost her but, in the long run, she considered that it could prove to be money well-spent, if she could get some guidance as to the right path to take in her straitened circumstances.

A similarly desperate situation was going on in the house of Jasper and Belinda Haygarth. They lived in a detached house, situated at the junction of the Downsway Road with The Green, then surrounded still further by a narrow lane that joined the aforementioned roads, creating a triangle, and it was in this triangle that their house was perched, isolated from other residences and aptly named "Three-Ways House".

They had started a textiles business when times were booming, and had made a fair bit of money from it; enough, certainly, to relocate to this postcard-pretty village, away from the urban sprawl that they had so hated. Times had changed, however, and the business was now struggling to break even, let alone make a profit, and was in a state where they had to decide if it was possible to revitalise it, or just walk away from it and cut their losses.

Belinda had had the temerity to start making a shopping list, and ask Jasper if there was anything he needed, at a point where he was contemplating the yawning financial abyss, and thus drawing out of him an unexpected tirade about her spendthrift ways, and how she was going to have to learn to live a more frugal life for the foreseeable future.

'That's all you ever do; spend, spend, spend! How on earth

do you think we're going to cope with virtually no income, when you just let it run through your fingers like sand?' he yelled, quite unreasonably, in Belinda's opinion.

'I'm going out to get some *food*!' she stated, more loudly than she had intended. 'If I don't buy any, what do you propose to live on? Cockroach stew and cobwebs? You know I'll get as many things on special offer or reduced as I can find, and we don't exactly live high on the hog these days, do we?'

His reply was unreasonable and illogical, but he couldn't help himself. 'Why the hell are you always buying food? How on earth do we manage to get through so much of the stuff when there's only the two of us?'

'I go once a week to the supermarket, and always when I know they're going to be reducing things, and the reason I'm 'always buying food', as you put it, is because eating is a daily occurrence, and I emptied my emergency store cupboard some time ago. We don't have any food stockpiled like we used to. And anyway, you eat like a horse. I honestly believe you've got hollow legs. I've never known anyone to pack away as much as you do; and three times a day to boot.

'You spend little enough time on the business these days. Why don't you get up off your well-fed arse and dig up that back garden? That way, we could at least grow some of our own stuff. And no, it won't be ready for some time, but later is better than never.' With that sobering suggestion, that he actually do something practical, instead of moaning all the time, his wife flounced out of the house, just in time to miss his indignant protest at the size of his backside, and the voraciousness of his appetite.

Belinda's mind was more concerned with how she could take something appetising to the hall tomorrow for next to no outlay. If she could find a pack of bacon offcuts, maybe she could make an egg and bacon quiche. That always went down well and wouldn't cost her much, if she bought own brand eggs (hopefully near their sell-by date and reduced to clear) and flour, and bought a pack of bacon off-cuts, which may even be reduced too. It was certainly the right time of day for the supermarket employees to be swanning round the store with their price-guns. She just might strike lucky.

She drove off, determined to do her best to spend as little as possible, and to prod her husband to make a start on growing their own food. The latter was not an instant solution, but if he never started, the idea would never come to fruition.

In the house anachronistically named Khartoum, Maude Asquith was also going through her own store cupboards, to gather together the ingredients she would need for the jam tarts and madeleines she intended to bake on Saturday morning, fresh for the party later in the day.

She was an elderly spinster who still lived in the house she had been born in, and in which her father had also first drawn breath, as had his father before him, his widow naming the house in memory of his honourable death in the ill-fated massacre of the Anglo-Egyptian Garrison in 1884-5.

The furniture bore witness to the lack of change that had locked the house in a time-warp in the latter years of Queen Victoria's reign, the family never having been wealthy, and believing that if an object was still functioning there was no need whatsoever to change it. Thus horsehair sofas still adorned her sitting room, and her dining room furniture was of the sturdy style that would probably withstand a nuclear attack.

The bedrooms were similarly furnished, with brass bedsteads, mahogany dressing tables and wardrobes, all lovingly polished by their current owner, and cherished in her memory as a sign of stability in the unchanging tenor of her life.

Not for Maude the fitted carpets and leather furniture of the modern sitting room; no chrome and glass dining table with chrome and leather chairs. It was not that she wouldn't have entertained the idea, had she been sufficiently well-off to consider such a vast change, more a case of always having to survive on limited resources, especially since her parents had died. The loss of their pensions to the household's running costs had been a major blow, as they had died within six months of each other, and she had found it hard to make ends meet ever since.

She soldiered on though, as she had been raised to, making do and mend; taking care of the good quality clothes that she had owned for years, and appearing to care not a fig for fashion, even if it was all an enormous bluff. Sometimes she used to sit and daydream about having untold riches and planning what she would do if she were ever in control of a fortune.

Fortunately, such idle and unrealistic daydreams did not occur too often, but were part of the reason that she, over the last year or two, had launched such a charm offensive on Lettice Keighley-Armstrong.

She had known Lettice slightly over the years and never really considered it worth wasting her time with such a curmudgeonly old grouse. In more recent times, however, she had begun to realise just how much Lettice was worth, after calling there once with the Christian Aid collecting box as a favour to the dear old vicar, who had been such a sweet old man that one could never say no to him.

On this occasion she had been asked in, to wait while Lettice looked for her purse and as she stood in the drawing room with the old woman pawing through her desk and enormous handbag, she had looked round at the dark furniture, and realised that it was not the same calibre as that which adorned her own home. Lettice's had been fine Georgian pieces, with a few touches of William III. There had even been a couple of medieval coffers placed in the window bays, lurking there darkly and expensively.

She had taken a peek into the dining room while Lettice had been thus occupied, and espied furniture that would fetch untold tens of thousands of pounds in the auction rooms, so rare were they, and of such antiquity.

The floors of both rooms were also covered in huge rugs that looked as if they had been woven from money, and by the time that Miss Keighley-Armstrong had located her battered old pigskin purse and carefully fed three pennies and six two-pence pieces through the slot of the collection box, Maude had decided that she had found a new best friend to cultivate.

The woman was, after all, unmarried, and had no family as far as she understood, and would need a good friend to whom she could leave all her earthly belongings. Why shouldn't that dear and trusted friend be Maude Asquith? She was only seventy-two to Lettice's eighty-five, and had much more time to have a real spree in the autumn of her life, before winter set in.

And so, began Operation Lettice, a charm offensive of such fervour and servility that Miss Keighley-Armstrong wasn't taken in for a minute, much preferring the comfortable old friendship she had with Violet Bingham, a relationship that had existed for what seemed like for ever now, and was in no danger of fading away.

Not realising that she had been rumbled right at the beginning of her plan and didn't have a choc-ice's chance in hell of being mentioned in Lettice's will, Maude put on her light spring coat, adjusted her hat in the hall mirror, and left home to make the short trek down Church Lane to 'Manor Gate' to ingratiate herself, once more, with the old woman.

As she crossed The Green, she noticed Wanda Warwick shaking a duster out of her front window, and waved to her, happy that she was on her way to a visit that might help her feather her own nest with some very fine down.

Wanda Warwick had been having a bit of a clean-up, and noticed the sprightly elderly woman crossing the road, her cream coat and fawn hat catching the brightness of the spring sunshine. At least she didn't seem to be on her way to see her, she thought as she waved with one hand and shook her duster furiously with the other. Company like that she could do without.

She simply didn't have the time for inane gossip and chatter. There were more important things going on in her life; like getting her small cottage clean and tidy for her appointment the next day with Krystal Yaxley. Then, on Sunday, she had a booth at a spring fair, which should bring in some much-needed funds, as her resources were running low. It had been a bad winter in her field of expertise, and she hoped the brightly optimistic weather would prompt people to seek her services now that winter was over and they could feel more positive about life, and optimistic about the future.

Closing the window, she surveyed her small sitting room, trying to adopt the eyes of a stranger to the little property. What impression did it give to an outsider? she wondered. Were there a tad too many dream-catchers hanging at the windows? Were the signs of the zodiac on the ceiling a bit over the top?

Remembering the state her kitchen was still in from the night before, she muttered, 'To hell with it! It's my home, and it should reflect my lifestyle, otherwise I might as well be living with someone, and spend most of my life compromising. This is how I like it, and if she doesn't like it, she can do one!'

Wanda was a white witch, or follower of Wicca, and lived her life accordingly. Nature must have picked up on this important thread running through her life, for as she turned fifty her features had become more prominent than in the earlier decades of her life, and her nose, with its hooked shape had lengthened, and her chin grown until, now, the unwary would immediately think of a witch on first sight of her, their impression only enhanced by the fact that she dyed her hair an unbecoming and unlikely jet black.

Her clothes were, by habit, black; her complexion pallid in the extreme, and she wore too much make-up, also a relic of her youth. She was quite an intimidating looking woman to anyone who did not know her, and had taken some time to be accepted into village life. After a few years, however, the other residents were used to her, and barely noticed how bizarre she looked when she went out in one of her black cloaks, looking for all the world as if she was off to either a Hallowe'en party or a Black Mass.

An hour later, having tackled the squalor awaiting her in the kitchen, she returned to the sitting room, mug of herbal tea in hand, to sort through her tarot cards and just get the feel of them again for her appointment tomorrow, for reading these cards was another of her eccentricities. She had not done a reading for at least three months, and felt that she needed to get to know her cards again by handling them so that they would fall right for her the next day.

As she sat shuffling, dealing, and laying out her tarot cards, wafts of lavender and herbs drifted down from tied bunches hanging from hooks on the central beam to tease her nostrils. Sitting thus in quiet contemplation, she let her mind wander to the reading she would do the next day. She knew very little about Krystal Yaxley, having had little to do with her since she and her family had settled in the village.

The first time she had spared a thought for her was when the news got out that her husband had walked out on her and their teenaged twin sons on New Year's Day, as if he had made a resolution to do so and not lost his nerve at the last minute. Both boys, she knew, were at university somewhere in the north of the country, and she imagined that Wanda's comfortable, almost charmed life had been absolutely shattered by the sudden departure of her husband and the family's only wage-earner.

Dealing the cards one more time, she tried to capture the right frame of mind for divination. The woman would need advice and help, and a little guidance from the cards would not go amiss in pointing out the right path to follow for the best outcome for her in the future.

In Manor Gate, once a rather grand gate house to the now demolished Georgian country house it had at one time, served Lettice Keighley-Armstrong sipped a cup of Darjeeling tea, relishing the spring-like weather, her French windows wide open, letting in the delicious fragrance of freshly mown grass. Lettice sniffed greedily as she heard the mower buzzing away in what she assumed was Colin Twentymen's rear garden. Very particular, he was, about the state of his garden; she often heard him at work in it, mowing, strimming, and trimming his hedges.

She relished days like today particularly, because she comprehended that she didn't have too many of them left. At eighty-five, she had no real health problems, but sometimes health was only skin-deep. Who knew what lay under the surface, gathering its strength to make an ambush? Many a friend of hers had died from an unexpected heart attack or a stroke. Even cancer camouflaged itself well until it was ready to reveal itself, ugly and gloating, as it spread to other parts of the body that had virtually no effective weapons to deal with it long term.

Every morning when she woke up she decided it was definitely a good day, simply because she had woken up at all, and though she showed most people the rough side of her tongue when dealing with them, it was not out of any innate bad temper; merely that she relished her own company, solitude being a friend that had never let her down. It was just part of her nature to be alone, and only the visits of her old friend Violet Bingham filled her with pleasure these days.

Her chair was turned towards the open French windows, so that she could watch the birds feasting at the feeders she had hung from the trees, within easy view of her armchair, this being one of her pleasures in life. With a sigh, she realised that spring was probably her favourite season, and mourned the fact that this one may be the last one she saw. This thought made her more determined than ever to enjoy every minute of it and not waste her time shut away with the doors all locked and the windows closed.

As she watched the birds and listened to their shrill exchange of opinions, her hands played idly with a string of dull stones that hung from her neck; an odd contrast with the quality of her old silk blouse. At each wrist were strings of the same dull stones, which had the look of childhood acquisitions, if not that of cheap holiday souvenirs, but she seemed inordinately fond of them and they must have held some special memory for her, for she was never seen without them.

Many who knew her had speculated about why she was so attached to such dreary baubles, when her mother had possessed such fine jewellery, made up especially from stones her husband had purchased during his years in South Africa, but none could come up with any explanation that would explain this fondness for such tawdry ornaments.

Her old black and white cat, previously taking a nap on the sofa, awoke, stretched luxuriously, then jumped to the floor and made his way over to the open doors. 'Well, hello to you, Mischief. Finally woke up, did you?'

The cat stared at her as she spoke to it, then turned to take a look out into the garden. Ignoring the birds – he was much too old even to think he could catch one nowadays, he turned back towards his mistress and made a brave attempt to jump into her lap.

Picking him up and plonking him on his goal, her hand automatically started to stroke his head, and she smiled at the loudness of his purr. He was getting on a bit, she thought, but he had been good company, and a much needed distraction when Daddy had finally died, and she was left totally on her own in the world. Maybe they'd both go to sleep one night and slip away together in the same night. That would be perfect, but very unlikely.

Turning her mind towards their new lady vicar, she smiled at how horrified she had been at the woman's appointment, being one of the first to get up and leave during the Induction service. But, give her her due: the woman had made a point of visiting her, to discuss any worries that might exist in her public disapproval, and had carried on visiting ever since.

Lettice's second thoughts had led her to thoroughly approve of Rev. Florrie. She now considered her a bright and enthusiastic girl to whose visits she now looked forward, and thought that she would do a lot of good in her calling, especially for women who had real problems.

Her persistence was the real reason she had agreed to go to the parish party, her insistence on a lift there and home again, just her way of letting Rev. Florrie know who was still in charge, and that she hadn't broken the old woman's spirit with her weekly visits that were becoming more and more of a pleasure, much to Lettice's surprise.

Heck! She wasn't getting soft in her extreme old age, was she? That would never do! As she came to this decision, she heard the tinkle of the old-fashioned pull doorbell, and pulled herself to her feet to answer it, rather hoping that it would be Rev. Florrie, for she felt a little of that young lady's company would be good for her, while she was still in such a good mood, herself.

'Hello, Maude!' she greeted her visitor with a grimace, her feelings of goodwill to all the world suddenly evaporating. 'I can't ask you in, I'm afraid; I'm very busy today with some paperwork from my solicitor. Unless it's something urgent, do you think you could call back another time?'

Maude Asquith smiled sycophantically at the old woman, and said that it didn't matter a jot. She was only a few minutes' walk away, and could pop over anytime without any inconvenience whatsoever. That said, she made an involuntary movement that resembled nothing more than a semi-curtsy, and turned from the door to return home.

'Thank the good Lord for that,' muttered Lettice under her breath as her visitor departed, having no idea how her off-the-cuff excuse had excited the spurned caller.

Maude hurried off back home, her stomach churning with excitement. Two years ago next month, it would be, since she had started to court the old woman. This talk of paperwork from a solicitor could mean she had achieved her objective. Never even contemplating that it might have been an out-and-out lie just to get rid of her, she had visions of Lettice drawing up a new will in her favour, and her mouth almost watered at the appetising thought of so much money.

While Colin Twentymen cultivated his garden at the rear of Carters Cottage, two other village residents sat at a table in the beer garden at the rear of The Druid's Head, stretching out their pints as long as they could. Both retired and both able to comprehend the attraction of each other's former professions, they spent as much time as they could in each other's company to avoid, what they referred to as, 'being stalked by all the old tabbies'. There was safety in numbers, they believed, and they were much more vulnerable to attack when they were alone.

Today being such a glorious and unseasonably warm day, they had met in The Druid's Head after a scratch lunch in their own homes. Money for a pint was one thing; money for a pub lunch was quite another, and completely out of the question financially. They were both pragmatic where money was concerned, and hated to waste it on unnecessary expenses like eating in the pub.

At the moment they were discussing their finances. Julius Twelvetrees, who resided at Bijou, The Green, and Toby Lattimer of Tresore in Coopers Lane, also retired and an avid collector of small but beautiful things, had found their pensions shrink in value over the years, and the current financial situation had more or less wiped out interest from savings which had made up part of their incomes in the past.

'There was a time when I could count on nine per cent on my savings, and some good dividends from my shares,' moaned Toby Lattimer, 'but the way things are at the moment, with everything seeming to get more expensive by the day, I've a real job just getting by on what my pension buys these days.'

'I know how you feel, but at least you could sell some of your bibelots, and you've got a load of antique furniture. I know they're mostly small pieces, but some of them are quite exquisite.'

'Perish the thought!' his compatriot in complaint exclaimed. 'And what about you? You're a retired jeweller, for heaven's sake. Surely you've got some old stock from your shop that you could hock to bring in a bob or two?'

'All gone, I'm afraid. I've been doing that for some time now, and I sold the very last bit just before Christmas. And I've still got that great pile of a house in Carsfold. That'll have to go. I can't keep that on any longer. It costs far too much to run; the heating bill alone would turn your stomach if I showed it to you.'

'Have you got any idea how a couple of old codgers like us could make a bob or two just to fill the larder?' asked Julius hopefully.

'Well, yes, I have had an idea occur to me, but a bit less of the 'old codgers' if you don't mind. Me, I'm in my prime, even if you are over the hill.' Toby was, in fact, sixty-six and Julius sixty-eight years of age.

'Come on, man, spit it out, and don't keep me in suspenders, as they say. I mean, apart from winning the Lottery or having a rich relative die and leave you the lot, what other chance is there of coming into a large sum of money?'

Toby merely tapped the side of his nose with an index finger and winked at his eager companion. 'All in good time, Julius, old chap. All in good time. What I will tell you is that it involves a bit of stake money, involves the currency market, and isn't entirely without risk.'

'You can forget that, then. Firstly, I haven't got any stake money and, secondly, if I had, I couldn't afford to risk it. Whatever it is, you'll have to go it alone, and maybe I'll join you, if it proves to be a success.' Julius was definitely out.

'Just sounding you out, old man: just sounding you out, that's all.'

From the little detached house next to the church, there was neither sound nor movement. Bonnie Fletcher fled the village each weekday morning in her little Peugeot, swearing that today would be the day that she missed her train, and returned every evening at about seven-thirty, tired and exasperated, after yet another day spent in the city.

Most weekends she spent in Market Darley where there was a little more nightlife than that provided by The Druid's Head, usually cadging sofas or a spare room from her old school-friends, with whom she socialised. There was no point in going out if she couldn't have a drink, and if she had to drive home, she might as well not go out at all.

Some residents wondered why she didn't just sell up and move to Market Darley, for that was where she spent two days of the week; the other five she commuted from there, so there seemed little point in her living in such an out of the way place as Shepford St Bernard. And this she wouldn't have done, unless her grandmother hadn't left her the cottage, after spending her last ten years in a nursing home.

Property prices were still falling in some areas, and this was definitely not the time to put a piece of prime real estate, such as her pretty village cottage, on to the market. She would put up with her rushed life, as it was only until the market picked up, and she could ask a fair price for a very desirable residence. Bonnie Fletcher considered that she had her head screwed on the right way, and could run her life with the maximum precision, if she just trusted her instincts.

Chapter Two

Friday morning – Market Darley

The door of the CID office in Market Darley was flung open with so much enthusiasm that it rebounded off the inside wall of the room, and DC Chris Roberts bounded in booming an enthusiastic, 'Morning, Guv. Morning Our Davey.'

The two men already in the office both looked up at him with disapproving expressions. 'That's "Sir" or "Inspector" to you, Roberts, as well you know,' this from DI Harry Falconer, the senior plain clothes officer who was almost at the end of his tether with this relative newcomer's inability to understand that he hated being called 'Guv'.

The extra-large man at the other desk patiently waited his turn to complain, and advised the new arrival, 'I'd prefer it if you'd call me Carmichael. Davey's only for family and very close friends.' DS Carmichael was similarly not enamoured of Roberts' informal manner of address.

DI Falconer and DS Carmichael had been working together for some time now, Falconer having joined the Force fresh from some years in the army, after completing a university degree. DS Carmichael had joined as a rookie in uniform, working his way up to his current position more by luck than by judgement.

DC Roberts had arrived on secondment the previous autumn, having secured a temporary transfer from Manchester to help his mother, who had suffered a stroke, and needed some assistance in her daily life while recuperating. His first assignment had been to go undercover as a mature student at the local college but, after an unfortunate incident that hospitalised him for some time, followed by a long period of convalescence, he had been preparing to return to work in the early February.

Unfortunately, a few days before he was due to resume his duties, his mother had suffered another and more catastrophic stroke, and had not survived. That had necessitated him seeking compassionate leave to deal with the paperwork, always a part of any death and, during this period, he had requested a permanent transfer to Market Darley, as he had inherited the family home on his mother's demise, and now needed time to go back to Manchester to give notice on his old digs and tidy up his affairs that end.

Thus, on this beautiful early March morning, he had re-entered their lives with his habitual breezy brashness. 'I'm back!' he announced unnecessarily, as if his returning presence was the most wonderful present they could ever receive, headed for the empty desk that had been prepared for him, and slumped down in the office chair as if he had only been gone for ten minutes.

'Doing anything special this weekend, then, Davey boy?' he asked Carmichael, his good natured face split with a broad, good-humoured grin.

'Please call me Carmichael,' replied the sergeant, making no attempt to answer the question.

'OK! Keep your hair on! I only asked if you've got anything planned for the weekend.'

As Carmichael composed his answer in his head, Falconer muttered, 'Sounds like a ruddy barber,' under his breath.

'As it happens, I am doing something rather special this weekend; tomorrow night, in fact,' Carmichael replied, his face lighting up as he remembered his plans for later.

'What's that then, my little sergeant?' asked Roberts, drawing a scowl from Falconer, and the admonition to show a little more respect for his senior officers.

'I'm going out with my family for the very belated wetting

210

of two babies' heads,' he informed the DC, his expression daring him to ask for more details.

'Oh yes, I remember now. Someone told me you'd become a father, and that *Detective Inspector Falconer* – I bet that was fun for all concerned – had delivered the new arrival. Congratulations to both of you. But whose is the other baby?'

Falconer didn't rise to the bait, and left it to Carmichael to provide any detail that the DC thought was his due. Carmichael obliged willingly, to avoid the topic of little Harriet's birth, simply announcing, 'My new little brother,' then buttoning his lip, as if there were a draught in the room, and he needed to keep his teeth warm.

With a widening of his eyes, Roberts let his mouth fall open and, before he gave himself time to think, asked, 'Good God! How old is your mother, for heaven's sake?' then, seeing the vast body of the DS start to rise from his chair, carried on without a break, with, 'All right! All right! I realise that was out of order. I was just surprised, that's all. What's his name?'

'Harry,' he replied, knowing exactly what was coming next.

'And your little one? A girl, I heard.'

'Harriet,' announced Carmichael, adopting an aggressive manner that dared Roberts to challenge anything he had just learnt.

Roberts, however, had the hide of a rhinoceros and commented, one index finger on his bottom lip, 'Oooh! Has the inspector been making house-calls then, or is all this just a coincidence, Inspector, *sir*?'

Falconer looked daggers at his newly returned DC, and explained that Carmichael had named his daughter after him because of the circumstances that had resulted in him delivering the baby. 'About Mrs Carmichael Senior's choice of name, I have no knowledge whatsoever, although I thought she usually favoured Shakespearean names. What's the story there, Sergeant?'

'Same old thing, sir, except this time she didn't go for a

character. She was all caught up with that speech about ... I dunno, something about "Cry God for Harry". There's no point in asking me. I don't read a lot of Shakespeare, but Mum's always been hooked in a strange sort of "watching the films" way.'

'But you said she'd named you 'Ralph', and only gave you a Shakespearean middle name.' Falconer had forgotten why this was. Roberts merely sat with his mouth open as this esoteric conversation unravelled before his very ears.

'I thought I told you she had a thing about Sir Ralph Richardson at the time, only she always pronounced it 'Raif'. God only knows why! And that's why I like to be known as Davey. *If* I've given my permission, that is,' he finished, with a glower at Roberts.

'What the hell are the rest of your family called, for goodness sake?' Roberts was, by now, fascinated, and wanted to follow through to the bitter end.

Taking this in good part, Carmichael began to enumerate his six siblings, quite enjoying the experience of somebody actually being interested in anything concerning him. 'The oldest is Romeo, but he's just known as Rome and he's a builder. Next there's Hamlet: known as Ham, and he works on a farm. Third is Mercutio, just called Merc, and he's a 'man with a van' – does all kinds of stuff.

'I'm next, then the two girls. Juliet's the eldest, and she's a hairdresser and beautician, and Imogen's a librarian. Now we've got little Harry to add to the mob as well.' As Carmichael finished, he smiled at the thought of his siblings, having long ago got over the initial embarrassment he had felt at his mother having another baby at her age.

'Blimey! What a tribe! Have you got any brother or sisters, Guv?'

'Sir,' Falconer corrected him.

'Sorry! Have you got any brothers and sisters, SIR?'

'No,' replied the inspector, with a note of finality in his

voice. 'Now, if we could get on with a little work before lunchtime, I'd be very grateful. Here, Roberts, I've got some crime figures in this folder for you to collate. Just hand them in to Bob Bryant on the desk when they're done. Thank you.'

As DC Roberts accepted the file handed to him and dipped his head towards his work, Falconer asked Carmichael what his exact plans were for this delayed celebration. Carmichael's expression of familial pride was a joy to see, and he explained, 'Merc's arranged a minibus taxi for them all to come over to Castle Farthing, and we're going to spend the evening in The Fisherman's Flies. Dad's babysitting – unheard of in the past – and Ma's coming with them all, as part of it is to celebrate Harry's birth. It should be a riot.'

'Not as much of a riot as your crazy wedding was, I hope.' Falconer still shuddered when he remembered the state the Carmichaels had got him into at that.

'Dunno, sir, but it should be a blast, and I'm not rostered to work on Sunday, so I can get over whatever happens at my own pace.'

'Can I come?' asked Roberts.

'No!' said Carmichael emphatically. 'It's family only,' and turned back to the paperwork on his desk.

Falconer sighed with relief, having, for a moment, wondered if the sergeant was going to extend an invitation to him as he had delivered young Harriet.

*

The Falconer Files

by

Andrea Frazer

For more information about **Andrea Frazer**
and other **Accent Press** titles
please visit

www.accentpress.co.uk